Brown Girl in the Ring

"Nalo Hopkinson's first novel, *Brown Girl in the Ring*, is simply triumphant."
—Dorothy Allison, author of *Bastard Out of Carolina*

"Hopkinson lives up to her advance billing."
—*New York Times Book Review*

"[Hopkinson] has created a vivid world of urban decay and startling, dangerous magic, where the human heart is both a physical and metaphorical key."
—*Publishers Weekly*

"It is great."
—Octavia E. Butler, author of *Parable of the Sower*

"An impressive debut precisely because of Hopkinson's fresh viewpoint."
—*Washington Post Book World*

"A parable of black feminist self-reliance, couched in poetic language and the structural conventions of classic SF."
—*Village Voice*

Skin Folk

"Everything is possible in her imagination."
—*Science Fiction Chronicle*

"Nalo Hopkinson, award-winning author of *Brown Girl in the Ring* and *Midnight Robber*, has released an impressive collection of short stories entitled *Skin Folk* . . . well crafted and brilliantly written."
—*Barnes & Noble*

The Salt Roads

"*The Salt Roads* succeeds impressively. . . ."
—*Locus*

"*The Salt Roads* is like nothing you've read before. . . . The characters' stories are heartbreaking and beautiful, living beyond the novel's pages. Hopkinson's writing is like a favorite song."
—Tananarive Due, American Book Award-winning author of *The Living Blood*

"With her conjurer's art, with daring and delightful audacity, Nalo Hopkinson reaches into the well of history."
—Sandra Jackson-Opoku, author of *The River Where Blood Is Born*

"Sexy, disturbing, touching, wildly comic. A tour de force from one of our most striking new voices in fiction."
—*Kirkus*, starred review

Tachyon Publications
1459 18th Street #139
San Francisco, CA 94107
415.285.5615
www.tachyonpublications.com
tachyon@tachyonpublications.com

Series Editor: Jacob Weisman
Project Editor: Jill Roberts

ISBN 13: 978-1-61696-198-5

Printed in the United States by Worzalla

First Edition: 2015
9 8 7 6 5 4 3 2 1

NALO HOPKINSON
Falling in Love with Hominids

FALLING IN LOVE
WITH HOMINIDS

NALO HOPKINSON

TACHYON || SAN FRANCISCO

Other books by Nalo Hopkinson

Novels
Brown Girl in the Ring (1998)
Midnight Robber (2000)
The Salt Roads (2003)
The New Moon's Arms (2007)
The Chaos (2012)
Sister Mine (2013)

Collections
Skin Folk (2001)
Report From Planet Midnight (2011)

Anthologies
Whispers from the Cotton Tree Root:
Caribbean Fabulist Fiction (2000)
Mojo: Conjure Stories (2003)
So Long Been Dreaming (2004)
Tesseracts Nine (2005, with Geoff Ryman)

CONTENTS

Foreword
Nalo Hopkinson

She got the which of what-she-did,
She hid the bell with a blot, she did,
But she fell in love with a hominid.
Where is the which of the what-she-did?
—"Ballad of the Lost C'Mell"
by Cordwainer Smith

I didn't used to like people much. When I was sixteen and depressed, keenly reactive to every injustice I witnessed or experienced, very aware of having no control over my life, and (I thought) powerless to do anything about all the evil, unhappiness, violence, and pain in the world, I had no hope for us as a species. We humans have spread over the face of this planet like a fungus, altering and destroying whole ecosystems and species, abusing and waging war on each other. If teenaged me thought about it too much, I was engulfed with despair.

Not to say that it was all bad. I had friends, there was good music in the world, my parents were involved in the arts and made sure to expose me and my brother to them. And there were books.

The title of this collection comes from my love of Cordwainer Smith's writing, especially his "Instrumentality of Mankind" stories. I loved his imagination, style, the poetry of his writing, his compassion. Loved his sensibility in writing about a racialized, manufactured underclass and telling some of the stories from their context. I'm black and female. I was born and for many years raised middle/creative class in the Caribbean, a region of the world which has had to be keenly aware of issues of race, class, gender, and privilege. You see the concerns reflected in much of our art and literature. I'd always loved reading science fiction and fantasy as well, and came to value the SF/F writers I found who could explicitly bring any of that into their writing in complicated ways. These are such human issues. I love and am fascinated by human beings. We are, all of us, capable simultaneously of such great good and such horrifying evil.

It's a bit of a trick to treat a collection such as this as though the stories were all conceived of and written at the same time, with a single unifying principle. In fact, they were written over the course of perhaps eight to ten years, for different editors, on different themes, and published in different venues. The only unifying element is me, the author. Thinking about the stories as one volume forced me to consider what I'm about. What are my passions and obsessions of which these stories might be emblematic? Well, so many things, really. But one of the progressions I've made is from being a depressed teenager who saw how powerless she was to change all the ills around her to being a mostly cheerful fifty-something who realizes there are all kinds of ways of working towards positive change. I am not as active in doing so as my conscience would have me be, but I am not at all passive, or powerless. And that's because I'm not alone. I've learned I can trust that humans in general will strive to make things better for themselves and their communities. Not all of us. Not always in principled, loving, or respectful ways. Often the direct opposite, in fact. But we're all on the same spinning ball of dirt, trying to live as best we can.

Yes, that's almost overweeningly Pollyana-ish, despite the fact that sometimes I just need to shake my fist at a mofo. I am not at all discounting all the pain, torture, and death we can and do inflict on others. As I hope will be clear from the stories that follow, I am not forgetting oppression, repression, abuse, genocide. I experience anger and outrage and despair. I see the ways in which science fiction is too often used to confirm people's complacency, to reassure them that it's okay for them not to act, because they are not the lone superhero who will fix the world's ills. And yet, humanity as a whole is not satisfied with complacency. So part of the work of these past few decades of my life has been the process of falling in love with hominids.

The Easthound

Whenever the canned Star Trek-*type computer voice of the Toronto subway system announces "Christie Station," I always hear "Crispy Station." I must have one day heard her announce the arrival of the easthound train; you know, the one that goes in the opposite direction of the westhound train?*

Oh, Black Betty, bam-ba-lam,
Oh, Black Betty, bam-ba-lam.

"The easthound bays at night," Jolly said.

Millie shivered. Bad luck to mention the easthound, and her twin bloody well knew it. God, she shouldn't even be thinking, "bloody." Millie put her hands to her mouth to stopper the words in so she wouldn't say them out loud.

"Easthound?" said Max. He pulled the worn black coat closer around his body. The coat had been getting tighter around him these past few months. Everyone could see it. "Uck the fuh is that easthound shit?"

Not what; he knew damned well what it was. He was asking Jolly what the hell she was doing bringing the easthound into their game of Loup-de-lou. Millie wanted to yell at Jolly too.

Jolly barely glanced at Max. She knelt in front of the fire, staring into it, re-twisting her dreads and separating them at the scalp where they were threatening to grow together. "It's my first line," she said. "You can play or not, no skin off my teeth."

They didn't talk about skin coming off, either. Jolly should be picking someone to come up with the next line of the game. But Jolly broke the rules when she damned well pleased. Loup-de-lou was her game, after all. She'd invented it. Someone had to come up with a first line. Then they picked the next person. That person had to continue the story by beginning with the last word or two of the line the last person said. And so on until someone closed the loup by ending the story with the first word or two of the very first line. Jolly was so thin. Millie had saved some of the chocolate bar she'd found to share with Jolly, but she knew that Jolly wouldn't take it. If you ate too much, you grew too quickly. Millie'd already eaten most of the chocolate, though. Couldn't help it. She was so hungry all the time!

Max hadn't answered Jolly. He took the bottle of vodka that Sai was holding and chugged down about a third of it. Nobody complained. That was his payment for finding the bottle in the first place. But could booze make you grow, too? Or did it keep you shrinky? Millie couldn't remember which. She fretfully watched Max's Adam's apple bob as he drank.

"The game?" Citron chirped up, reminding them. A twin of the flames of their fire danced in his green eyes. "We gonna play?"

Right. The game. Jolly bobbed her head yes. Sai, too. Millie said, "I'm in." Max sighed and shrugged his yes.

Max took up where Jolly had left off. "At night the easthound howls," he growled, "but only when there's no moon." He pointed at Citron.

A little clumsy, Millie thought, but a good second line.

Quickly, Citron picked it up with, "No moon is so bright as the easthound's eyes when it spies a plump rat on a garbage heap." He pointed at Millie.

Garbage heap? What kind of end bit was that? Didn't give her much with which to begin the new loup. Trust Citron to throw her a tough one. And that "eyes, spies" thing, too. A rhyme in the middle, instead of at the end. Clever bastard. Thinking furiously, Millie louped, "Garbage heaps high in the . . . cities of noonless night."

Jolly said, "You're cheating. It was 'garbage heap,' not 'garbage heaps.'" She gnawed a strip from the edge of her thumbnail, blew the crescented clipping from her lips into the fire.

"Chuh." Millie made a dismissive motion with her good hand. "You just don't want to have to continue on with 'noonless night.'" Smirking, she pointed at her twin.

Jolly started in on the nail of her index finger. "And you're just not very good at this game, are you, Millie?"

"Twins, stop it," Max told them.

"I didn't start it," Jolly countered, through chewed nail bits. Millie hated to see her bite her nails, and Jolly knew it.

Jolly stood and flounced closer to the fire. Over her back she spat the phrase, "Noonless night, a rat's bright fright, and blood in the bite all delight the easthound." The final two words were the two with which they'd begun. Game over. Jolly spat out a triumphant, "Loup!" First round to Jolly.

Sai slapped the palm of her hand down on the ground between the players. "Aw, jeez, Jolly! You didn't have to end it so soon, just cause you're mad at your sister! I was working on a great loup."

"Jolly's only showing off!" Millie said. Truth was, Jolly was right. Millie really wasn't much good at Loup-de-lou. It was only a stupid game, a distraction to take their minds off hunger, off being cold and scared, off watching everybody else and yourself every waking second for signs of sprouting. But Millie didn't want to be distracted. Taking your mind off things could kill you. She was only going along with the game to show the others that she wasn't getting cranky; getting loupy.

She rubbed the end of her handless wrist. Damp was making it achy. She reached for the bottle of vodka where Max had stood it upright in the crook of his crossed legs. "Nuh-uh-uh," he chided, pulling it out of her reach and passing it to Citron, who took two pulls at the bottle and coughed.

Max said to Millie, "You don't get any treats until you start a new game."

Jolly turned back from the fire, her grinning teeth the only thing that shone in her black silhouette.

"Wasn't me who spoiled that last one," Millie grumbled. But she leaned back on the packed earth, her good forearm and the one with the missing hand both lying flush against the soil. She considered how to begin. The ground was a little warmer tonight than it had been last night. Spring was coming. Soon, there'd be pungent wild leeks to pull up and eat from the river bank. She'd been craving their taste all through this frozen winter. Had been yearning for the sight and taste of green, growing things. Only she wouldn't eat too many of them. You couldn't ever eat your fill of anything, or that might bring out the Hound. Soon it'd be warm enough to sleep outside again. She thought of rats and garbage heaps, and slammed her mind's door shut on the picture. Millie liked sleeping with the air on her skin, even though it was dangerous out of doors. It felt more dangerous indoors, what with everybody growing up.

And then she knew how to start the loup. She said, "The river swells in May's spring tide."

Jolly strode back from the fire and took the vodka from Max. "That's a really good one." She offered the bottle to her twin.

Millie found herself smiling as she took it. Jolly was quick to speak her mind, whether scorn or praise. Millie could never stay mad at her for long. Millie drank through her smile, feeling the vodka burn its trail down. With her stump she pointed at Jolly and waited to hear how Jolly would Loup-de-lou with the words "spring tide."

"The spring's May tide is deep and wide," louped Jolly. She was breaking the rules again; three words, not two, and she'd added a "the" at the top, and changed the order around! People shouldn't change stuff, it was bad! Millie was about to protest when a quavery howl crazed the crisp night, then disappeared like a sob into silence.

"Shit!" hissed Sai. She leapt up and began kicking dirt onto the fire to douse it. The others stood too.

"Race you to the house!" yelled a gleeful Jolly, already halfway there at a run.

Barking with forced laughter, the others followed her. Millie, who was almost as quick as Jolly, reached the disintegrating cement steps of the house a split second before Jolly pushed in through the door, yelling "I win!" as loudly as she could. The others tumbled in behind Millie, shoving and giggling.

Sai hissed, "Sshh!" Loud noises weren't a good idea.

With a chuckle in her voice, Jolly replied, "Oh, chill, we're fine. Remember how Churchy used to say that loud noises chased away ghosts?"

Everyone went silent. They were probably all thinking the same thing; that maybe Churchy was a ghost now. Millie whispered, "We have to keep quiet, or the easthound will hear us."

"Bite me," said Max. "There's no such thing as an easthound." His voice was deeper than it had been last week. No use pretending. He was growing up. Millie put a bit more distance between him and her. Max really was getting too old. If he didn't do the right thing soon and leave on his own, they'd have to kick him out. Hopefully before something ugly happened.

Citron closed the door behind them. It was dark in the house. Millie tried to listen beyond the door to the outside. That had been no wolf howling, and they all knew it. She tried to rub away the pain in her wrist. "Do we have any aspirin?"

Sai replied, "I'm sorry. I took the last two yesterday."

Citron sat with a thump on the floor and started to sob. "I hate this," he said slurrily. "I'm cold and I'm scared and there's no bread left, and it smells of mildew in here—"

"You're just drunk," Millie told him.

"—and Millie's cranky all the time," Citron continued with a glare at Millie, "and Sai farts in her sleep, and Max's boots don't fit him any more. He's growing up."

"Shut up!" said Max. He grabbed Citron by the shoulders, dragged him to his feet, and started to shake him. "Shut up!" His voice broke on the "up" and ended in a little squeak. It should have been funny, but now he had Citron up against the wall and was choking him. Jolly and Sai yanked at Max's hands. They told him over and over to stop, but he wouldn't. The creepiest thing was, Citron wasn't making any sound. He couldn't. He couldn't get any air. He scrabbled at Max's hands, trying to pull them off his neck.

Millie knew she had to do something quickly. She slammed the bottle of vodka across Max's back, like christening a ship. She'd seen it on tv, when tvs still worked. When you could still plug one in and have juice flow through the wires to make funny cartoon creatures move behind the screen, and your mom wouldn't sprout in front of your eyes and eat your dad and bite your hand off.

Millie'd thought the bottle would shatter. But maybe the glass was too thick, because though it whacked Max's back with a solid thump, it didn't break. Max dropped to the floor like he'd been shot. Jolly put her hands to her mouth. Startled at what she herself had done, Millie dropped the bottle. It exploded when it hit the floor, right near Max's head. Vodka fountained up and out, and then Max was whimpering and rolling around in the booze and broken glass. There were dark smears under him.

"Ow! Jesus! Ow!" He peered up to see who had hit him. Millie moved closer to Jolly.

"Max." Citron's voice was hoarse. He reached a hand out to Max. "Get out of the glass, dude. Can you stand up?"

Millie couldn't believe it. "Citron, he just tried to kill you!"

"I shouldn't have talked about growing up. Jolly, can you find the candles? It's dark in here. Come on, Max." Citron pulled Max to his feet.

Max came up mad. He shook broken glass off his leather jacket, and stood towering over Millie. Was his chest thicker than it had been? Was that hair shadowing his chin? Millie whimpered and cowered away. Jolly put herself between Millie and Max. "Don't be a big old bully," she said to Max. "Picking on the one-hand girl. Don't be a dog."

It was like a light came back on in Max's eyes. He looked at Jolly, then at Millie. "You hurt me, Millie. I wouldn't hurt you," he said to Millie. "Even if . . ."

"If . . . that thing was happening to you," Jolly interrupted him, "you wouldn't care who you were hurting. Besides, you were choking Citron, so don't give us that innocent look and go on about not hurting people."

Max's eyes welled up. They glistened in the candlelight. "I'll go," he said drunkenly. His voice sounded high, like the boy he was ceasing to be. "Soon. I'll go away. I promise."

"When?" Millie asked softly. They all heard her, though. Citron looked at her with big, wet doe eyes.

Max swallowed. "Tomorrow. No. A week."

"Three days," Jolly told him. "Two more sleeps."

Max made a small sound in his throat. He wiped his hand over his face. "Three days," he agreed. Jolly nodded, firmly.

After that, no one wanted to play Loup-de-lou any more. They didn't bother with candles. They all went to their own places, against the walls so they could keep an eye on each other. Millie and Jolly had the best place, together near the window. That way, if anything bad happened, Jolly could boost Millie out the window. There used to be a low bookcase under that window. They'd burned the wood months ago, for cooking with. The books that had been on it were piled up to one side, and Jolly'd scavenged a pile of old clothes for a bed. Jolly rummaged around under the clothes. She pulled out the gold necklace that their mom had given her for passing French. Jolly only wore it to sleep. She fumbled with the clasp, dropped the necklace, swore under her breath. She found the necklace again and put it on successfully this time. She kissed Millie on the forehead. "Sleep tight, Mills."

Millie said, "My wrist hurts too much. Come with me tomorrow to see if the kids two streets over have any painkillers?"

"Sure, honey." Warrens kept their distance from each other, for fear of becoming targets if somebody in someone else's warren sprouted. "But try to get some sleep, okay?" Jolly lay down and was asleep almost immediately, her breathing quick and shallow.

Millie remained sitting with her back against the wall. Max lay on the other side of the room, using his coat as a blanket. Was he sleeping, or just lying there, listening?

She used to like Max. Weeks after the world had gone mad, he'd found her and Jolly hiding under the porch of somebody's house. They were dirty and hungry, and the stench of rotting meat from inside the house was drawing flies. Jolly had managed to keep Millie alive that long, but Millie was delirious with pain, and the place where her hand had been bitten off had started smelling funny. Max had brought them clean water. He'd searched and bargained with the other warrens of hiding kids until he found morphine and antibiotics for Millie. He was the one who'd told them that it looked like only adults were getting sick.

But now Millie was scared of him. She sat awake half the night, watching Max. Once, he shifted and snorted, and the hairs on Millie's arms stood on end. She shoved herself right up close against Jolly. But Max just grumbled and rolled over and kept sleeping. He didn't change. Not this time. Millie watched him a little longer, until she couldn't keep her eyes open. She curled up beside Jolly. Jolly was scrawny, her skin downy with the peach fuzz that Sai said came from starvation. Most of them had it. Nobody wanted to grow up and change, but Jolly needed to eat a little more, just a little. Millie stared into the dark and worried. She didn't know when she fell asleep. She woke when first light was making the window into a glowing blue square. She was cold. Millie reached to put her arm around Jolly. Her arm landed on wadded-up clothing with nobody in it. "She's gone," said Citron.

"Whuh?" Millie rolled over, sat up. She was still tired. "She gone to check the traps?" Jolly barely ate, but she was best at catching gamey squirrels, feral cats, and the occasional raccoon.

"I dunno. I woke up just as the door was closing behind her. She let in a draft."

Millie leapt to her feet. "It was Max! He sprouted! He ate her!"

Citron leapt up too. He pulled her into a hug. "Sh. It wasn't Max. Look, he's still sleeping."

He was. Millie could see him huddled under his coat.

"See?" said Citron. "Now hush. You're going to wake him and Sai up."

"Oh god, I was so scared for a moment." She was lying; she never stopped being scared. She sobbed and let Citron keep hugging her, but not for long. Things could sneak up on you while you were busy making snot and getting hugs to make you feel better. Millie swallowed back the rest of her tears. She pulled out of Citron's arms. "Thanks." She went and checked beside Jolly's side of the bed. Jolly's jacket wasn't there. Neither was her penguin. Ah. "She's gone to find aspirin for me." Millie sighed with relief and guilt. "She took her penguin to trade with. That's almost her most favorite thing ever."

"Next to you, you mean."

"I suppose so. I come first, then her necklace, then the penguin." Jolly'd found the ceramic penguin a long time ago when they'd been scavenging in the wreckage of a drug store. The penguin stood on a circular base, the whole thing about ten inches tall. Its beak was broken, but when you twisted the white base, music played out of it. Jolly had kept it carefully since, wrapped in a torn blouse. She played it once a week and on special occasions. Twisted the base twice only, let the penguin do a slow turn to the few notes of tinny song. Churchy had told them that penguin was from a movie called *Madagascar*. She'd been old enough to remember old-time stuff like that. It was soon after that that they'd had to kill her.

Millie stared at her and Jolly's sleeping place. There was something . . . "She didn't take socks. Her feet must be freezing." She picked up the pair of socks with the fewest holes in it. "We have to go find her."

"You go," Citron replied. "It's cold out, and I want to get some more sleep."

"You know we're not supposed to go anywhere on our own!"

"Yeah, but we do. Lots of times."

"Except me. I always have someone with me."

"Right. Like that's any safer than being alone. I'm going back to bed." He yawned and turned away.

Millie fought the urge to yell at him. Instead she said, "I claim leader."

Citron stopped. "Aw, come on, Millie."

But Millie was determined. "Leader. One of us might be in danger, so I claim leader. So you have to be my follower."

He looked skywards and sighed. "Fine. Where?"

That meant she was leader. You asked the leader what to do, and the leader told you. Usually everyone asked Jolly what to do, or Max. Now that she had an excuse to go to Jolly, Millie stopped feeling as though something had gnawed away the pit of her stomach. She yanked her coat out of the pile of clothing that was her bed and shrugged it on. "Button me," she said to Citron, biting back the "please." Leaders didn't say please. They just gave orders. That was the right way to do it.

Citron concentrated hard on the buttons, not looking in Millie's eyes as he did them up. He started in the middle, buttoned down to the last button just below her hips, then stood up to do the buttons at her chest. He held the fabric away from her, so it wouldn't touch her body at all. His fingers didn't touch her, but still her chest felt tingly as Citron did up the top buttons. She knew he was blushing, even though you couldn't tell on his dark face. Hers neither. If it had been Max doing this, his face would have lit up like a strawberry. They found strawberries growing sometimes, in summer.

Leaders didn't blush. Millie straightened up and looked at Citron. He had such a baby face. If he was lucky, he'd never sprout. She'd heard that some people didn't. Max said it was too soon to tell, because the pandemic had only started two years ago, but Millie liked to hope that some kids would avoid the horrible thing. No temper getting worse and worse. No changing all of a sudden into something different and scary. Millie wondered briefly what happened to the ones who didn't sprout, who just got old. Food for the easthound, probably. "Maybe we should go . . ." Millie began to ask, then remembered herself. Leaders didn't ask, they told. "We're going over by the grocery first," she told Citron. "Maybe she's just checking her traps."

"She took her music box to check her traps?"

"Doesn't matter. That's where we're going to go." She stuffed Jolly's socks into her coat pocket, then shoved her shoulder against the damp-swollen door and stepped out into the watery light of an early spring morning. The sun made her blink.

Citron asked, "Shouldn't we get those two to come along with us? You know, so there's more of us?"

"No," growled Millie. "Just now you wanted me to go all alone, but now you want company?"

"But who does trading this early in the morning?"

"We're not going to wake Max and Sai, okay? We'll find her ourselves!"

Citron frowned. Millie shivered. It was so cold out that her nose-hairs froze together when she breathed in. Like scattered pins, tiny, shiny daggers of frost edged the sidewalk slabs and the new spring leaves of the small maple tree that grew outside their squat. Trust Jolly to make her get out of a warm bed to go looking for her on a morning like this. She picked up three solid throwing rocks. They were gritty with dirt and the cold of them burned her fingers. She stuffed them into her jacket pocket, on top of Jolly's socks. Citron had the baseball bat he carried everywhere. Millie turned up her collar and stuck her hand into her jeans pocket. "C'mon."

Jolly'd put a new batch of traps over by that old grocery store. The roof was caved in. There was no food in the grocery any more, or soap, or cough medicine. Everything had been scavenged by the nearby warrens of kids, but animals sometimes made nests and shit in the junk that was left. Jolly'd caught a dog once. A gaunt poodle with dirty, matted hair. But they didn't eat dogs, ever. You were what you ate. They'd only killed it in an orgy of fury and frustration that had swelled over them like a river.

Black Betty had a child,
Bam-ba-lam,
That child's gone wild,
Bam-ba-lam.

Really, it was Millie who'd started it, back before everything went wrong, two winters ago. They'd been at home. Jolly sitting on the living room floor that early evening, texting with her friends, occasionally giggling at something one of them said. Millie and Dad on the couch, sharing a bowl of raspberries. All of them watching some old-time cartoon movie on tv about animals that could do Kung Fu. Waiting for Mum to come home from work. Because then they would order pizza. It was pizza night. Dad getting a text message on his phone. Dad holding the phone down by his knee to make out the words, even though his eyesight was just fine, he said. Jolly watching them, waiting to hear if it was Mum, if she'd be home soon. Millie leaning closer to Dad and squinting at the tiny message in the phone's window. Mouthing the words silently. Then frowning. Saying, "Mum says she's coming home on the easthound train?" Dad falling out laughing. Eastbound, sweetie.

There hadn't been an easthound before that. It was Millie who'd called it, who'd made it be. Jolly'd told her that wasn't true, that she didn't make the pandemic just by reading a word wrong, that the world didn't work that way. But the world didn't work any more the way it used to, so what did Jolly know? Even if she was older than Millie.

Jolly and Millie's family had assigned adjectives to the girls early on in their lives. Millie was The Younger One. (By twenty-eight and three-quarter minutes. The midwife had been worried that Mum would need a C-section to get Millie out.) Jolly was The Kidder. She liked jokes and games. She'd come up with Loup-de-lou to help keep Millie's mind off the agony when she'd lost her hand. Millie'd still been able to feel the missing hand there, on the end of her wrist, and pain wouldn't let her sleep or rest, and all the adults in the world were sprouting and trying to kill off the kids, and Max was making her and Jolly and Citron move to a new hiding place every few days, until he and Jolly figured out the thing about sprinkling peppermint oil to hide their scent trails so that sprouteds couldn't track them. That was back before Sai had joined them, and then Churchy. Back before Churchy had sprouted on them one night in the dark as they were all sharing half a stale bread loaf and a big liter bottle of flat cola, and Max and Citron and Sai had grabbed anything heavy or sharp they could find and waled away at the thing that had been Churchy just seconds before, until it lay still on the ground, all pulpy and bloody. And the whole time, Jolly had stayed near still-weak Millie, brandishing a heavy frying pan and muttering, "It's okay, Mills. I won't let her get you."

The feeling was coming back, like her hand was still there. Her wrist had settled into a throbbing ache. She hoped it wasn't getting infected again.

Watchfully, they walked down their side street and turned onto the main street in the direction of the old grocery store. They walked up the middle of the empty road. That way, if a sprouted came out of one of the shops or alleyways, they might have time to see it before it attacked.

The burger place, the gas station, the little shoe repair place on the corner; Millie tried to remember what stores like that had been like before. When they'd had unbroken windows and unempty shelves. When there'd been people shopping in them and adults running them, back when adults used to be just grown-up people suspicious of packs of schoolkids in their stores, not howling, sharp-toothed child-killers with dank, stringy fur and paws instead of hands. Ravenous monsters that grew and grew so quickly that you could watch it happen, if you were stupid enough to stick around. Their teeth, hair and claws lengthened, their bodies getting bigger and heavier minute by minute, until they could no longer eat quickly enough to keep up with the growth, and they weakened and died a few days after they'd sprouted.

Jolly wasn't tending to her traps. Millie swallowed. "Okay, so we'll go check with the warren over on Patel Street. They usually have aspirin and stuff." She walked in silence, except for the worry voice in her head.

Citron said, "That tree's going to have to start over."

"What?" Millie realized she'd stopped at the traffic light out of habit, because it had gone to red. She was such an idiot. And so was Citron, for just going along with her. She started walking again. Citron tagged along, always just a little behind.

"The maple tree," he puffed. When you never had enough to eat, you got tired quickly. "The one outside our place. It put its leaves out too early, and now the frost has killed them. It'll have to start over."

"Whatever." Then she felt guilty for being so crabby with him. What could she say to make nice? "Uh, that was a nice line you made in Loup-de-lou last night. The one with eyes and spies in it."

Citron smiled at her. "Thanks. It wasn't quite right, though. Sprouteds have bleedy red eyes, not shiny ones."

"But your line wasn't about sprouteds. It was about the . . . the easthound." She looked all around and behind her. Nothing.

"Thing is," Citron replied, so quietly that Millie almost didn't hear him, "we're all the easthound."

Instantly, Millie swatted the back of his head. "Shut up!"

"Ow!"

"Just shut up! Take that back! It's not true!"

"Stop making such a racket, willya?"

"So stop being such a loser!" She was sweating in her jacket, her skinny knees trembling. So hungry all the time. So scared.

Citron's eyes widened. "Millie—!"

He was looking behind her. She turned, hand fumbling in her jacket pocket for her rocks. The sprouted bowled her over while her hand was still snagged in her pocket. Thick, curling fur and snarling and teeth as long as her pinkie. It grabbed her. Its paws were like catcher's mitts with claws in them. It howled and briefly let her go. It's in pain, she thought wonderingly, even as she fought her hand out of her pocket and tried to get out from under the sprouted. All that quick growing. It must hurt them. The sprouted snapped at her face, missed. They were fast and strong when they first sprouted, but clumsy in their ever-changing bodies. The sprouted set its jaws in her chest. Through her coat and sweater, its teeth tore into her skin. Pain. Teeth sliding along her ribs. Millie tried to wrestle the head off her. She got her fingers deep into the fur around its neck. Then an impact jerked the sprouted's head sideways. Citron and his baseball bat, screaming, "Die, die, die!" as he beat the sprouted. It leapt for him. It was already bigger. Millie rolled to her feet, looking around for anything she could use as a weapon. Citron was keeping the sprouted at bay, just barely, by swinging his bat at it. It advanced on him, howling in pain with every step forward.

Sai seemed to come out of nowhere. She had the piece of rebar she carried whenever she went out. The three of them raged at the sprouted, screaming and hitting. Millie kicked and kicked. The sprouted screamed back, in pain or fury. Its eyes were all bleedy. It swatted Citron aside, but he got up and came at it again. Finally it wasn't fighting any more. They kept hitting it until they were sure it was dead. Even after Sai and Citron had stopped, Millie stomped the sprouted. With each stomp she grunted, in thick animal rage at herself for letting it sneak up on her, for leaving the warren without her knife. Out of the corner of her eye she could see a few kids that had crept out from other warrens to see what the racket was about. She didn't care. She stomped.

"Millie! Millie!" It was Citron. "It's dead!"

Millie gave the bloody lump of hair and bone and flesh one more kick, then stood panting. Just a second to catch her breath, then they could keep looking for Jolly. They couldn't stay there long. A dead sprouted could draw others. If one sprouted was bad, a feeding frenzy of them was worse.

Sai was gulping, sobbing. She looked at them with stricken eyes. "I woke up and I called to Max and he didn't answer, and when I went over and lifted his coat," Sai burst into gusts of weeping, "there was only part of his head and one arm there. And bones. Not even much blood." Sai clutched herself and shuddered. "While we were sleeping, a sprouted came in and killed Max and ate most of him, even licked up his blood, and we didn't wake up! I thought it had eaten all of you! I thought it was coming back for me!"

Something gleamed white in the broken mess of the sprouted's corpse. Millie leaned over to see better, fighting not to gag on the smell of blood and worse. She had to crouch closer. There was lots of blood on the thing lying in the curve of the sprouted's body, but with chilly clarity, Millie recognized it. It was the circular base of Jolly's musical penguin. Millie looked over at Citron and Sai. "Run," she told them. The tears coursing down her face felt cool. Because her skin was so hot now.

"What?" asked Sai. "Why?"

Millie straightened. Her legs were shaking so much they barely held her up. That small pop she'd felt when she pulled on the sprouted's neck. "A sprouted didn't come into our squat. It was already in there." She opened her hand to show them the thing she'd pulled off the sprouted's throat in her battle with it; Jolly's gold necklace. Instinct often led sprouteds to return to where the people they loved were. Jolly had run away to protect the rest of her warren from herself. "Bloody run!" Millie yelled at them. "Go find another squat! Somewhere I won't look for you! Don't you get it? I'm her twin!"

First Citron's face then Sai's went blank with shock as they understood what Millie was saying. Citron sobbed, once. It might have been the word, "Bye." He grabbed Sai's arm. The two of them stumbled away. The other kids that had come out to gawk had disappeared back to their warrens. Millie turned her back so she couldn't see what direction Sai and Citron were moving in, but she could hear them, more keenly than she'd ever been able to hear. She could smell them. The easthound could track them. The downy starvation fuzz on Millie's arm was already coarser. The pain in her handless wrist spiked. She looked at it. It was aching because the hand was starting to grow in again. There were tiny fingers on the end of it now. And she needed to eat so badly.

When had Jolly sprouted? Probably way more than twenty-eight and three-quarter minutes ago. Citron and Sai's only chance was that Millie had always done everything later than her twin.

Still clutching Jolly's necklace, she began to run, too; in a different direction. Leeks, she told the sprouting Hound, fresh leeks. You like those, right? Not blood and still-warm, still-screaming flesh. You like leeks. The Hound wasn't fully come into itself yet. It was almost believing her that leeks would satisfy its hunger. And it didn't understand that she couldn't swim. You're thirsty too, right? she told it.

It was.

Faster, faster, faster, Millie sped towards the river, where the spring tide was running deep and wide.

> *That child's gone wild.*
> *Oh, Black Betty, bam-ba-lam.*

Loup.

Soul Case

In Jamaican parlance, "soul case" refers to the human body. Around the world you can find folk tales in which a wizard may remove his soul (the source of his vulnerability and the seat of his power) from his body and place it into another vessel for safe-keeping. Maronnage was the historical practice in the Caribbean of Africans rejecting slavery and retreating into the wilderness to create their own temporary autonomous zones. The term comes from the word "maroon," which is derived from the Spanish word "cimarron," which means "escaped animal." Interesting to have one's ancestors described as such. This next story contains the first scene that came to me when I began writing my novel Blackheart Man, *in which I created a maroon community and gave it the ability to develop unmolested for a couple hundred years before the slave owners tried to reclaim the humans they perceived to be theirs by right. I used literary magic to create the maroon nation of Chynchin, but in 1605, real Africans founded the free society of Palmares in Brazil, a quilombo (maroon nation) which thrived for eighty-nine years before the Portuguese army waged war on it and destroyed it. In my story, Acotiren's name is an homage to director Carlos Diegues's film* Quilombo, *which uses the iconography of Afro-Caribbean spirituality to tell a tale of ancient Palmares.*

Moments after the sun's bottom lip cleared the horizon, the brigade charged down the hill. Kima stood with the rest of the Garfun, ready to give back blow for blow.

The pistoleers descended towards the waiting village compong. Their silence unnerved. Only the paddy thump of the camels' wide feet made any sound. Compong people murmured, stepped back. But Mother Letty gestured to the Garfuns defending them to stand still. So they did. Kima felt her palm slippery on her sharpened hoe.

The pistoleers advanced upon them in five rows; some tens of impeccably uniformed men and women posting up and down in unison on their camels. Each row but the last comprised seven gangly camels, each camel ridden by a soldier, each soldier kitted out a la zouave, in identical and pristine red-and-navy with clean white shirts. Near on four muskets for each of them, and powder, carried by a small boy running beside each camel. There were only twelve muskets in the compong.

Now the first rows of camels stepped onto the pitch road that led into the village. The road was easily wide enough for seven camels across. The cool morning sun had not yet made the surface of the pitch sticky. The camels didn't even break stride. Kima made a noise of dismay. Where was the strong science that the three witches had promised them? Weeks and weeks they'd had the villagers carting reeking black pitch from the deep sink of it that lay in the gully, re-warming it on fires, mixing it with stones and spreading it into this road that led from nowhere to the entrance of the compong, and stopped abruptly there. Had they done nothing but create a smooth paved surface by which the army could enter and destroy them?

From her position at the head of the Garfuns, the black witch, the Obe Acotiren, showed no doubt. She only pursed her lips and grunted, once. Standing beside her, white Mother Letty and the Taino witch Maridowa did not even that. The three should have been behind the Garfuns, where they could be protected. If the villagers lost their Knowledgeables, they would be at the mercy of the whites' fish magic. Yet there the three stood and watched. Acotiren even had her baby grandson cotched on her hip. So the Garfuns took their cue from the three women. Like them, they kept their ground, ready but still.

"Twice five," whispered Mother Letty. "Twice six." She was counting the soldiers as they stepped onto the black road. Kima thought it little comfort to know exactly how many soldiers had come to kill them, but she found herself counting silently along with Mother Letty.

The leading edge of the army was almost upon them, scant yards from the entrance to the compong. Camels covered almost the full length of the road. A few of the Garfuns made ready to charge. "Hold," said Mother Letty. Her voice cut through the pounding of the camels. They held.

Maridowa turned her wide, brown face to the Garfuns and grinned. "Just a little more," she said. She was merry at strange times, the young Taino witch was.

The soldiers had their muskets at the ready. The barrels gleamed in the sun. The Garfuns' muskets were dull and scorched. "So many of them," whispered Kima. She raised her hoe, cocked it ready to strike. Beside her, the white boy Carter whimpered, but clutched his cutlass at the ready, a grim look on his face. He'd said he would rather die than be pressganged onto the ships once more as a sailor. He had fourteen years. If he survived this, the village would let him join the boys to be circumcised; let him become a man.

Thrice six . . .

The thrice seventh haughty camel stepped smartly onto the battlefield, a little ahead of its fellows. "That will do it," pronounced the Obe Acotiren. It wasn't quite a question.

The pitch went liquid. It was that quick. Camels began to flounder, then to sink. The villagers gasped, talked excitedly to each other. They had laid the pitch only four fingers deep! How then was it swallowing entire camels and riders?

The pitch swamp had not a care for what was possible and what not. It sucked the brigade into its greedy gullet like a pig gobbling slops. Camels mawed in dismay, the pitch snapping their narrow ankles as they tried to clamber out. They sank more quickly than their lighter riders. Soldier men and women clawed at each other, stepped on each other's heads and shoulders to fight free of the melted pitch. To no avail. The last hoarse scream was swallowed by the pitch in scarce the time it took the Obe Acotiren's fifth grandchild—the fat brown boy just past his toddling age, his older sisters and brothers having long since joined the Garfun fighters—to slip from her arms and go running for his favourite mango tree.

The black face of the road of tar was smooth and flat again, as though the army had never been.

One meager row of uniformed soldiers stared back at the Garfuns from the other side of the pitch. Their weapons hung unused from their hands. Then, together, they slapped their camels into a turn, and galloped hard for the foot of the hill.

All but one, who remained a-camelback at the bank of the river of pitch.

The pistoleer slid off her beast. She stood on the edge of where her fellows, suffocated, were slowly hardening. She bent her knees slightly, curling her upper body around her belly. Fists held out in front of her, she screamed full throat at the villagers; a raw howl of grief that used all the air in her lungs, and that went on long after she should have had none remaining. She seemed like to spit those very lungs up. Her camel watched her disinterestedly for a while, then began to wander up the hill. It stopped to crop yellow hog plums from a scraggly tree.

On the hill above, the general sounded the retreat. In vain; most of his army had already dispersed. (Over the next few weeks, many of them would straggle into Garfun compongs—some with their camels—begging asylum. This they would be granted. It was a good land, but mostly harsh scrub. It needed many to tend it.)

Some few of the Garfuns probed the pitch with their weapons. They did not penetrate. Cautiously, the Garfuns stepped onto the pitch. It was hard once more, and held them easily. They began to dance and laugh, to call for their children and their families to join them. Soon there was a celebration on the flat pitch road. An old matron tried to show Carter the steps of her dance. He did his best to follow her, laughing at his own clumsiness.

The Obe Acotiren watched the soldier woman, who had collapsed onto her knees now, her scream hiccoughing into sobs. While the army was becoming tar beneath the feet of the villagers, Acotiren had pushed through the crowd and fetched her fearless grandchild from the first branch of the mango tree. He'd fallen out of it thrice before, but every day returned to try again. She hitched him up onto her hip. He clamped his legs at her waist and fisted up a handful of her garment at the shoulder. He brought the fist happily to his mouth.

Acotiren's face bore a calm, stern sadness. "Never you mind," Kima heard her mutter in the direction of the grieving woman. "What we do today going to come back on us, and more besides." Maridowa glanced at the Obe, but said nothing.

Then Acotiren produced her obi bag from wherever she had had it hidden on her person, and tossed it onto the pitch. Mother Letty started forward. "Tiren, no!" cried Mother Letty, her face anguished.

She was too late to intercept the obi bag. It landed on the road. It was a small thing, no bigger than a guinea fowl's egg. It should have simply bounced and rolled. Instead, it sank instantly, as though it weighed as much in itself as the whole tarred army together.

Maridowa was dancing on the road, and hadn't noticed what was happening. It was Kima who saw it all. Acotiren pressed her lips together, then smiled a bright smile at her grandchild. "Come," she said. "Make I show you how to climb a mango tree."

Tranquil, as though she hadn't just tossed her soul case away to be embalmed forever in tar, she turned her back to go and play with the boy, leaving Mother Letty kneeling there, tears coursing through the lines on her ancient face as she watched her friend go.

In less than a year Acotiren was frail and bent. There was no more climbing trees for her. Her eyes had grown crystalline with cataracts, her hands tremulous, her body sere and unmuscled. One morning she walked into the bush to die, and never came out again. But by then her daughter's child, Acotiren's fifth grandchild, was so sure-footed from skinning up gru-gru bef palms and mamapom trees with his nana that he never, ever fell. Wherever he could plant his feet, he could go. His friends called him Goat.

Message in a Bottle

Size matters. The message may be the medium, but children are small.

"Whatcha doing, Kamla?" I peer down at the chubby-fingered kid who has dug her brown toes into the sand of the beach. I try to look relaxed, indulgent. She's only a child, about four years old, though that outsize head she's got looks strangely adult. It bobs around on her neck as her muscles fight for control. The adoption centre had told Babette and Sunil that their new daughter checked out perfectly healthy otherwise.

Kamla squints back up at me. She gravely considers my question, then holds her hand out, palm up, and opens it like an origami puzzle box. "I'm finding shells," she says. The shell she proffers has a tiny hermit crab sticking out of it. Its delicate body has been crushed like a ball of paper in her tight fist. The crab is most unequivocally dead.

I've managed to live a good many decades as an adult without having children in my life. I don't hate them, though I know that every childless person is supposed to say that so as not to be pecked to death by the righteous breeders of the flock. But I truly don't hate children. I just don't understand them. They seem like another species. I'll help a lost child find a parent, or give a boost to a little body struggling to get a drink from a water fountain—same as I'd do for a puppy or a kitten—but I've never had the urge to be a father. My home is also my studio, and it's a warren of tangled cables, jury-rigged networked computers, and piles of books about as stable as playing-card houses. Plus bins full of old newspaper clippings, bones of dead animals, rusted metal I picked up on the street, whatever. I don't throw anything away if it looks the least bit interesting. You never know when it might come in handy as part of an installation piece. The chaos has a certain nest-like comfort to it.

Gently, I take the dead hermit crab in its shell from Kamla's hand. She doesn't seem disturbed by my claiming her toy. "It's wrong," she tells me in her lisping child's voice. "Want to find more."

She begins to look around again, searching the sand. This is the other reason children creep me out. They don't yet grok that delicate, all-important boundary between the animate and inanimate. It's all one to them. Takes them a while to figure out that travelling from the land of the living to the land of the dead is a one-way trip.

I drop the deceased crab from a shaking hand. "No, Kamla," I say. "It's time to go in for lunch now."

I reach for her little brown fist. She pulls it away from me and curls it tightly towards her chest. She frowns up at me with that enfranchised hauteur that is the province of kings and four-year-olds. She shakes her head. "No, don't want lunch yet. Have to look for shells."

They say that play is the work of children. Kamla starts scurrying across the sand, intent on her task. But I'm responsible to Kamla's mother, not to Kamla. I promised to watch the child for an hour while Babette prepared lunch. Babs and Sunil have looked tired, desperate and drawn for a while now. Since they adopted Kamla.

There's still about twenty minutes left in my tenure as Kamla's sitter. I'm counting every minute. I run after her. She's already a good hundred yards away, stuffing shells down the front of her bright green bathing suit as quickly as she can. When I catch up with her, she won't come.

Fifteen minutes left with her. Finally, I have to pick her up. Fish-slippery in my arms, she struggles, her black hair whipping across her face as she shakes her head, "No! No!"

I haul her bodily back to the cottage, to Babette. By then, Kamla is loudly shrieking her distress, and the neighbours are watching from their quaint summer cottages. I dump Kamla into her mother's arms. Babette's expression as she takes the child blends frustration with concern. She cradles the back of Kamla's head. Kamla is prone to painful whiplash injuries.

Lunch consists of store-bought cornmeal muffins served with hot dogs cut into fingerjoint-sized pieces, and bright orange carrot sticks. The muffins have a sticky-fake sweetness. Rage forgotten, Kamla devours her meal with a contented, tuneless singing. She has slopped grape juice down the front of her bathing suit. She looks at me over the top of her cup. It's a calm, ancient gaze, and it unnerves me utterly.

Babette has slushed her grape juice and mine with vodka and lots of ice. "Remember Purple Cows?" she asks. "How sick we got on them at Frosh Week in first year?"

"What's Frosh Week?" asks Kamla.

"It's the first week of university, love. University is big people's school."

"Yes, I do know what a university is," pipes the child. Sometimes Kamla speaks in oddly complete sentences. "But what in the world is a frosh?"

"It's short for freshman," I tell her. "Those are people going to university for the first time."

"Oh." She returns to trying to stab her hot dog chunks with a sharp spear of carrot. Over the top of her head, I smile vaguely at Babette. I sip at the awful drink, gulp down my carrot sticks and sausages. As soon as my plate is empty, I make my excuses. Babette's eyes look sad as she waves me goodbye from the kitchen table. Sunil is only able to come up to their summer cottage on weekends. When he does so, Babs tells me that he sleeps most of the weekend away, too exhausted from his job to talk much to her, or to play with Kamla on the beach.

On my way out the door, I stop to look back. Kamla is sitting in Babette's lap. There's a purple Kamla-sized handprint on Babette's stained, yellow T-shirt. Kamla is slurping down more grape juice, and doesn't look up as I leave.

———

When I reached the age where my friends were starting to spawn like frogs in springtime—or whenever the hell frogs spawn—my unwillingness to do the same became more of a problem. Out on a date once with Sula, a lissom giraffe of a woman with a tongue just as supple, I mentioned that I didn't intend to have kids. She frowned. Had I ever seen her do that before?

"Really?" she said. "Don't you care about passing on your legacy?"

"You mean my surname?"

She laughed uncomfortably. "You know what I mean."

"I really don't. I'm not a king and I'm never going to be rich. I'm not going to leave behind much wealth for someone to inherit. It's not like I'm building an empire."

She made a face as though someone had dropped a mouse in her butter churn. "What are you going to do with your life, then?"

"Well," I chuckled, trying to make a joke of it, "I guess I'm going to go home and put a gun to my head, since I'm clearly no use to myself or anyone else."

Now she looked like she was smelling something rotten. "Oh, don't be morbid," she snapped.

"Huh? It's morbid to not want kids?"

"No, it's morbid to think your life has so little value that you might as well kill yourself."

"Oh, come on, Sula!"

I'd raised my voice above the low-level chatter in the restaurant. The couple at the table closest to us glanced our way. I sighed and continued: "My life has tons of value. I just happen to think it consists of more than my genetic material. Don't you?"

"I guess." But she pulled her hand away from mine. She fidgeted with her napkin in her lap. For the rest of dinner, she seemed distracted. She didn't meet my eye often, though we chatted pleasantly enough. I told her about this bunch of Sioux activists, how they'd been protesting against a university whose archaeology department had dug up one of their ancestral burial sites. I'm Rosebud Sioux on my mum's side. When the director of the department refused to reconsider, these guys had gone one night to the graveyard where his great-grandmother was buried. They'd dug up her remains, laid out all the bones, labelled them with little tags. They did jail time, but the university returned their ancestors' remains to the band council.

Sula's only response to the story was, "Don't you think the living are more important?" That night's sex was great. Sula rode me hard and put me away wet. But she wouldn't stay the night. I curled into the damp spot when she'd left, warming it with my heat. We saw each other two or three times after that, but the zing had gone out of it.

Babette and Sunil began talking about moving away from St. John's. Kamla was about to move up a grade in school. Her parents hoped she'd make new friends in a new school. Well, any friends, really. Kids tended to tease Kamla, call her names.

Babette found a job before Sunil did. She was offered a post teaching digital design at the Emily Carr Institute in Vancouver. Construction was booming there, so Sunil found work pretty easily afterwards. When she heard they were moving, Kamla threw many kinds of fits. She didn't want to leave the ocean. Sunil pointed out that there would be ocean in Vancouver. But Kamla stamped her foot. "I want this ocean right here. Don't you understand?" Sunil and Babette had made their decision, though, and Kamla was just a kid. The whole family packed up kit and caboodle in a move that Babette later told me was the most tiring thing she'd ever done.

On the phone, Babette tells me, "A week after we got here, we took Kamla down to Wreck Beach. The seals come in real close to shore, you know? You can see them peeking at you as they hide in the waves. We thought Kamla would love it."

"Did she?" I ask, only half-listening. I'm thinking about my imminent date with Cecilia, who I've been seeing for a few months now. She is lush and brown. It takes both of my hands to hold one of her breasts, and when we spoon at night, her belly fits warm in my palm like a bowl of hot soup on a cold day.

"You know what Kamla did?" Babette asks, bringing me back from my jism-damp haze. I hear the inhale and "tsp" sound of someone smoking a cigarette. Babette had started smoking again during the move. "She poked around in the sand for a few minutes, then she told us we were stupid and bad and she wasn't going to talk to us any more. Sulked the rest of the day, and wouldn't eat her dinner that night. She's still sulking now, months later."

That's another thing about kids: their single-mindedness. They latch onto an idea like a bulldog at a rabbit hole, and before you know it, you're arranging your whole life around their likes and dislikes. They're supposed to be your insurance for the future; you know, to carry your name on, and shit? My mother's been after me to breed, but I'm making my own legacy, thank you very much. A body of art I can point to and document. I'm finally supporting myself sort of decently through a combination of exhibition fees, teaching and speaking gigs. I want to ask Cecilia to move in with me, but every time I come close to doing so, I hear Sula's words in my head: *No children? Well, what are you going to do with yourself, then?* I don't know whether Cecilia wants kids, and I'm afraid to ask.

"Greg?" says Babette's voice through the telephone. "You still there?"

"Yeah. Sorry. Mind wandering."

"I'm worried about Kamla."

"Because she's upset about the move? I'm sure she'll come around. She's making friends in school, isn't she?"

"Not really. The other day, the class bully called her Baby Bobber. For the way her head moves."

I suppress a snort of laughter. It's not funny. Poor kid. "What did you do?"

"We had the school contact his parents. But it's not just that she doesn't have many friends. She's making our lives hell with this obsession for Bradley's Cove. And she's not growing."

"You mean she's, like, emotionally immature?" *Or intellectually?* I think.

"No, physically. We figure she's about eight, but she's not much bigger than a five-year-old."

"Have you taken her to the doctor?"

"Yeah. They're running some tests."

Cecilia can jerry-rig a computer network together in a matter of minutes. We geekspeak at each other all the time. When we're out in public, people fall silent in linguistic bafflement around us.

"They say Kamla's fine," Babette tells me, "and we should just put more protein in her diet."

Cecilia and I are going to go shopping for a new motherboard for her, then we're going to take blankets and pillows to the abandoned train out in the old rail yards and hump like bunnies till we both come screaming. Maybe she'll wear those white stockings under her clothes. The sight of the gap of naked brown thigh between the tops of the stockings and her underwear always makes me hard.

Babette says, "There's this protein drink for kids. Makes her pee bright yellow."

The other thing about becoming a parent? It becomes perfectly normal to discuss your child's excreta with anyone who'll sit still for five minutes. When we were in art school together, Babette used to talk about gigabytes, Cronenberg and post-humanism.

I can hear someone else ringing through on the line. It's probably Cecilia. I mutter a quick reassurance at Babette and get her off the phone.

Kamla never does get over her obsession with the beach, and with shells. By the time she is nine, she's accumulated a library's worth of reference books with names like *Molluscs of the Eastern Seaboard*, and *Seashells: Nature's Wonder*. She continues to grow slowly. At ten years old, people mistake her for six. Sunil and Babette send her for test after test.

"She's got a full set of adult teeth," Babette tells me as we sit in a coffee shop on Churchill Square. "And all the bones in her skull are fused."

"That sounds dangerous," I say.

"No, it happens to all of us once we've stopped growing. Her head's fully grown, even if the rest of her isn't. I guess that's something. You gonna eat those fries?"

Babette's come home to visit relatives. She's quit smoking, and she's six months pregnant. If she'd waited two more months, the airline wouldn't have let her travel until the baby was born. "Those symptoms of Kamla's," says Babette, "they're all part of the DGS."

The papers have dubbed it "Delayed Growth Syndrome." Its official name is Diaz Syndrome, after the doctor who first identified it. There are thousands of kids with Kamla's condition. It's a brand new disorder. Researchers have no clue what's causing it, or if the bodies of the kids with it will ever achieve full adulthood. Their brains, however, are way ahead of their bodies. All the kids who've tested positive for DGS are scarily smart.

"Kamla seems to be healthy," Babette tells me. "Physically, anyway. It's her emotional state I'm worried about."

I say, "I'm gonna have some dessert. You want anything?"

"Yeah, something crunchy with meringue and caramel. I want it to be so sweet that the roof of my mouth tries to crawl away from it."

Cecilia's doing tech support for somebody's office today. Weekend rates. My mum's keeping an eye on our son Russ, who's two and a half. Yesterday we caught him scooping up ants into his mouth from an anthill he'd found in the backyard. He was giggling at the way they tickled his tongue, chomping down on them as they scurried about. His mouth was full of anthill mud. He didn't even notice that he was being bitten until Cecilia and I asked him. That's when he started crying in pain, and he was inconsolable for half an hour. I call him our creepy little alien child. We kinda had him by accident, me and Cece. She didn't want kids any more than I did, but when we found out she was pregnant, we both got . . . curious, I guess.

Curious to see what this particular life adventure would be; how our small brown child might change a world that desperately needs some change. We sort of dared each other to go through with it, and now here we are. Baby's not about changing anyone's world but ours just yet, though. We've both learned the real meaning of sleep deprivation. That morning when he was so constipated that trying to shit made him scream in pain, I called Babette in panic. Turns out poo and pee are really damned important, especially when you're responsible for the life of a small, helpless being that can barely do anything else. Russ gurgles with helpless laughter when I blow raspberries on his tummy. And there's a spot on his neck, just under his ear, that smells sweet, even when the rest of him is stinky. He's a perfect specimen; all his bits are in proportion. The next time I meet Babette for lunch I ask Babette what new thing is bothering her about her kid, if not the delayed growth.

"She gets along fine with me and Sunil, you know? I feel like I can talk to her about anything. But she gets very frustrated with kids her age. She wants to play all these elaborate games, and some of them don't understand. Then she gets angry. She came stomping home from a friend's place the other day and went straight to her room. When I looked in on her, she was sitting looking in her mirror. There were tears running down her cheeks. 'I bloody hate being a kid,' she said to me. 'The other kids are stupid, and my hand-eye coordination sucks.'"

"She said that her hand-eye coordination sucked? That sounds almost too . . ."

"Yeah, I know. Too grown up for a ten-year-old. She probably had to grow up quickly, being an adoptee."

"You ever find out where she came from before you took her?"

Babette shakes her head. She's eaten all of her pavlova and half of my carrot cake.

It just so happens that I have a show opening at Eastern Edge while Babette and Sunil are in town. "The Excavations," I call it. It was Russ's anthill escapade that gave me the idea. I've trucked in about half a ton of dirt left over from a local archaeological dig. I wish I could have gotten it directly from Mexico, but I couldn't afford the permit for doing that. I seeded the soil with the kinds of present-day historical artifacts that the researchers tossed aside in their zeal to get to the iconic past of the native peoples of the region: a rubber boot that had once belonged to a Mayan Zapatista from Chiapas; a large plastic jug that used to hold bleach, and that had been refitted as a bucket for a small child to tote water in; a scrap of hand-woven blanket with brown stains on it. People who enter the exhibition get basic excavation tools. When they pull something free of the soil, it triggers a story about the artifact on the monitors above. Sunil is coming to the opening. Babette has decided to stay at her relatives' place and nap. Six months along in her pregnancy, she's sleepy a lot.

I'm holding court in the gallery, Cecilia striding around the catwalk above me, doing a last check of all the connections, when Sunil walks in. He's brought Kamla. She doesn't alarm me any more. She's just a kid. As I watch her grow up, I get some idea of what Russ's growing years will be like. In a way, she's his advance guard.

Kamla scurries in ahead of her dad, right up to me, her head wobbling as though her neck is a column of gelatin. She sticks out her hand. "Hey, Greg," she says. "Long time." Behind her, Sunil gives me a bashful smile.

I reach down to shake the hand of what appears to be a six-year-old.

"Uh, hey," I say. Okay, I lied a little bit. I still don't really know how to talk to kids.

"This looks cool," she tells me, gazing around. "What do we do?" She squats down and starts sifting soil through her fingers.

"Kamla, you mustn't touch the art," says Sunil.

I say, "Actually, it's okay. That's exactly what I want people to do."

Kamla flashes me a grateful glance. I give her a small spade and take her through the exhibition. She digs up artifact after artifact, watches the stories about them on the video displays, asks me questions. I get so caught up talking to her about my project that I forget how young she is. She seems really interested. Most of the other people are here because they're friends of mine, or because it's cool to be able to say that you went to an art opening last weekend. The gallery owner has to drag me away to be interviewed by the guy from *Art(ext)/e*. I grin at Kamla and leave her digging happily in the dirt.

While I'm talking to the interviewer, Kamla comes running up to me, Sunil behind her yelling, "Kamla! Don't interrupt!"

She ignores him, throws her mushroom-shaped body full tilt into my arms, and gives me a whole body hug. "It was you!" she says. "It was you!" She's clutching something in one dirt-encrusted fist. The guy from *Art(ext)/e* kinda freezes up at the sight of Kamla. But he catches himself, pastes the smile back on, motions his camerawoman to take a picture.

"I'm so sorry," Sunil says. "When she gets an idea in her head . . ."

"Yeah, I know. What'd you find, chick?" I ask Kamla. She opens her palm to show me. It's a shell. I shake my head. "Honestly? I barely remember putting that in there. Some of the artifacts are 'blanks' that trigger no stories. The dig where I got it from used to be underwater a few centuries ago."

"It's perfect!" says Kamla, squeezing me hard.

Perfect like she isn't. Damn.

"I've been looking everywhere for this!" she tells me.

"What, is it rare or something?" I ask her.

She rears back in my arms so that she can look at me properly. "You have no idea," she says. "I'm going to keep this so safe. It'll never get out of my sight again."

"Kamla!" scolds Sunil. "That is part of Greg's exhibition. It's staying right here with him."

The dismay on Kamla's face would make a stone weep. It's obvious that it hadn't even occurred to her that I mightn't let her have the shell. Her eyes start to well up.

"Don't cry," I tell her. "It's just an old shell. Of course you can take it."

"You shouldn't indulge her," Sunil says. "You'll spoil her."

I hitch Kamla up on my hip, on that bone adults have that seems tailor-made for cotching a child's butt on. "Let's call it her reward for asking some really smart questions about the exhibition."

Sunil sighs. Kamla's practically glowing, she's so happy. My heart warms to her smile.

When the phone rings at my home many hours later, it takes me a while to orient myself. It's 3:05 a.m. by the clock by our bedside. "Hello?" I mumble into the phone. I should have known better than to have that fifth whiskey at the opening. My mouth feels and tastes like the plains of the Serengeti, complete with lion spoor.

"Greg?" The person is whispering. "Is this Greg?"

It's a second or so before I recognise the voice. "Kamla? What's wrong? Is your mum okay?"

"They're fine. Everyone's asleep."

"Like you should be. Why the fuck are you calling me at this hour?" I ask, forgetting that I'm talking to a child. Something about Kamla's delivery makes it easy to forget.

"I've been on the Net. Listen, can you come get me? The story's about to break. It's all over Twitter and YouTube already. It'll be on the morning news here in a few hours. Goddamned Miles. We told them he was always running his mouth off."

"What? Told who? Kamla, what's going on?"

Cecilia is awake beside me. She's turned on the bedside lamp. *Who?* she mouths. I make my lips mime a soundless *Kamla*.

"It's a long story," Kamla says. "Please, can you just come get me? You need to know about this. And I need another adult to talk to, someone who isn't my caretaker."

Whatever's going on, she really sounds upset. "Okay, I'll be there soon."

Kamla gives me the address, and I hang up. I tell Cecilia what's going on.

"You should just let Babs and Sunil know that she's disturbed about something," she says. "Maybe it's another symptom of that DGS."

"I'll talk to them after Kamla tells me what's going on," I say. "I promised her to hear her out first."

"You sure that's wise? She's a child, Greg. Probably she just had a nightmare."

Feeding our child has made Cecilia's breasts sit lower on her rib cage. Her hips stretch out the nylon of her nightgown. Through the translucent fabric I can see the shadow of pubic hair and the valley that the curves of her thighs make. Her eyes are full of sleep, and her hair is a tousled mess, and she's so beautiful I could tumble her right now. But there's this frightened kid waiting to talk to me. I kiss Cecilia goodbye and promise to call her as soon as I've learned more.

Kamla's waiting for me outside the house when I pull up in my car. The night air is a little chilly, and she's a lonely, shivering silhouette against the front door. She makes to come in the passenger side of the car, but I motion her around to my side. "We're going to leave a note for your parents first," I tell her. I have one already prepared. "And we're just going sit right here in the car and talk."

"We can leave a note," she replies, "but we have to be away from here long enough so you can hear the whole story. I can't have Sunil and Babette charging to the rescue right now."

I've never heard her call her parents by their first names; Babs and Sunil aren't into that kind of thing. Her face in her weirdly adult head looks calm, decisive. I find myself acquiescing. So I slip the note under the front door. It tells Babette and Sunil that Kamla's with me, that everything's all right. I leave them my cell phone number, though I'm pretty sure that Babette already has it.

Kamla gets into the car. She quietly closes the door. We drive. I keep glancing over at her, but for a few minutes, she doesn't say anything. I'm just about to ask her what was so urgent that she needed to pull a stunt like this when she says, "Your installation had a certain antique brio to it, Greg. Really charming. My orig—I mean, I have a colleague whose particular interest is in the nascent identity politics as expressed by artists of the twentieth and twenty-first centuries, and how that expression was the progenitor of current speciesism."

"Have you been reading your mum's theory books?"

"No," she replies. There was so much bitterness in that one word. "I'm just a freak. Your kid's almost three, right?"

"Yeah."

"In a blink of an eye, barely a decade from now, his body will be entering puberty. He'll start getting erections, having sexual thoughts."

"I don't want to think about all that right now," I say. "I'm still too freaked that he's begun making poo-poo jokes. Kamla, is this the thing you wanted to tell me? Cause I'm not getting it."

"A decade from now, I'll have the body of a seven-year-old."

"You can't know that. There aren't any DGS kids who've reached their twenties yet."

"I know. I'm the oldest of them, by a few weeks."

Another thing she can't know.

"But we're all well past the age where normal children have achieved adolescence."

Goggling at her, I almost drive through a red light. I slam on the brakes. The car jolts to a halt. "What? What kind of shit is that? You're ten years old. A precocious ten, yes, but only ten."

"Go in there." She points into the parking lot of a nearby grocery store. "It won't be open for another three hours."

I pull into the lot and park. "If the cops come by and see us," I say, "I could be in a lot of shit. They'll think I'm some degenerate Indian perv with a thing for little girls."

Shit. I shouldn't be talking to a ten-year-old this way. Kamla always makes me forget. It's that big head, those big words.

"DGS people do get abused," she tells me. "Just like real children do."

"You *are* a real child!"

She glares at me, then looks sad. She says, "Sunil and Babette are going to have to move soon. It's so hard for me to keep up this pretence. I've managed to smartmouth so much at school and in our neighbourhood that it's become uncomfortable to live there anymore."

My eyes have become accustomed enough to the dark that I can see the silent tears running down her cheeks. I want to hold her to me, to comfort her, but I'm afraid of how that will look if the cops show up. Besides, I'm getting the skin-crawly feeling that comes when you realise that someone with whom you've been making pleasant conversation is as mad as a hatter. "I'm taking you back home," I whisper. I start turning the key in the ignition.

"Please!" She puts a hand on my wrist. "Greg, please hear me out. I'll make it quick. I just don't know how to convince you."

I take my hand off the key. "Just tell me," I said. "Whatever it is, your parents love you. You can work it out."

She leans back against the passenger side door and curls her knees up to her chest, a little ball of misery. "Okay. Let me get it all out before you say anything else, all right?"

"All right."

"They grew us from cells from our originals; ten of us per original. They used a viral injection technique to put extra-long tails on one of the strands of our DNA. You need more telomeres to slow down aging."

The scientific jargon exiting smoothly from the mouth of a child could have been comic. But I had goose bumps. She didn't appear to be repeating something she'd memorised.

"Each batch of ten yielded on average four viable blastocytes. They implanted those in womb donors. Two-thirds of them took. Most of those went to full term and were delivered. Had to be C-sections, of course. Our huge skulls presented too much of a risk for our birth mothers. We were usually four years old before we were strong enough to lift our own heads, and that was with a lot of physiotherapy. They treated us really well; best education, kept us fully informed from the start of what they wanted from us."

"Which was?" I whisper, terrified to hear the answer.

"Wait. You said you would." She continues her story. "Any of us could back out if we wanted to. Ours is a society that you would probably find strange, but we do have moral codes. Any of us who didn't want to make the journey could opt to undergo surgical procedures to correct some of the physical changes. Bones and muscles would lengthen, and they would reach puberty normally and thereafter age like regular people. They'll never achieve full adult height, and there'll always be something a little bit odd about their features, but it probably won't be so bad.

"But a few of us were excited by the idea, the crazy, wonderful idea, and we decided to go through with it. They waited until we were age thirteen for us to confirm our choice. In many cultures, that used to be the age when you were allowed to begin making adult decisions."

"You're ten, Kamla."

"I'm twenty-three, though my body won't start producing adult sex hormones for another fifty years. I won't attain my full growth till I'm in my early hundreds. I can expect—"

"You're delusional," I whisper.

"I'm from your future," she says. God. The child's been watching too many B-movies. She continues, "They wanted to send us here and back as full adults, but do you have any idea what the freight costs would have been? The insurance? Arts grants are hard to get in my world, too. The gallery had to scale the budget way back."

"Gallery?"

"National gallery. Hush. Let me talk. They sent small people instead. Clones of the originals, with their personalities superimposed onto our own. They sent back children who weren't children."

I start the car. I'm taking her back home right now. She needs help; therapy, or something. The sky's beginning to brighten. She doesn't try to stop me this time.

Glumly, she goes on. "The weird thing is, even though this body isn't interested in adult sex, I *remember* what it was like, remember enjoying it. It's those implanted memories from my original."

I'm edging past the speed limit in my hurry to get her back to her parents. I make myself slow down a little.

"Those of us living in extremely conservative or extremely poor places are having a difficult time. We stay in touch with them by email and cell phone, and we have our own closed Facebook group, but not all of us have access to computer technology. We've never been able to figure out what happened to Kemi. Some of us were never adopted, had to make our own way as street kids. Never old enough to be granted adult freedoms. So many lost. This fucking project better have been worth it."

I decide to keep her talking. "What project, Kamla?"

"It's so *hard* to pretend you don't have an adult brain! Do you know what it's like turning in schoolwork that's at a grade-five level, when we all have PhD's in our heads? We figured that one of us would crack, but we hoped it'd be later, when we'd reached what your world would consider the age of majority."

We're cruising past a newspaper box. I look through its plastic window to see the headline: "I'M FROM THE FUTURE," SAYS BOBBLE-HEADED BOY. Ah. One of our more erudite news organs.

Oh, Christ. They all have this delusion. All the DGS kids. For a crazy half-second, I find myself wondering whether Sunil and Babette can return Kamla to the adoption centre. And I'm guiltily grateful that Russ, as far as we can tell, is normal.

"Human beings, we're becoming increasingly post-human," Kamla says. She's staring at the headline, too. "Things change so quickly. Total technological upheaval of society every five to eight years. Difficult to keep up, to connect amongst the generations. By the time your Russ is a teenager, you probably won't understand his world at all."

She's hit on the thing that really scares me about kids. This brave new world that Cecilia and I are trying to make for our son? For the generations to follow us? We won't know how to live in it.

Kamla says, "Art helps us know how to do change. That's made it very valuable to us."

"Thank heaven for that," I say, humouring her. "Maybe I'd like your world."

She sits up in her seat, buckles herself in. Shit. I should have made her do that the minute she got in the car. I have one of those heart-in-the-mouth moments that I have often, now that I'm a parent. "In my world," she says, "what you do would be obsolete." She sniggers a little. "Video monitors! I'd never seen a real one, only minibeams disguised to mimic ancient tech. Us DGSers have all become anthropologists here in the past, as well as curators."

"Wait; you're a what?"

"I'm a curator, Greg. I'm trying to tell you; our national gallery is having a giant retrospective; tens of thousands of works of art from all over the world, and all over the world's history. They sent us back to retrieve some of the pieces that had been destroyed. Expensive enough to send living biomaterial back; their grant wasn't enough to pay for returning us to our time. So we're going to *grow* our way there. Those of us that survive."

There are more cars out on the road, more brakes squealing, more horns honking. "I'm not going to miss mass transit when I finally get home," she says. "Your world stinks."

"Yeah, it does." We're nearly to her parents' place. From my side, I lock her door. Of course she notices. She just glances at the sound. She looks like she's being taken to her death.

"I didn't know it until yesterday," she tells me, "but it was you I came for. That installation."

And now the too-clever bloody child has me where I live. Though I know it's all air pie and Kamla is as nutty as a fruitcake, my heart's performing a tympanum of joy. "My installation's going to be in the retrospective?" I ask. Even as the words come out of my mouth, I'm embarrassed at how eager I sound, at how this little girl, as children will, has dug her way into my psyche and found the thing which will make me respond to her.

She gasps and puts her hand to her mouth. "Oh, Greg! I'm so sorry; not you, the shell!"

My heart suicides, the brief, hallucinatory hope dashed. "The shell?"

"Yes. In the culture where I live, speciesism has become a defining concept through which we understand what it means to be human animals. Not every culture or subculture ascribes to it, but the art world of my culture certainly does." She's got her teacher voice on again. She does sound like a bloody curator. "Human beings aren't the only ones who make art," she says.

All right. Familiar territory. "Okay, perhaps. Bower birds make pretty nests to attract a mate. Cetaceans sing to each other. But we're the only ones who make art *mean*; who make it comment on our everyday reality."

From the corner of my eye, I see her shake her oversized head. "No. We don't always know what they're saying, we can't always know the reality on which they're commenting. Who knows what a sea cucumber thinks of the conditions of its particular stretch of ocean floor?"

A sea cucumber? We've just turned onto her parents' street. She'll be out of my hands soon. Poor Babette.

"Every shell is different," she says.

My perverse brain instantly puts it to the tune of "Every Sperm Is Sacred."

She continues, "Every shell is a life journal, made out of the very substance of its creator, and left as a record of what it thought, even if we can't understand exactly what it thought. Sometimes interpretation is a trap. Sometimes we need to simply observe."

"And you've come all this way to take that . . . shell back?" I can see it sticking out of the chest pocket of her fleece shirt.

"It's difficult to explain to you, because you don't have the background, and I don't have the time to teach you. I specialise in shell formations. I mean, that's Vanda's specialty. She's the curator whose memories I'm carrying. Of its kind, the mollusc that made this shell is a genius. The unique conformation of the whorls of its shell expresses a set of concepts that haven't been explored before by the other artists of its species. After this one, all the others will draw on and riff off its expression of its world. They're the derivatives, but this is the original. In our world, it was lost."

Barmy. Loony. "So how did you know that it even existed, then? Did the snail or slug that lived inside it take pictures or something?" I've descended into cruelty. I'm still smarting that Kamla hasn't picked me, my work. My legacy doesn't get to go to the future.

She gives me a wry smile, as though she understands.

I pull up outside the house, start leaning on the horn. Over the noise, she shouts, "The creature didn't take a picture. You did."

Fuck, fuck, fuck. With my precious video camera. I'd videotaped every artifact with which I'd seeded the soil that went onto the gallery floor. I didn't tell her that.

She nods. "Not all the tape survived, so we didn't know who had recorded it, or where the shell had come from. But we had an idea where the recording had come from."

Lights are coming on in the house. Kamla looks over there and sighs. "I haven't entirely convinced you, have I?"

"No," I say regretfully. But damn it, a part of me still hopes that it's all true.

"They're probably going to institutionalise me. All of us."

The front door opens. Sunil is running out to the car, a gravid Babette following more slowly.

"You have to help me, Greg. Please? We're going to outlive all our captors. We will get out. But in the meantime . . ."

She pulls the shell out of her pocket, offers it to me on her tiny palm. "Please keep it safe for me?"

She opens the car door. "It's your ticket to the future," she says, and gets out of the car to greet her parents.

I lied. I fucking hate kids.

The Smile on the Face

Innocent young ladies of Niger will sometimes mess around with tigers.

There was a young lady . . .

"Geez, who gives a damn what a . . . what? What a laidly worm is, anyway?" Gilla muttered. She was curled up on the couch, school library book on her knees.

"Mm?" said her mother, peering at the computer monitor. She made a noise of impatience and hit a key on the keyboard a few times.

"Nothing, Mum. Just I don't know what this book's talking about." Boring old school assignment. Gilla wanted to go and get ready for Patricia's party, but Mum had said she should finish her reading first.

"Did you say, 'laidly worm'?" her mother asked. Her fingers were clicking away at the keyboard again now. Gilla wished she could type that quickly. But that would mean practising, and she wasn't about to do any more of that than she had to.

"Yeah." Damn. If Mum had heard that, she'd probably heard her say, "shit," too.

"It's a type of dragon."

Looks like she wasn't going to pay attention to the other word that Gilla had used. This time, anyway. "So why don't they just call it that?" Gilla asked her.

"It's a special type. It doesn't have wings, so it just crawls along the ground. Its skin oozes all the time. Guess that protects it when it crawls, like a slug's slime."

"Yuck, Mum!"

Gilla's mother smiled, even as she was writing. "Well, you wanted to know."

"No, I didn't. I just have to know, for school."

"A laidly worm's always ravenous and it makes a noise like a cow in gastric distress."

Gilla giggled. Her mother stopped typing and finally looked at her. "You know, I guess you could think of it as a larval dragon. Maybe it eats and eats so it'll have enough energy to moult into the flying kind. What a cool idea. I'll have to look into it." She turned back to her work. "Why do you have to know about it? What're you reading?"

"This lady in the story? Some guy wanted to marry her, but she didn't like him, so he put her in his dungeon . . ."

". . . and came after her one night in the form of a laidly worm to eat her," Gilla's mother finished. "You're learning about Margaret of Antioch?"

Gilla boggled at her. "Saint Margaret, yeah. How'd you know?"

"How?" Her mother swivelled the rickety steno chair round to face Gilla and grinned, brushing a tangle of dreadlocks back from her face. "Sweetie, this is your mother, remember? The professor of African and Middle Eastern Studies?"

"Oh." And her point? Gilla could tell that her face had that "huh?" look. Mum probably could see it too, 'cause she said:

"Gilla, Antioch was in ancient Turkey. In the Middle East?"

"Oh yeah, right. Mum, can I get micro-braids?"

Now it was her mum looking like, "huh?" "What in the world are those, Gilla?"

Well, at least she was interested. It wasn't a "no" straight off the bat. "These tiny braid extensions, right? Maybe only four or five strands per braid. And they're straight, not like . . . Anyway, Kashy says that the hairdressing salon across from school does them. They braid the extensions right into your own hair, any colour you want, as long as you want them to be, and they can style them just like that. Kashy says it only takes a few hours, and you can wear them in for six weeks."

Her mum came over, put her warm palms gently on either side of Gilla's face and looked seriously into her eyes. Gilla hated when she did that, like she was still a little kid. "You want to tame your hair," her mother said. Self-consciously, Gilla pulled away from her mum's hands, smoothed back the cloudy mass that she'd tied out of the way with a bandanna so that she could do her homework without getting hair in her eyes, in her mouth, up her nose. Her mum continued, "You want hair that lies down and plays dead, and you want to pay a lot of money for it, and you want to do it every six weeks."

Gilla pulled her face away. The book slid off her knee to the floor. "Mum, why do you always have to make everything sound so horrible?" Some of her hair had slipped out of the bandanna; it always did. Gilla could see three or four black sprigs of it dancing at the edge of her vision, tickling her forehead. She untied the bandanna and furiously retied it, capturing as much of the bushy mess as she could and binding it tightly with the cloth.

Her mother just shook her head at her. "Stop being such a drama queen. How much do micro-braids cost?"

Gilla was ashamed to tell her now, but she named a figure, a few bucks less than the sign in the salon window had said. Her mother just raised one eyebrow at her.

"That, my girl, is three months of your allowance."

Well, yeah. She'd been hoping that Mum and Dad would pay for the braids. Guess not.

"Tell you what; you save up for it, then you can have them."

Gilla grinned.

"But," her mother continued, "you have to continue buying your bus tickets while you're saving."

Gilla stopped grinning.

"Don't look so glum. If you make your own lunch to take every day, it shouldn't be so bad. Now, finish reading the rest of the story."

And Mum was back at her computer again, tap-tap-tap. Gilla pouted at her back but didn't say anything, 'cause really, she was kind of pleased. She was going to get micro-braids! She hated soggy, made-the-night-before sandwiches, but it'd be worth it. She ignored the little voice in her mind that was saying, "every six weeks?" and went back to her reading.

"Euw, gross."

"Now what?" her mother asked.

"This guy? This, like, laidly worm guy thing? It *eats* Saint Margaret, and then she's in his stomach; like, *inside* him! And she prays to Jesus, and she's sooo holy that the wooden cross around her neck turns back into a tree, and it puts its roots into the ground *through* the dragon guy thing, and its branches bust him open and he dies, and out she comes!"

"Presto bingo," her mum laughs, "Instant patron saint of childbirth!"

"Why?" But Gilla thought about that one a little bit, and she figured she might know why. "Never mind, don't tell me. So they made her a saint because she killed the dragon guy thing?"

"Well yes, they sainted her eventually, after a bunch of people tortured and executed her for refusing to marry that man. She was a convert to Christianity, and she said she'd refused him because he wasn't a Christian. But some people think that she wasn't a Christian any more either, at least not by the end."

"Huh?" Was Kashy ever gonna show up? It was almost time for the party to start.

"That thing about the wooden cross turning back into a living tree? That's not a very Christian symbol, that sprouting tree. A dead tree made into the shape of a cross, yes. But not a living, magical tree. That's a pagan symbol. Maybe Margaret of Antioch was the one who commanded the piece of wood around her neck to sprout again. Maybe the story is telling us that when Christianity failed her, she claimed her power as a wood witch. I think that Margaret of Antioch was a hamadryad."

"A cobra?" That much they had learned in school. Gilla knew the word "hamadryad."

Her mother laughed. "Yeah, a king cobra is a type of hamadryad, but I'm talking about the original meaning. A hamadryad was a female spirit whose soul resided in a tree. A druid is a man, a tree wizard. A hamadryad is a woman; a tree witch, I guess you could say. But where druids lived outside of trees and learned everything they could about them, a hamadryad doesn't need a class to learn about it. She just *is* a tree."

Creepy. Gilla glanced out the window to where black branches beckoned, clothed obscenely in tiny spring leaves. She didn't want to talk about trees.

The doorbell rang. "Oh," said Gilla. "That must be Kashy!" She sprang up to get the door, throwing her textbook aside again.

There was a young lady of Niger . . .

"It kind of creaks sometimes, y'know?" Gilla enquired of Kashy's reflection in the mirror.

In response, Kashy just tugged harder at Gilla's hair. "Hold still, girl. Lemme see what I can do with this. And shut up with that weirdness. You're always going on about that tree. Creeps me out."

Gilla sighed, resigned, and leaned back in the chair. "Okay. Only don't pull it too tight, okay? Gives me a headache." When Kashy had a makeover jones on her, there was nothing to do but submit and hope you could wash the goop off your face and unstick your hair from the mousse before you had to go outdoors and risk scaring the pigeons. That last experiment of Kashy's with the "natural" lipstick had been such a disaster. Gilla had been left looking as though she'd been eating fried chicken and had forgotten to wash the grease off her mouth. It had been months ago, but Foster was still giggling over it.

Gilla crossed her arms. Then she checked out the mirror and saw how that looked, how it made her breasts puff out. She remembered

Roger in the schoolyard, pointing at her the first day back at school in September and bellowing, "Boobies!" She put her arms on the rests of the chair instead. She sucked her stomach in and took a quick glance in the mirror to see if that made her look slimmer. Fat chance. Really fat. It did make her breasts jut again, though; oh, goody. She couldn't win. She sighed once more and slumped a little in the chair, smushing both bust and belly into a lumpy mass.

"And straighten up, okay?" Kashy said. "I can't reach the front of your head with you sitting hunched over like that." Kashy's hands were busy, sectioning Gilla's thick black hair into four and twisting each section into plaits.

"That tree," Gilla replied. "The one in the front yard."

Kashy just rolled her perfectly made-up eyes. "Okay, so tell me again about that wormy old cherry tree."

"I don't like it. I'm trying to sleep at night, and all I can hear is it creaking and groaning and . . . *talking* to itself all night!"

"Talking!" Kashy giggled. "So now it's talking to you?"

"Yes. Swaying. Its branches rubbing against each other. Muttering and whispering at me, night after night. I hate that tree. I've always hated it. I wish Mum or Dad would cut it down." Gilla sighed. Since she'd started ninth grade two years ago, Gilla sighed a lot. That's when her body, already sprouting with puberty, had laid down fat pads on her chest, belly and thighs. When her high, round butt had gotten rounder. When her budding breasts had swelled even bigger than her mother's. And when she'd started hearing the tree at night.

"What's it say?" Kashy asked. Her angular brown face stared curiously at Gilla in the mirror.

Gilla looked at Kashy, how she had every hair in place, how her shoulders were slim and how the contours of the tight sweater showed off her friend's tiny, pointy breasts. Gilla and Kashy used to be able to wear each other's clothes, until two years ago.

"Don't make fun of me."

"I'm not." Kashy's voice was serious; the look on her face, too. "I know it's been bothering you. What do you hear the tree saying?"

"It . . . it talks about the itchy places it can't reach, where its bark has gone knotty. It talks about the taste of soil, all gritty and brown. It says it likes the feeling of worms sliding in and amongst its roots in the wet, dark earth."

"Gah! You're making this up!"

"I'm not!" Gilla stormed out of her chair, pulling her hair out of Kashy's hands. "If you're not going to believe me, then don't ask, okay?"

"Okay, okay, I believe you!" Kashy shrugged her shoulders, threw her palms skyward in a gesture of defeat. "Slimy old worms feel good, just"—she reached out and slid her hands briskly up and down Gilla's bare arms—"rubbing up against you!" And she laughed, that perfect Kashy laugh, like tiny, friendly bells.

Gilla found herself laughing too. "Well, that's what it says!"

"All right, girl. What else does it say?"

At first Gilla didn't answer. She was too busy shaking her hair free of the plaits, puffing it up with her hands into a kinky black cloud. "I'm just going to wear it like this to the party, okay? I'll tie it back with my bandanna and let it poof out behind me. That's the easiest thing." *I'm never going to look like you, Kashy. Not any more.* In the upper grades at school, everybody who hung out together looked alike. The skinny glam girls hung with the skinny glam girls. The goth guys and girls hung out in back of the school and shared clove cigarettes and black lipstick. The fat girls clumped together. How long would Kashy stay tight with her? Turning so she couldn't see her own plump, gravid body in the mirror, she dared to look at her friend. Kashy was biting her bottom lip, looking contrite.

"I'm sorry," she said. "I shouldn't have laughed at you."

"It's okay." Gilla took a cotton ball from off the dresser, doused it in cold cream, started scraping the makeup off her face. She figured she'd keep the eyeliner on. At least she had pretty eyes, big and brown and sparkly. She muttered at Kashy, "It says it likes stretching and growing, reaching for the light."

Who went for a ride . . .

"Bye, Mum!" Gilla and Kashy surged out the front door. Gilla closed it behind her, then, standing on her doorstep with her friend, took a deep breath and turned to face the cherry tree. Half its branches were dead. The remaining twisted ones made a mockery of the tree's spring finery of new green leaves. It crouched on the front lawn, gnarling at them. It stood between them and the curb, and the walkway was super long. They'd have to walk under the tree's grasping branches the whole way.

The sun was slowly diving down the sky, casting a soft orange light on everything. Daylean, Dad called it; that time between the two worlds of day and night when anything could happen. Usually Gilla liked this time of day best. Today she scowled at the cherry tree and told Kashy, "Mum says women used to live in the trees."

"What, like, in tree houses? Your mum says the weirdest things, Gilla."

"No. They used to be the spirits of the trees. When the trees died, so did they."

"Well, this one's almost dead, and it can't get you. And you're going to have to walk past it to reach the street, and I know you want to go to that party, so take my hand and come on."

Gilla held tight to her friend's firm, confident hand. She could feel the clammy dampness of her own palm. "Okay," Kashy said, "on three, we're gonna run all the way to the curb, all right? One, two, three!"

And they were off, screeching and giggling, Gilla doing her best to stay upright in her new wedgies, the first thing even close to high heels that her parents had ever let her wear. Gilla risked a glance sideways. Kashy looked graceful and coltish. Her breasts didn't bounce. Gilla put on her broadest smile, screeched extra loud to let the world know how much fun she was having, and galumphed her way to streetside. As she and Kashy drew level with the tree, she felt the tiniest "bonk" on her head. She couldn't brush whatever it was off right away, 'cause she needed her hands to keep her balance. Laughing desperately from all this funfunfun, she ran. They made it safely to the curb. Kashy bent, panting, to catch her breath. For all that she looked so trim, she had no wind at all. Gilla swam twice a week and was on the volleyball team, and that little run had barely even given her a glow. She started searching with her hands for whatever had fallen in her hair.

It was smooth, roundish. It had a stem. She pulled it out and looked at it. A perfect cherry. So soon? She could have sworn that the tree hadn't even blossomed yet. "Hah!" she yelled at the witchy old tree. She brandished the cherry at it. "A peace offering? So you admit defeat, huh?" In elation at having gotten past the tree, she forgot who in the story had been eater and who eaten. "Well, you can't eat me, 'cause I'm gonna eat YOU!" And she popped the cherry into her mouth, bursting its sweet roundness between her teeth. The first cherry of the season. It tasted wonderful, until a hearty slap on her shoulder made her gulp.

"Hey, girl," Foster's voice said, "you look great! You too, of course, Kashy."

Gilla didn't answer. She put horrified hands to her mouth. Foster, big old goofy Foster with his twinkly eyes and his too-baggy sweat-shirt, gently took the shoulder that he'd slapped so carelessly seconds before. "You okay, Gilla?"

Kashy looked on in concern.

Gilla swallowed. Found her voice. "Jesus fuck, Foster! You made me swallow it!"

Seeing that she was all right, Foster grinned his silly grin. "And you know what Roger says about girls who swallow!"

"No, man; you made me swallow the cherry pit!" Oh, God; what was going to happen now?

"Oo, scary," Foster said. "It's gonna grow into a tree inside you, and then you'll be sooorry!" He made cartoon monster fingers in Gilla's face and mugged at her. Kashy burst out laughing. Gilla too. Lightly, she slapped Foster's hands away. Yeah, it was only an old tree.

"C'mon," she said. "Let's go to this party already."

They went and grabbed their bikes out of her parents' garage. It was a challenge riding in those wedge heels, but at least she was wearing pants, unlike Kashy, who seemed to have perfected how to ride in a tight skirt with her knees decently together, as she perfected every- thing to do with her appearance. Gilla did her best to look dignified without dumping the bike.

"I can't wait to start driving lessons," Kashy complained. "I'm getting all sweaty. I'm going to have to do my makeup all over again when I get to Patricia's place." She perched on her bike like a princess in her carriage, and neither Gilla nor Foster could persuade her to move any faster than a crawl. Gilla swore that if Kashy could, she would have ridden sidesaddle in her little skirt.

All the way there, Foster, Gilla and Kashy argued over what type of cobra a hamadryad was. Gilla was sure she remembered one thing: hamadryads had inflatable hoods just below their heads. She tried to ignore how the ride was making the back of her neck sticky. The underside of the triangular mass of her hair was glued uncomfortably to her skin.

Who went for a ride on a tiger . . .

They could hear music coming from Patricia's house. The three of them locked their bikes to the fence and headed inside. Gilla sur- reptitiously tugged the hem of her blouse down over her hips. But Kashy'd known her too long. Her eyes followed the movement of Gilla's hands, and she sighed. "I wish I had a butt like yours," Kashy said.

"What? You crazy?"

"Naw, man. Look how nice your pants fit you. Mine always sag in the behind."

Foster chuckled. "Yeah, sometimes I wish I had a butt like Gilla's too."

Gilla looked at him, baffled. Beneath those baggy pants Foster always wore, he had a fine behind; strong and shapely. She'd seen him in swim trunks.

Foster made grabbing motions at the air. "Wish I had it right here, warm and solid in between these two hands."

Kashy hooted. Gilla reached up and swatted Foster on the back of the head. He ducked, grinning. All three of them were laughing as they stepped into the house.

After the coolness of the spring air outside, the first step into the warmth and artificial lighting of Patricia's place was a shock. "Hey there, folks," said Patricia's dad. "Welcome. Let me just take your jackets, and you head right on in to the living room."

"Jeez," Gilla muttered to Foster once they'd handed off their jackets. "The 'rents aren't going to hang around, are they? That'd be such a total drag."

In the living room were some of their friends from school, lounging on the chairs and the floor, laughing and talking and drinking bright red punch out of plastic glasses. Everybody was on their best behaviour, since Patricia's parents were still around. Boring. Gilla elbowed Foster once they were out of Mr. Bright's earshot. "Try not to be too obvious about ogling Tanya, okay? She's been making goo-goo eyes at you all term."

He put a hand to his chest, looked mock innocent. "Who, me?" He gave a wave of his hand and went off to say hi to some of his buddies.

Patricia's mother was serving around mini patties on a tray. She wore stretch pants that made her big butt look bigger than ever when she bent over to offer the tray, and even through her heavy sweatshirt Gilla could make out where her large breasts didn't quite fit into her bra but exploded up over the top of it. Shit. Gilla'd forgotten to check how she looked in her new blouse. She'd have to get to the bathroom soon. Betcha a bunch of the other girls were already lined up outside it, waiting to fix their hair, their makeup, readjust their pantyhose, renew their "natural" lipstick.

Patricia, looking awkward but sweet in a little flowered dress, grinned at them and beckoned them over. Gilla smoothed her hair back, sucked her gut in, and started to head over towards her, picking her way carefully in her wedgies.

She nearly toppled as a hand grabbed her ankle. "Hey, big girl. Mind where you put that foot. Wouldn't want you to step on my leg and break it."

Gilla felt her face heat with embarrassment. She yanked her leg out of Roger's grip and lost her balance. Kashy had to steady her. Roger chuckled. "Getting a little top heavy there, Gilla?" he said. His buddies Karl and Haygood, lounging near him, snickered.

Karl was obviously trying to look up Kashy's skirt. Kashy smoothed it down over her thighs, glared at him, and led the way to where Patricia was sitting. "Come on, girl," she whispered to Gilla. "The best thing is to ignore them."

Cannot ignore them all your days. Gilla smiled her too-bright smile, hugged Patricia and kissed her cheek. "Mum and Dad are going soon," Patricia whispered at them. "They promised me."

"They'd better," Kashy said.

"God, I know," Patricia groaned. "They'd better not embarrass me like this too much longer." She went to greet some new arrivals.

Gilla perched on the couch with Kashy, trying to find a position that didn't make her tummy bulge, trying to keep her mind on the small talk. Where was Foster? Oh, in the corner. Tanya was sitting way close to him, tugging at her necklace and smiling deeply into his eyes. Foster had his "I'm such a stud" smile on.

Mr. Bright came in with a tray of drinks. He pecked his chubby wife on the lips as she went by. He turned and contemplated her when her back was to him. He was smiling when he turned back. The smile lingered happily on his face long after the kiss was over.

Are you any less than she? Well, she certainly was, thank heaven. With any luck, it'd be a few years before she was as round as Mrs. Bright. And what was this "less than she" business, anyway? Who talked like that? Gilla took a glass of punch from Mr. Bright's tray and sucked it down, trying to pay attention to Jahanara and Kashy talking about whether 14 karat gold was better for necklaces than 18 karat.

"Mum," said Patricia from over by the door. "Dad?"

Her mother laughed nervously. "Yes, we're going, we're going. You have the phone number at the Hamptons' house?"

"Yesss, Mum," Patricia hissed. "See you later, okay?" She grabbed their coats from the hallway closet, all but bustled them out the door.

"We'll be back by 2 a.m.!" her dad yelled over his shoulder. Everyone sat still until they heard that lovely noise, the sound of the car starting up and driving off down the street.

Foster got up, took the CD out of the stereo player. Thank God. Any more of that kiddie pop, and Gilla'd thought she'd probably barf. Foster grinned around to everyone, produced another CD from his chest pocket and put it into the CD player. A jungle mix started up. People cheered and started dancing. Patricia turned out all the lights but the one in the hallway.

And now Gilla needed to pee. Which meant she had to pass the clot of people stuck all over Roger again. Well, she really needed to check on that blouse, anyway. She'd just make sure she was far from Roger's grasping hands. She stood, tugged at the hem of her blouse so it was covering her bum again. *Reach those shoulders tall too, strong one. Stretch now.* When had she started talking to herself like that? But it was good advice. She fluffed up her hair, drew herself up straight and walked with as much dignity as she could in the direction of the bathroom.

Roger and Gilla had been the first in their class to hit puberty. Roger's voice had deepened into a raspy bass, and his shoulders, chest and arms had broadened with muscle. He'd shot up about a foot in the past few months, it seemed. He sauntered rather than walked and he always seemed to be braying an opinion on everything, the more insulting the better. Gilla flicked a glance at him. In one huge hand he had a paper napkin which he'd piled with three patties, two huge slices of black rum cake and a couple of slices of ham. He was pushing the food into his mouth as he brayed some boasty something at his buddies. He seemed barely aware of his own chewing and swallowing. Probably took a lot of feeding to keep that growing body going. He was handsome, though. Had a broad baby face with nice full lips and the beginnings of a goatee. People were willing to hang with him just in hopes that he would pay attention to them, so why did he need to spend his time making Gilla's life miserable?

Oops, shit. Shouldn't even have thought it, 'cause now he'd noticed her noticing. He caught and held her gaze, and still looking at her, leaned over and murmured something at the knot of people gathered around him. The group burst out laughing. "No, really?" said Clarissa in a high, witchy voice. Gilla put her head down and surged out of the room, not stopping until she was up the stairs to the second floor and inside the bathroom. She stayed in there for as long as she dared.

When she came out, Clarissa was in the second floor hallway. Gilla said, "Bathroom's free now."

"Did you really let them do that to you?"

"Huh?" In confusion, Gilla met Clarissa's eyes. Clarissa's cheeks were flushed and she had a bright, knowing look on her face.

"Roger told us. How you let him suck on your . . ." Clarissa bit on her bottom lip. Her cheeks got even pinker. "Then you let Haygood do it too. Don't you, like, feel like a total slut now?"

"But I didn't . . ."

"Oh, come on, Gilla. We all saw how you were looking at Roger."

Liar! Can such a liar live? The thought hissed through Gilla, strong as someone whispering in her ear.

"You know," Clarissa said, "You're even kinda pretty. If you just lost some weight, you wouldn't have to throw yourself at all those guys like that."

Gilla felt her face go hot. Her mouth filled with saliva. She was suddenly very aware of little things: the bite of her bra into her skin, where it was trying to contain her fat, swingy breasts; the hard, lumpy memory of the cherry pit slipping down her throat; the bristly triangular hedge of her hair, bobbing at the base of her neck and swelling to cover her ears. Her mouth fell open, but no words came out.

"He doesn't even really like you, you know." Clarissa smirked at her and sauntered past her into the bathroom.

She couldn't, she mustn't still be there when Clarissa got out of the bathroom. In the awkward wedge heels, she clattered her way down the stairs like an elephant, her mind a jumble. Once in the downstairs hallway, she didn't head back towards the happy, warm sound of laughter and music in the living room, but shoved her way out the front door.

It was even darker out there, despite the porch light being on. Foster was out on the porch, leaning against the railing and whispering with someone. Tanya, shivering in the short sundress she was wearing, was staring wide-eyed at Foster and hanging on every word. "And then," Foster said, gesturing with his long arms, "I grabbed the ball from him, and I . . ." He turned, saw Gilla. "Hey girl, what's up?"

Tanya looked at her like she was the insurance salesman who'd interrupted her dinner.

"I, Foster," stammered Gilla. "What's 'calumny' mean?"

"Huh?" He pushed himself upright, looking concerned. "Scuse me, Tanya, okay?"

"All right," Tanya said sulkily. She went inside.

Gilla stood in the cold, shivering. *That liar! He has no right!*

Foster asked again, "What's wrong?"

"Calumny. What's it mean?" she repeated.

"I dunno. Why?"

"I think it means a lie, a really bad one." *He and his toadies. If you find a nest of vipers, should you not root it out?* "It just came to me, you know?" Her thoughts were whipping and thrashing in the storm in her head. *We never gave them our favour!*

Foster came and put a hand on her shoulder, looked into her eyes. "Gilla, who's telling lies? You gonna tell me what's going on?"

The warmth of her friend's palm through the cloth of her blouse brought her back to herself. "Damn, it's cold out here!"

Something funny happened to Foster's face. He hesitated, then opened his arms to her. "Here," he said.

Blinking with surprise, Gilla stepped into the hug. She stopped shivering. They stood there for a few seconds, Gilla wondering what, what? Should she put her arms around him too? Were they still just friends? Was he just warming her up because she was cold? Did he like her? Well of course he liked her, he hung out with her and Kashy during lunch period at school almost every day. Lots of the guys gave him shit for that. But did he like her like *that*? Did she want him to? *By your own choice, never by another's.* What was she supposed to do now? And what was with all these weird things she seemed to be thinking all of a sudden?

"Um, Gilla?"

"Yeah?"

"Could you get off my foot now?"

The laughter that bubbled from her tasted like cherries in the back of her throat. She stepped off poor Foster's abused toes, leaned her head into his shoulder, giggling. "Oh, Foster. Why didn't you just say I was hurting you?"

Foster was giggling too, his voice high with embarrassment. "I didn't know what to say, or what was the right thing to do, or what."

"You and me both."

"I haven't held too many girls like that before. I mean, only when I'm sure they want me to."

Now Gilla backed up so she could look at him better. "Really? What about Tanya?"

He looked sheepish, and kind of sullen. "Yeah, I bet she'd like that. She's nice, you know? Only . . ."

"Only what?" Gilla sat on the rail beside Foster.

"She just kinda sits there, like a sponge. I talk and I talk, and she just soaks it all up. She doesn't say anything interesting back, she doesn't tell me about anything she does, she just wants me to entertain her. Saniya was like that too, and Kristen," he said, naming a couple of his short-lived school romances. "I like girls, you know? A lot. I just want one with a brain in her head. You and Kashy got more going on than that, right? More fun hanging with you guys."

"So?" said Gilla, wondering what she was going to say.

"So what?"

"So what about Kashy?" She stumbled over her friend's name, because what she was really thinking was, *What about me?* Did she even like Foster like that?

"Oh, look," drawled a way too familiar voice. "It's the faggot and the fat girl."

Roger, Karl and Haywood had just come lumbering out of the house. Haywood snickered. Gilla froze.

"Oh, give it up, Roger," Foster drawled back. He lounged against the railing again. "It's so fucking tired. Every time you don't know what to say—which, my friend, is often—you call somebody 'faggot.'"

Haywood and Karl, their grins uncertain, glanced from Roger to Foster and back again. Foster got an evil smile, put a considering finger to his chin. "You ever hear of the pot calling the kettle black?"

At that, Karl and Haywood started to howl with laughter. Roger growled. That was the only way to describe the sound coming out of his mouth. Karl and Foster touched their fists together. "Good one, man. Good one," Karl said. Foster grinned at him.

But Roger elbowed past Karl and stood chest to chest with Foster, his arms crossed in front of him, almost like he was afraid to let his body touch Foster's. Roger glared at Foster, who stayed lounging calmly on the railing with a smirk on his face, looking Roger straight in the face. "And you know both our mothers ugly like duppy too, so you can't come at me with that one either. You know that's true, man; you know it."

Before he had even finished speaking, Haywood and Karl had cracked up laughing. Then, to Gilla's amazement, Roger's lips started to twitch. He grinned, slapped Foster on the back, shook his hand. "A'ight man, a'ight," said Roger. "You got me." Foster grinned, mock-punched Roger on the shoulder.

"We're going out back for a smoke," Haywood said. "You coming, Foster?"

"Yeah man, yeah. Gilla, catch you later, okay?" The four of them slouched off together, Roger trailing a little. Just before they rounded the corner of the house, Roger looked back at Gilla. He pursed his lips together and smooched at her silently. Then they were gone. Gilla stood there, hugging herself, cold again.

She crept back inside. The lights were all off, except for a couple of candles over by the stereo. Someone had moved the dinner table with the food on it over there too, to clear the floor. A knot of people were dancing right in the centre of the living room. There was Clarissa, with Jim. Clarissa was jigging about, trying to look cool. Bet she didn't even know she wasn't on the beat. "Rock on," Gilla whispered.

The television was on, the sound inaudible over the music. A few people huddled on the floor around it, watching a skinny blonde chick drop-kick bad guys. The blue light from the tv flickered over their faces like cold flame.

On the couches all around the room, couples were necking. Gilla tried to make out Kashy's form, but it was too dark to really see if she was there. Gilla scouted the room out until she spied an empty lone chair. She went and perched on it, bobbed her head to the music and tapped her foot, pretending to have a good time.

She sighed. Sometimes she hated parties. She wanted to go and get a slice of that black rum cake. It was her favourite. But people would see her eating. She slouched protectively over her belly and stared across the room at the television. The programme had changed. Now it was an old-time movie or some shit, with guys and girls on a beach. Their bathing suits were in this ancient style, and the girls' hair, my God. One of them wore hers in this weird puffy 'do. To Gilla's eye, she looked a little chunky, too. How had she gotten a part in this movie? The actors started dancing on the beach, this bizarre kind of shimmy thing. The people watching the television started pointing and laughing. Gilla heard Hussain's voice say, "No, don't change the channel! That's Frankie Avalon and Annette Funicello!" Yeah, Hussain *would* know crap like that.

"Gilla, move your butt over! Make some room!" It was Kashy, shoving her hips onto the same chair that Gilla was on. Gilla giggled and shifted over for her. They each cotched on the chair, not quite fitting. "Guess what?" Kashy said. "Remi just asked me out!"

Remi was *fine*; he was just Kashy's height when she was in heels, lean and broad-shouldered with big brown eyes, strong hands, and those smooth East African looks. The knot that had been in Gilla's throat all night got harder. She swallowed around it and made her mouth smile. But she never got to mumble insincere congratulations to her friend, because just then . . .

They came back . . .

Roger strode in with his posse, all laughing so loudly that Gilla could hear them over the music. Foster shot Gilla a grin that made her toes feel all warm. Kashy looked at her funny, a slight smile on her face. Roger went and stood smirking at the television. On the screen, the chunky chick and the funny-looking guy in the old-fashioned bathing suits and haircuts were playing Postman in a phone booth with their friends. Postman! Stupid kid game.

They came back . . .
They came back from the ride . . .

Gilla wondered how she'd gotten herself into this. Roger had grabbed Clarissa, hugged her tight to him, announced that he wanted to play Postman, and in two twos Clarissa and Roger's servile friends had put the lights on and herded everybody into an old-fashioned game of Postman. Girls in the living room, guys stationed in closets all over the house, and Clarissa and Hussain playing . . .

"Postman!" yelled Hussain. "I've got a message for Kashy!" He was enjoying the hell out of this. That was a neat plan Hussain had come up with to avoid kissing any girls. Gilla had a hunch that females weren't his type.

"It's Remi!" Kashy whispered. She sprang to her feet. "I bet it's Remi!" She glowed at Gilla, and followed Hussain off to find her "message" in some closet or bathroom somewhere and neck with him.

Left sitting hunched over on the hard chair, Gilla glared at their departing backs. She thought about how Roger's friends fell over themselves to do anything he said, and tried to figure out where she'd learned the word "servile." The voice no longer seemed like a different voice in her head now, just her own. But it knew words she didn't know, things she'd never experienced, like how it felt to unfurl your leaves to the bright taste of the sun, and the empty screaming space in the air as a sister died, her bark and pith chopped through to make ships or firewood.

"That's some crazy shit," she muttered to herself.

"Postman!" chirped Clarissa. Her eyes sparkled and her colour was high. Yeah, bet she'd been off lipping at some "messages" of her own. Lipping. Now there was another weird word. "Postman for Gilla!" said Clarissa.

Gilla's heart started to thunk like an axe chopping through wood. She stood. "What. . . ?"

Clarissa smirked at her. "Postman for you, hot stuff. You coming, or not?" And then she was off up the stairs and into the depths of Mr. and Mrs. Bright's house.

Who could it be? Who wanted to kiss her? Gilla felt tiny dots of clammy sweat spring out under her eyes. Maybe Remi? No, no. He liked Kashy. Maybe, please, maybe Foster?

Clarissa was leading her on a winding route. They passed a hallway closet. Muffled chuckles and thumps came from inside. "No, wait," murmured a male voice. "Let *me* take it off." Then they went by the bathroom. The giggles that wriggled out from under the bathroom door came from two female voices.

"There is no time so sap-sweet as the spring bacchanalia," Gilla heard herself saying.

Clarissa just kept walking. "You are *so* weird," she said over her shoulder.

They passed a closed bedroom door. Then came to another bedroom. Its door was closed, too, but Clarissa just slammed it open. "Postman!" she yelled.

The wriggling on the bed resolved itself into Patricia Bright and Haygood, entwined. Gilla didn't know where to look. At least their clothes were still on, sort of. Patricia looked up from under Haygood's armpit with a self-satisfied smile. "Jeez, I'm having an intimate birthday moment here."

"Sorry," said Clarissa, sounding not the least bit sorry, "but Gilla's got a date." She pointed towards the closet door.

"Have a gooood time, killa Gilla," Clarissa told her. Haygood snickered.

Gilla felt cold. "In there?" she asked Clarissa.

"Yup," Clarissa chirruped. "Your special treat." She turned on her heel and headed out the bedroom door, yelling, "Who needs the Postman?"

"You gonna be okay, Gilla?" Patricia asked. She looked concerned.

"Yeah, I'll be fine. Who's in there?"

Patricia smiled. "That's half the fun, silly; not knowing."

Haygood just leered at her. Gilla made a face at him.

"Go on and enjoy yourself," Patricia said. "If you need help, you can always let us know, okay?"

"Okay." Gilla was rooted where she stood. Patricia and Haygood were kissing again, ignoring her.

She could go back into the living room. She didn't have to do this. But . . . who? Remembering the warm cloak of Foster's arms around her, heavy as a carpet of fall leaves, Gilla found herself walking towards the closet. She pulled the door open, tried to peer in. A hand reached out and yanked her inside.

With the lady inside . . .

Hangers reached like twigs in the dark to catch in Gilla's hair. Clothing tangled her in it. A heavy body pushed her back against a wall. Blind, Gilla reached her arms out, tried to feel who it was. Strong hands pushed hers away, started squeezing her breasts, her belly. "Fat girl . . ." oozed a voice.

Roger. Gilla hissed, fought. He was so strong! His face was on hers now, his lips at her lips. The awful thing was, his breath tasted lovely. Unable to do anything else, she turned her mouth away from his. That put his mouth right at her ear. With warm, damp breath he said, "You know you want it, Gilla. Come on. Just relax." The words crawled into her ears. His laugh was mocking.

And the smile on the face . . .

Gilla's hair bristled at the base of her neck. She pushed at Roger, tried to knee him in the groin, but he just shoved her legs apart and laughed. "Girl, you know this is the only way a thick girl like you is going to get any play. You know it."

She knew it. She was only good for this. Thighs too heavy—*But must not a trunk be strong to bear the weight?*—belly too round—*Should the fruits of the tree be sere and wasted, then?*—hair too nappy—*A well-leafed tree is a healthy tree.* The words, her own words, whirled around and around in her head. What? What?

Simply this: you must fight those who would make free with you. Win or lose, you must fight.

A taste like summer cherries rose in Gilla's mouth again. Kashy envied her shape, her strength.

The back of Gilla's neck tingled. The sensation unfurled down her spine. She gathered power from the core of her, from that muscled, padded belly, and elbowed Roger high in the stomach. "No!" she roared, a fiery breath. The wind whuffed out of Roger. He tumbled back against the opposite wall, slid bonelessly down to the ground. Gilla fell onto her hands and knees, solidly centred on all fours. Her toes, her fingers flexed. She wasn't surprised to feel her limbs flesh themselves into four knotted appendages, backwards-crooked and strong as wood. She'd sprouted claws, too. She tapped them impatiently.

"Oh, God," moaned Roger. He tried to pull his feet up against his body, further away from her. "Gilla, what the hell? Is that you?"

Foster had liked holding her. He found her beautiful. With a tickling ripple, the thought clothed Gilla in scales, head to toe. When she looked down at her new dragon feet, she could see the scales twinkling, cherry-red. She lashed her new tail, sending clothing and hangers flying. Roger whimpered, "I'm sorry."

Testing out her bunchy, branchy limbs, Gilla took an experimental step closer to Roger. He began to sob.

And you? asked the deep, fruity voice in her mind. *What say you of you?*

Gilla considered, licking her lips. Roger smelled like meat. *I think I'm all those things that Kashy and Foster like about me. I'm a good friend.*

Yes.

I'm pretty. No, I'm beautiful.

Yes.

I'm good to hold.

Yes.

I bike hard.

Yes.

I run like the wind.

Yes.

I use my brain—well, sometimes.

(A smile to the voice this time). *Yes.*

I use my lungs.

Yes!

Gilla inhaled a deep breath of musty closet and Roger's fear-sweat. Her sigh made her chest creak like tall trees in a gentle breeze, and she felt her ribs unfurling into batlike wings. They filled the remaining closet space. "Please," whispered Roger. "Please."

"Hey, Rog?" called Haygood. "You must be having a real good time in there, if you're begging for more."

"Please, *what?!*" roared Gilla. At the nape of her neck, her hama-dryad hood flared open. She exhaled a hot wind. Her breath smelled like cherry pie, which made her giggle. She was having a good time, even if Roger wasn't.

The giggles erupted as small gouts of flame. One of them lit the hem of Roger's sweater. "Please don't!" he yelled, beating out the fire with his hands. "God, Gilla; stop!"

Patricia's voice came from beyond the door. "That doesn't sound too good," she said to Haygood. "Hey, Gil?" she shouted. "You okay in there?"

Roger scrabbled to his feet. "Whaddya mean, is *Gilla* okay? Get me out of here! She's turned into some kind of monster!" He started banging on the inside of the closet door.

A polyester dress was beginning to char. No biggie. Gilla flapped it out with a wing. But it *was* getting close in the closet, and Haygood and Patricia were yanking on the door. Gilla swung her head towards it. Roger cringed. Gilla ignored him. She nosed the door open and stepped outside. Roger pushed past her. "Fuck, Haygood; get her!"

Haygood's shirt was off, his jeans zipper not done up all the way. His lips looked swollen. He peered suspiciously at Gilla. "Why?" he asked Roger. "What's she doing?"

Patricia was still wriggling her dress down over her hips. Her hair was a mess. "Yeah," she said to Roger, "what's the big problem? You didn't hurt her, did you?" She turned to Gilla, put a hand on her scaly left foreshoulder. "You okay, girl?"

What in the world was going on? Why weren't they scared? "Uh," replied Gilla. "I dunno. How do I look?"

Patricia frowned. "Same as ever," she said, just as Kashy and Foster burst into the room.

"We heard yelling," Kashy said, panting. "What's up? Roger, you been bugging Gilla again?"

Foster took Gilla's paw. "Did he mess with you?"

"What the fuck's the matter with everyone?" Roger was nearly screeching. "Can't you see? She's some kind of dragon, or something!"

That was the last straw. Gilla started to laugh. Great belly laughs that started from her middle and came guffawing through her snout. Good thing there was no fire this time, 'cause Gilla didn't know if she could have stopped it. She laughed so hard that the cherry pit she'd swallowed came back up. "Urp," she said, spitting it into her hand. Her hand. She was back to normal now.

She grinned at Roger. He goggled. "How'd you do that?" he demanded.

Gilla ignored him. Her schoolmates had started coming into the room from all over the house to see what the racket was. "Yeah, he messed with me," Gilla said, so they could all hear. "Roger sent the Postman for me even though he doesn't like me and he knows I don't like him, and then he stuck his hand down my bra."

"What a creep," muttered Clarissa's boyfriend Jim.

Foster stepped up to Roger, glaring. "What is your problem, man?" Roger stuck his chest out and tried to glare back, but he couldn't meet Foster's eyes. He kept sneaking nervous peeks around Foster at Gilla.

Clarissa snickered at Gilla. "So what's the big deal? You do it with him all the time, anyway."

Oh, enough of this ill-favoured chit. Weirdly, the voice felt like it was coming from Gilla's palm now. The hand where she held the cherry pit. But it still sounded and felt like her own thoughts. Gilla stalked over to Clarissa. "You don't believe that Roger attacked me?"

Clarissa made a face of disgust. "I believe that you're so fat and ugly that you'll go with anybody, 'cause nobody would have you."

"That's dumb," said Kashy. "How could she go with anybody, if nobody would have her?"

"I'll have her," said Foster. He looked shyly at Gilla. Then his face flushed. "I mean, I'd like, I mean . . ." No one could hear the end of the sentence, because they were laughing so hard. Except Roger, Karl and Haygood.

Gilla put her arms around Foster, afraid still that she'd misunderstood. But he hugged back, hard. Gilla felt all warm. Foster was such a goof. "Clarissa," said Gilla, "if something bad ever happens to you and nobody will believe your side of the story, you can talk to me. Because I know what it's like."

Clarissa reddened. Roger swore and stomped out of the room. Haygood and Karl followed him.

Gilla regarded the cherry pit in the palm of her hand. Considered. Then she put it in her mouth again and swallowed it down.

"Why'd you do that?" Foster asked.

"Just felt like it."

"A tree'll grow inside you," he teased.

Gilla chuckled. "I wish. Hey, I never did get a real Postman message." She nodded towards the closet. "D'you wanna?"

Foster ducked his head, took her hand. "Yeah."

Gilla led the way, grinning.

> *They came back from the ride*
> *With the lady inside,*
> *And a smile on the face of the tiger.*

Left Foot, Right

In her award-winning short story "Travels with the Snow Queen," Kelly Link writes that fairy tale heroines often seem to have difficulties with their feet; too-tight glass slippers, being forced to dance in red-hot iron shoes, having one foot stuck to a loaf of bread, et cetera. While I was writing this next story, I really began to feel that Kelly was right.

"Allyuh have this in a size 9?" Jenna puts the shiny red patent shoe down on the counter. Well, it used to be shiny. She's been wearing it everywhere, and now it's dulled by dust. It's the left side of a high-heeled pump, pointy-toed, with large shiny fake rhinestones decorating the toe box. Each stone is a different size and colour, in a different cheap plastic setting. The red veneer has stripped off the heel of the shoe. It curls up off the white plastic heel base in strips. Jenna's heart clenches. It's exactly the kind of tacky, blinged-out accessory that Zuleika loves—loved—to wear.

The girl behind the counter is wearing a straw baseball cap, its peak pulled down low over her face. The girl asks, in a puzzled voice, "But don't you bought exactly the same shoes last week?"

And the week before that, thinks Jenna. *And the one before that.* "I lost them," she replies. "At least, I lost the right side"—she nearly chokes on the half truth—"so I want to replace them." All around her, other salespeople help other customers. The people in the store zip past Jenna, half-seen, half-heard. This year's soca road march roars through the store's sound system. Last month, Jenna loved it. Now, any happy music makes her vexed.

"Jeez, what's the matter with you *now*?" the girl says. Jenna startles, guiltily. She risks a look at the shoe store girl's face. She hadn't really done so before. She has been avoiding eye contact with people lately, afraid that if anyone's two eyes make four with hers, the fury in hers will burn the heart out of the core of them.

But the girl isn't looking at Jenna. With one hand, she is curling the peak of her cap to protect her eyes against the sun's glare through the store windows. Only her small, round mouth shows. She seems to be peering into the display on the cash register. She slaps the side of the cash register. "Damned thing. It's like every time I touch it, the network goes down."

"Oh," says Jenna. "Is not me you were talking to, then?"

The girl laughs, a childlike sound, like small dinner bells tinkling. "No. Unless it have something the matter with you too. Is there?"

Jenna turns away, pretends to be checking out the rows of men's running shoes, each one more aerodynamically fantastical than the last, like race cars. "No, not me. About the shoes?"

"Sure." The girl takes the pump from Jenna. Her fingertips are cool when they brush Jenna's hand. "What a shame you can't replace just one side. Though you really wore this one down in just a week. You need both sides, left and right." The girl inspects the inside of the shoe, in that mysterious way that people who sell shoes do. "You say you want a size nine? But you take more like an eight, right?"

"How you know that?"

"I remember from last time you were in the store. Feet are so important, you don't find?"

Jenna doesn't remember seeing the girl in the store before. But the details of her life have been a little hazy the past few weeks. Everything seems dusted with unreality. Her, standing in a shoe shop, doing something as ordinary as buying a pair of shoes. Her standing at all, instead of floundering.

The shoe shop girl's body sinks lower and lower. Jenna is confused until the girl comes out from behind the counter. She's really short. She has been standing on something in order to reach the cash register. Her arms and legs are plump, foreshortened. The hems of her jeans are rolled up. Her body is pleasantly rotund.

The girl glances at Jenna's feet. At least, that's where Jenna thinks she's looking. Jenna's seeing the girl from above, so it's hard to tell. In addition to the straw cap, the girl's twisty black hair is in thousands of tiny plaits that keep falling over her face. She must have been looking at Jenna's feet, because she says, "Yup. Size eight. Don't it?"

Jenna stares down at the top of the girl's head. She says, "Yes, but the pumps run small." The girl is wearing cute yellow moccasins that look hand-sewn. She didn't get those at this discount shoe outlet. Her feet are tiny; the toe boxes of her moccasins sag a little. Her toes don't quite fill them up. Jenna curls her own toes under. Her feet feel unfamiliar in her plain white washekongs, the tennis shoes she used to wear so often, before her world fell in. Now she only wears two sides of shoes when she needs to fake normal. Or when she needs to take the red pump off to show the people in the shoe store. The blisters on the sole of her right foot are uncomfortable cushions against the canvas-lined foam inside the shoe. Although she'd scrubbed the right foot bottom before putting the washekong on, she hadn't been able to get all of the weeks of ground-in dirt out. The heel of her left foot, imprisoned most of the time in the red high heel, has become a stranger to the ground. Going completely flat-footed like this makes the shortened tendons in her left ankle stretch and twang.

The girl hands the shoe back to her and says, "I going in the back to see if we have any more of these." She disappears amongst the high rows of shoe shelves. She walks jerkily, with a strange rise and fall motion.

Jenna sits on one of the benches in the middle of the store. She slips off her left-side tennis shoe and slides her left foot back into the destroyed pump. The height of it makes her instep ache, and her foot slides around a little in the too-big shoe. When she'd borrowed Zuleika's pumps without asking, she'd only planned to wear them out to the club that one night. The discomfort of the red shoe feels needful and good. It will be even more so when she can remove the right side washekong, feel dirt and hot asphalt and rocks with her bare right foot. She waits for the girl to bring the replacement pumps. The girl returns, hop-drop, hop-drop, carrying a shoe box.

Jenna doesn't want to be in the shop, fully shod, a second longer. She takes the box from the girl, almost grabbing it. "These are fine," she says, and stumps, hop-drop, hop-drop, to the cash register. She starts taking money out of her purse.

Behind her, the girl calls, "You don't want to try them on first?"

"Don't need to," Jenna replies. "I know how they fit."

The girl gets back behind the counter and clambers up onto whatever she'd been standing on. She sighs. "This job," she says to Jenna, "so much standing on your feet all the time. I not used to it."

Jenna isn't paying the girl a lot of attention. Instead, she's texting her father to come and get her. She doesn't drive at the moment. May never drive again.

The girl rings up the purchase. Her plaits have fallen into her eyes once more. When she leans forward to give Jenna her change, her breath smells like pepper shrimp. Jenna's tummy rumbles. But she knows she won't eat. Maybe some ginger tea. The smell of almost any food makes her stomach knot these past few weeks.

The girl pats Jenna's hand and says something to her. Jenna can't hear it clearly over the sound of her grumbling stomach. Embarrassed, she mumbles an impatient "thank you" at the girl, grabs the shopping bag with the shoes in it, and quickly leaves the store. After the air-conditioned chill of the store, the tropical blast of the outdoors heat is like surfacing from the river depths to sweet, scorching air. She kicks off the single tennis shoe. She stuffs it into the shopping bag with the new pair of pumps.

What the girl said, it had sounded like "Is Eowyn Sinead."

Jenna doesn't know anybody with those names.

Daddy texts back that he'll meet her at the Savannah, by the ice cream man. He means the ice cream truck that has been at the same side of the Savannah since Jenna and Zuleika were young. Jenna likes soursop ice cream. Zuleika liked rum and raisin. One Sunday when they were both still little, their parents had brought Jenna and Zuleika to the Savannah. Jenna had nagged Zuleika for a taste of her ice cream until Mummy ordered Zuleika to let her try it. A sulking Zuleika gave Jenna her cone. Jenna tasted it, spat it out, and dropped the cone. So Daddy made Jenna give Zuleika her ice cream, which made Jenna bawl. But Zuleika wanted her rum and raisin. She pouted and threw Jenna's ice cream as far as she could. It landed in the hair of a lady that was walking in front of them. Jenna was unhappy, Mummy and Daddy were unhappy, the lady was unhappy, and Zuleika was unhappy.

Jenna remembers the odd satisfaction she had felt through her misery. Except that then Zuleika wouldn't talk to her or play with her for the rest of the day. Jenna smiles. It probably hadn't helped that she had followed Zuleika around the whole rest of that day, nagging her for her attention.

Jenna turns off her phone so no one else can call her. Her boyfriend Clarence tried for a while, came to visit her a couple of times after the accident, but Jenna wouldn't talk to him. She didn't dare open her mouth, for fear of drowning him in screams that would start and never, ever stop. Clarence eventually gave up. The doctors say that Jenna is well enough to return to school. She doesn't know what she will say to Clarence when she sees him there.

As Jenna is crossing the street, she walks with her bare right foot on tiptoe. That almost matches the height of the high heel on her left foot, so it isn't so obvious that one foot is bare. But she can't keep that up for long, not any more. After more than a fortnight of walking with her right foot on tiptoe, the foot has rebelled. Her toes cramp painfully, so she lowers her bare heel to the ground. She steps in a patch of sun-melted tar, but she barely feels the burn. Her foot bottom has developed too much callous for it to bother her much. People in the street make wide berths around her in her tattered one-side shoe. They figure she is homeless, or mad, or both. She doesn't care. She makes her way to the 300-acre Savannah. Not too many people walking or jogging the footpath yet, not in the daytime heat.

But the food trucks are in full swing, vending oyster cocktail, roast corn, pholourie, doubles. Jenna ducks past the ice cream man, hoping he won't see her and ask how she's doing. He knows—knew—Jenna and Zuleika well. He had watched them grow up.

The poui trees are in full bloom. They carpet the grass with yellow and pink blossoms. Jenna steps over a cricket wicket discarded on the ground, and goes around a bunch of navy-uniformed school girls liming on the grass under the trees. A couple of them are eating rotis. They all stop their chatting long enough to stare at her. Once she passes them, they whoop with laughter.

Jenna doesn't know how she will manage school next week.

She finds a bench not too far from the ice cream man, where she can see Daddy when he comes. She sits and puts the shoe bag on her lap. She clutches the folded top of it tightly. She doesn't put the new shoes on. She never has. They aren't for her. She was wearing the left side of Zuleika's shoes when she surfaced. She has to give Zuleika a good pair of the shoes in return for the ones she took without permission.

For a few minutes, Jenna rests her aching feet. Then she realizes that the air is beginning to cool. The sun will be going down soon. Jenna texts her father again, tells him never mind, that she will come home on her own later. He tries to insist. She refuses. Then she turns the phone off. Is better like this, anyway. Her parents are doing their best. Looking after Jenna, asking after her. Doing their grieving in private. Some days, Jenna can't bear the burden of their forgiveness.

She can't take neither bus nor taxi half-shod the way she is. She gets up off the bench, wincing at the separate pains in her feet. She starts walking. Clop, thump. Clop, thump. One shoe off, and one shoe on.

It's dark when she gets to the right place on the highway. The sight of the torn-apart metal guard rail sets her blood boiling so, till she nearly feels warm enough for the first time in almost a month. Anger is the only thing hotting her up nowadays. When are they going to fix it?

She lets herself through the space between the twisted pieces of metal and starts clambering down the embankment. Below her, the river whispers and chuckles. A few times, she loses her footing in the pebbles and sparse scrub grass of the dry red earth of the embankment, and slides a little way down. She could hold onto clumps of grass to try to stop her skid, but why? Instead, she digs in the heel of Zuleika's remaining pump. Above her, cars whoosh by along the highway. But the closer she gets to the tiny patch of wild between the highway and the river, the more the traffic sounds feel muffled, less important. The moonlight helps her to see her way, but she doesn't need it. She knows the route, every rock, every hillock of grass. She has been here every night for a few weeks now, as soon as the bleeding stopped and the hospital discharged her.

Tiny glowing dots of fireflies prick the darkness open here and there all around her. Jenna's skin pimples in the cool evening breeze. The sobbing river flows past, just ahead of her.

At the shore line, Jenna gets to her knees. "Zuleika!" she yells. She sits back on her heels in the chilly riverbank mud, clutching the shoe bag in her lap, and waits. The heel of the red shoe pokes into her backside, but the mud feels good on the blistered sole of the other, bare foot.

"Zuleika!"

Nothing.

"I sorry about your fucking shoes, all right?"

Nothing.

She gets the new shoes out of their box. She tosses them into the water. They sink. She waits. She is waiting for the frogs in the reeds to stop chirping. For the sucking pit of grief in her chest to fill in.

For Zuleika to forgive her.

When none of that happens—just like it hasn't happened every other time she's come down here—she sighs and stands up. The heel of the left shoe sinks down into the mud. She pulls it out with a sucking sound.

The river isn't the only thing weeping. Someone is crying, over there in the dark, where the mangroves cluster thicker together. Jenna heads, hop-drop, towards the sound. There are tiny footprints in the muddy soil. They lead away from the crying, towards the direction of the embankment. In the dark, Jenna can't make out how far they go. But she can tell where they came from, so she follows the footprints backwards.

There's a child sitting on a big rock by the waterside. The child is the one crying. It is wearing a huge panama hat. To keep from burning in the moonshine? Jenna doesn't laugh at her own joke. The child is wearing jeans rolled up at the ankles, a too-big t-shirt. It has its legs tucked up and its chin on its knees, propping sorrow. In the moonlight, Jenna can see the yellow moccasins on its tiny feet. It's the girl from the shoe store.

When she gets near enough, Jenna says, "What you doing out here? Something wrong?"

"I was trying to catch crabs," the girl replies. "I like them too bad."

Jenna remembers the seafood smell on the girl's breath. "Trying to catch them how?"

"With my hands, nuh?"

"You went wading in this water at night, with nobody around? This water not good," says Jenna. It takes people, she doesn't say. Sure enough, now that she's closer, she can see that the girl is sopping wet. Water is running off her clothes and streaming down the sides of the rock.

"Mummy don't have time for me," the girl replies. "I been trying to catch my dinner myself, but . . ." the girl starts sobbing again. "My feet hurt so much! All that standing in the shoe store, all day. Every time I put my feet down, is like I walking on nails. I keep flinching when I step, and frightening off the crabs-them."

Poor thing. Something small releases inside Jenna, like the easing of a stitch. She squishes through the mud and sits on the rock beside the girl. She puts the bag with the empty shoe box in it down on the rock. "I know how it feel when your feet paining you," she says.

Whimpering, the girl leans closer to Jenna. The smell of seafood makes Jenna's tummy grumble again. Jenna thinks she could comfort the girl with a hug. She doesn't do it, though. Since last month, she doesn't have any business with comfort. But the girl won't stop crying, her shoulders jerking with the force of her sorrow. Unwillingly, Jenna asks, "You want me help you catch the crabs?"

The girl doesn't lift her panama-hatted head, but her crying noise stops. "You would do that for me?" she asks, sounding so young. She's only a child!

"You would have to show me how," Jenna replies. "And how old you are, anyway?"

The girl says, "You have to put your feet in the water, slow-slow and quiet, so the crabs don't know you're there. You have to stay crouched over, ready to grab them when they come up."

Jenna doesn't want to put her feet back into the river that had swallowed her and Zuleika not too long ago. She still has nightmares of escaping through the open driver's side window, of her head feeling light from holding her breath in. Only in her dreams, Zuleika doesn't let go when she grabs Jenna's right foot.

Jenna whispers so the child won't hear her talking to Zuleika. "I told you to undo your seatbelt, don't it? When we started sinking, I told you. You should have come with me. But all you did was scream."

In Jenna's dreams, she isn't able to kick her leg free of Zuleika's panicked hold. In Jenna's dreams, river weed comes pouring out of Zuleika's hand and wraps itself around Jenna's right ankle, and doesn't let go. In Jenna's dreams, she drowns with her sister. Every night, she drowns.

But she's promised the shoe shop child. "Okay," says Jenna. "Just until your mummy comes." She briefly wonders why a little girl is working in a shoe store, why she's hunting for crabs alone down by the river at night, but she doesn't wonder for too long. The world has become strange, and she is no longer part of it.

Jenna takes off the mashed-up left-side shoe and puts it on the rock. She wiggles her toes. Night air slips through the spaces between them. It feels odd. She had put that shoe back on after Zuleika's funeral.

She eases herself down off the rock. Now she's standing, both feet bare, on the riverbank. Her feet are squishing up mud. The left foot sinks a little farther into the mud than the right one. In front of her, black as oil, the roiling river giggles.

She can't do this. Jenna turns to walk back to solid land, to leave the child to wait there alone for its mother.

"Don't be frightened," says the child.

"I not frightened," Jenna replies. She is, but not of the water. Truth to tell, she wants nothing more than to sink down into the river, to join Zuleika. She wants it so badly, but she knows she can't. Can't make her parents lose two daughters to the river in less than a month. And she loves the sweet air. Heaven help her, but she loves it more than she loves her sister.

The child says, "You have to walk slow, keep your eyes peeled on the river bottom. When you see a crab, you reach down and grab it with your two hands."

"And what if it pinch me?"

"They small. They can't pinch hard."

Jenna tries it. She slides her feet along in the shallows. The moonlight lends its glow to the water there. After a minute or two of squinting, she can make out the river bottom. At first, Jenna's feet hurt every time she takes a step, but pretty soon the chilly river water numbs them. A crab scuttles sideways in front of her. Jenna pounces. Splashes. Misses. She falls into the shallow water. She's wet to the waist. The child laughs, and Jenna finds herself smiling, just a little. Jenna picks herself up. "Lemme try again."

She misses the second time, too. At the third fall, she laughs at herself. And at the fourth. By the fifth missed crab, she and the child are shrieking with merriment.

The child points. "There! Look another one!"

Jenna leaps for the splayed, scuttling crab. She catches it. She's holding it by its hard-shelled body. Its claws wave around and scrabble at her hand, but the crab is too small to do any damage. Jenna rises with it, triumphant, from the river bed. She whoops in glee, and the child applauds. Jenna realises that she's stopped thinking of the child as a girl. Really, she doesn't know whether it's a girl or a boy. She wades closer to the bank with her catch. "What I do with it now?" she asks.

The child hesitates. Then slowly, it removes the large panama hat that's been obscuring its face. It turns the hat over, bowl-like, and holds it out. "I put them in here," it says.

It has no face. Just a small bump where a nose should be, and that perfectly bowed mouth. Jenna is startled for a second, but she recovers. Not polite to stare. Anyway, in a world gone strange, why make a fuss about a missing pair of eyes and a nose with no holes? Jenna drops the crab into the hat the child holds out. Immediately, the child grabs the live crab up and rips into it with tiny, sharp teeth. It spits out a mouthful of broken shell. "You could catch more, please? I so hungry."

Jenna splashes about some more. She catches crabs, and she laughs giddily. Before this, the river has been making fun of her. Now, it is chortling with her. Jenna catches crabs and drops them into the child's hat. Jenna is shivering, belly deep. Maybe from being cold and wet, maybe from giggling so hard. The child smiles and eats and pats its full belly. Jenna pats her empty one. She goes closer to the shore. "Let me have one," she says to the child. She holds her hand out.

The child turns its blank face towards the sound of her voice. "You eat salt, or you eat fresh?" it asks.

"You have salt?" Jenna asks. "I would prefer that over eating it fresh."

"I don't have any."

Why does the child sound so happy about that? Jenna doesn't have patience with gladness nowadays. She has stopped hanging out with her friends and them from since. They would probably just want to go to the club, to dress up nice, to lime. Jenna doesn't want to do any of that any more. Dressing up leads to borrowing your sister's shoes without permission. It leads to quarreling over the shoes in the car on the way to the club. It leads to your sister losing control of the steering wheel and driving the car off the road into the river.

Jenna's eyes overflow. She has become used to the quick spurt of tears, as though someone has squeezed lime juice into her eyes.

Gently, the child says, "And look the salt right there so." It nods approvingly and hands over a particularly big crab. Jenna snatches it. She pulls off a gundy claw. With her teeth, she cracks it open. Crab juice and moist meat fall into her mouth. She sucks the rest of the meat out of the claw. She's so hungry that she barely chews before swallowing. As she eats, she cries salt tears onto the food, seasoning it. She fills her belly.

Jenna stops eating when she notices that the child is trying to reach for its own moccasined feet. Its arms are too short. The child says, softly, "I wish I could take these shoes off." It turns its smooth face in Jenna's direction, and smiles. "She had them with her in the car that night. She was going to give them to you, Mummy. As a present for me."

Jenna's mind goes still, like the space between one breath and the next. Somehow, she is out of the water and sitting on the rock beside the child. Gently, she touches one of the child's infant-fat legs. The child doesn't protest. Just leans back on its hands, its face upturned towards hers. Jenna lifts the child's small, lumpy foot. She loosens the lace on the moccasin and eases it off. The tiny yellow shoe sits in her palm, an empty shell. The child's foot is cold. Jenna cups the foot to warm it, and removes the other shoe. She looks at the two baby feet that fit easily in her hand. The child's strange gait makes sense now. Its feet are turned backwards.

Jenna gasps and pulls the child onto her lap. She curls her arms around it and holds its cold body close to hers. The other life she'd lost that night. The one only she and her older sister had known about.

The child snuggles against her. It puts one hand to its mouth and contentedly sucks its thumb. Jenna rocks it. She says, "I didn't even self tell Clarence yet, you know." The child grunts and keeps sucking its thumb. Jenna continues, "I sixteen. He fifteen. I was trying to think whether I was ready to grow up so fast."

The child sucks its thumb.

Jenna takes a breath that fills her lungs so deeply that it hurts. "Part of me was relieved to lose you." Her breath catches. "Zuleika *drowned*. And part of me was glad!" Jenna rocks the child and bawls. "I sorry," she says. "I so sorry." After a while, she is quiet. Time passes, a peaceful space of forever.

The child takes its thumb out of its mouth. It says, "Is her own she need."

Jenna is puzzled. "What?"

"Is that I was trying to tell you in the store. She don't want new shoes. She have the right side shoe already. You have to give her back the left side one. The one you been wearing."

Jenna surprises herself with a low yip of laughter. All this laughing tonight, like a language she'd forgotten. "I didn't even self think of that."

The child replies, "I have to go now."

Jenna sighs. "Yes, I know." She takes the child's blank, unwritten face in her hands and kisses it.

The child stands and pulls off its t-shirt and jeans. Its body is as featureless as its face. Jenna puts its hat back on. The child says, "You could keep my shoes instead, if you want." It eases itself down off the rock and toddles towards the water, away from life. But in the mud, the imprints of its feet are turned towards Jenna. The child enters the river. Knee deep, it stops and looks back at her. It calls out, "Auntie say she will look after me!"

Jenna waves. "Tell her thanks!"

Her child nods and waves back. It dives into the water, panama hat and all.

Jenna is still holding the tiny, wet moccasins. Gently, she squeezes the water from them. She slips them into the front pocket of her jeans. She goes and picks up the destroyed left pump from the rock. She kisses it. She yells, "Zuleika! Look your shoe here!" She raises her arm, meaning to fling the shoe into the river.

But there. In the very middle of the water; a rising, rolling semicircle, like a half-submerged truck tyre. Blacker than the blackness around. Swallowing light. The back of Jenna's neck prickles. Muscles in her calves jump; her running muscles. She makes herself remain still, though.

The fat, rolling pipe of blackness extends into a snakelike tail that wriggles over to the shore. The tail is un-bifurcated, its tip as big around as her wrist. The tip is coiled around a red patent pump, the matching right side to the shoe that Jenna is holding. In a whisper, Jenna asks, "Zuleika?" The tail tip slaps up onto the bank, splashing Jenna with mud.

Zuleika rises godlike from the river. Jenna whimpers and runs behind the rock.

Zuleika's upper half is still wearing the red sequined minidress, now in shreds, that she'd worn to go dancing the night of the accident. Moonlight makes the sequins twinkle, where they aren't hidden by river weed that has become tangled in them. The weed dangles and drips. Zuleika's lower half has become that snakelike tail. At her middle, the tail is as thick around as her waist. She floats upright. Her tail waves on the surface of the water. It extends as far upriver as Jenna can see in the moonlight.

Jenna's douen child clambers from where she'd been hidden behind Zuleika's back. The child climbs to sit on Zuleika's shoulders. It knots its fingers into the snares of Zuleika's hair. The water hasn't damaged its hat. Is the child smiling, or baring its teeth? Jenna can't tell.

Zuleika raises the whole length of her tail, and Jenna quails at the sheer mass of it, blacker than black against the night sky. Zuleika smashes her tail against the water's surface. The vast wave of sound, echoing up the river, hurts Jenna's ears. Jenna hears cars screeching to a halt on the highway, horns bleating. Jenna puts her hands against her ears and cowers. Not another crash. Please.

But there is no sound of collision. A couple of car doors slam. A couple of voices ask each other what the rass that sound was. Mama d'lo Zuleika hovers calmly in the water. The few trees must be hiding her from view, because soon, car doors slam again. Cars start up and drive off. Zuleika, Jenna, and the douen child are alone again.

Jenna finds that she's still holding the left-side shoe. She gathers her courage. She comes out from behind the rock. She says to her sister, "This is yours." She holds the shoe out to Zuleika.

Zuleika's tail-tip comes flying out of the darkness and grabs the shoe from Jenna. She hugs both once-shiny red shoes—the dusty one and the waterlogged one—to her breast.

The wetness in Jenna's own eyes makes the moon break up and shimmer like its own reflection on the water. "I miss you," she says.

Zuleika smiles gently. Carrying her niece or nephew, Zuleika sinks back beneath the water.

Jenna's hands are cold. She slides them into the front pockets of her jeans. One hand touches the child's shoes. The other touches her cell phone. She brings it out. It's wet, but for a wonder, it's still working. She texts her mother, says she will be home soon. She calls another number. "Clarence, you busy? You could come and give me a lift home? I by the river. You know where. No, I'm all right. I love you, too. Have something I need to tell you. Don't worry, I said!"

She still has her washekongs. She rinses her feet in the river and puts them on. She collects the empty shoe box and the plastic shopping bag. She climbs up the embankment to the roadside to wait for her boyfriend.

Old Habits

I was thinking about the notion of ghosts being the souls of people whose physical lives are ended, but who for some reason remain stuck, unable to move on to the next plane of existence.

Ghost malls are sadder than living people malls, even though malls of the living are already pretty damned sad places to be. And let me get this out of the way right now, before we go any further: I'm dead, okay? I'm fucking dead. This is not going to be one of those stories where the surprise twist is *and he was dead!* I'm not a bloody surprise twist. I'm just a guy who wanted to buy a necktie to wear at his son's high school graduation.

I wander through the Sears department store for a bit, past a pyramid of shiny boxes with action heroes peeking out of their cellophane windows, another one of hard-bodied girl dolls with permanently pointed toes and tight pink clothing, past a rack of identical women's cashmere sweaters in different colours: purple, black, red and green. The sign on the rack reads, 30% off, today only! It's Christmas season. Everywhere I wander, I'm followed by elevator music versions of the usual hoary Christmas classics. Funny, a ghost being haunted by music.

I make a right at the perfume counter. It's kind of a relief to no longer be able to smell it before I see it, to no longer have to hold my breath to avoid inhaling the migraine-inducing esters cloying the air around it.

Black Anchor Ohsweygian is lying on the ground by the White Shoulders perfume display. Actually, she's rolling around, her long grey hair in her eyes, her face contorted, yelling. I can't hear her; she's on the clock. Her hands slap ineffectually at the air, trying to fight off the invisible security guard who did her in. Her outer black skirt is up around her thighs, revealing underneath it a beige skirt, and under that a flower print one, and under that a baggy pair of jeans. She's wearing down-at-heel construction boots. They're too big for her; as I watch, she kicks out and one of the boots flies off, exposing layers of torn socks and a flash of puffy, bruised ankle. The boot wings right through me. I don't even flinch when I see it coming. I've lost the habit.

Now Black Anchor's face is being crushed down onto the hard tile floor, her features compressed. She's told me that the security guard knelt on her head to hold her down. One arm is trapped under her, the other one flailing. It won't be long now. I shouldn't watch. It's her private moment. We all have them, us ghosts. Once a day, we die all over again. You get used to it, but it's not really polite to watch someone re-dying their last moments of true contact with the world. For some of us, that moment becomes precious, a treasured thing. Jimmy would go ballistic if he ever caught me watching him choke on a piece of steak in the Surf 'N' Turf restaurant up on the third floor. Black doesn't mind sharing her death with me, though. She's told me I can watch as often as I like. I used to do it out of prurient curiosity, but now I watch because I just feel a person should have someone who cares about them with them when they die. I like Black. I can't touch her to comfort her. Can't even whisper to her. Not while she's still alive, which she just barely is right now. In a few seconds she'll be able to hear and see me, to know that I am here, bearing witness. But we still won't be able to touch. If we try, it'll be like two drifts of smoke melting into and through each other. That may be the true tragedy of being a ghost.

Black Anchor's squinched face has flushed an unpleasant shade of red. Her arm flops to the ground. Her rusty shopping cart has tumbled over beside her, spilling overused white plastic shopping bags, knotted shut and stuffed so full the bags are torn in places. In the bags are Black Anchor's worldly possessions. She pulls the darnedest things out of those bags to entertain Baby Boo with. I mean, why in the world did Black Anchor used to carry a pair of diving goggles with her as she trudged year in year out up and down the city streets, pushing her disintegrating shopping cart in front of her? She won't tell me or Jimmy why she has the goggles. Says a lady has to have some secrets.

I go and sit by Black Anchor's head. I hope, for the umpteenth time, that I've passed through the security guard that killed her. I hope he can feel me doing so, even just the tiniest bit, and it's making him shudder. Goose walking on his grave. Maybe he'll die in this mall too, someday, and become a ghost. Have to look Black Anchor in the eye.

A little "tuh" of exhaled breath puffs out of her. Every day, she breathes her last one more time. Her body relaxes. Her face stops looking squished against the floor. She opens her eyes, sees me sitting there. She smiles. "That was a good one," she says. "I think the guard had had hummus for lunch. I think I smelled chick peas and parsley on his breath." In her mouth, I can see the blackened stump that is all that was left of one rotted-out front tooth.

I return her smile. In those few seconds of pseudo-life she goes on the clock every day, Black Anchor tries to capture one more sensory detail from all she has left of the real world. "You are so fucking crazy," I tell her. "Wanna go for a walk?"

"Sure. I've clocked out for the day." The usual ghost joke. She sits up. By the time we get to our feet, her bundle buggy is upright again, her belongings crammed back into it. Her boot is back on her foot. It happens like that every time. I've never been able to catch the moment when it changes. Black pushes her creaky bundle buggy in front of her. We walk out of the south entrance of Sears, the one that leads right into the mall. Cheerful canned music follows us, exulting about the comforts of chestnuts and open fires.

Quigley's standing in front of the jewellery shop, peering in at the display. He does that a lot, especially at Christmas time and Valentine's Day, when the fanciest diamond rings get displayed in the window.

The day Quigley kicked it had been a February 13. He'd been in the mall shopping for an engagement ring for his girl. He was going to put it in a big box of fancy chocolates, surprise her with it on Valentine's Day. But then he had that final asthma attack, right there in the mall's west elevator. Quigley's twenty-four years old. Was twenty-four years old. Will be twenty-four years old for a long, long time now. Perhaps forever. He still carries around that box of expensive chocolates he bought before he stopped breathing. It's in one of those chi-chi little paper shopping bags, the kind with the flat bottom and the twisted paper handles.

Quigley waves sadly at us. He has pushed his waving hand through the handles of the gift bag. The bag bumps against his forearm. We wave back. Black murmurs, "He's brooding. He doesn't get over it, he'll find himself stepping outside."

There's a rumour among the mall ghosts; kind of an urban legend or maybe spectral legend that we whisper amongst ourselves when we're telling each other stories to keep the boredom at bay. There was this guy, apparently, this ghost guy before my time, who got so stir-crazy that he yanked open one of the big glass doors that leads to the outside. He stepped into the blackness that is all we can see beyond the mall doors. People say that once he was outside, they couldn't see him any longer. They say he shouted, once. Some people say it was a shout of joy. Some of them think it was agony, or terror. Jimmy says the shout sounded more like surprise to him. Whatever it was, the guy never came back. Jimmy says we lose one like that every few years. Once it was an eight-year-old girl. Everyone felt bad about that one. They still get into arguments about which one of them failed to keep an eye on her.

What that story tells me; we can touch the doors to the outside. Not everything in this mall is intangible to us.

I'm with Black Anchor Ohsweygian and Jimmy Lee around one of the square vinyl-topped tables in the food court; the kind with rounded-off edges that seats four. Like everywhere else in the mall, the food court seems deserted except for the ghosts. But there's food under the heat lamps and in the warming trays. Overcooked battered shrimp at the Cap'n Jack's counter; floppy, grey beef slices in gravy at Meat 'n' Taters; soggy broccoli florets at China Munch. The food levels go down and are replenished constantly during the day. To us, it's like plastic dollhouse food. We see the steam curling up from the warming trays, but there's no sound of cooking, no food smells. Kitty's standing in front of Mega Burger. I think she's staring at the shiny metal milk shake dispenser.

Jimmy and Black Anchor and I are sitting on those hard plastic seats that are bolted to food court tables. We're playing "Things I Miss." Kind of sitting, anyway. Sitting on surfaces is one of those habits that's hard to break. We can't feel the chairs under our butts, but we still try to sit on them. Jimmy Lee's aim isn't so good; he's actually sunk about two inches into his chair. But then, he's a tall guy; maybe it helps him not have to lean over to see eye to ghost eye with me and Black Anchor. Baby Boo has decided to join us today. He—I've decided to call him "he"—is lying on his back on the food court table, swaddled in his yellow blanket and onesie. He's mumbling at his little fist and staring from one to the other of us as we speak. Baby Boo doesn't quite have the hang of the laws of physics; he'd died too young to learn many of them. He's suspended in mid-air, about a hand's breadth above the table.

Things we miss, now that we're ghosts:

Jimmy says, "Really good cigars. Drawing the smoke of them into my lungs, holding it there, letting it out through my nose." All us mall ghosts, our chests rose and fell in their remembered rhythms, but no air went in and out.

Black Anchor Ohsweygian stares at her thin, wrinkled fingers on the table top. She says, "The sweet musk of beets, fragrant as blood-soaked earth."

"Vanilla milk shakes," I say, thinking of Kitty over there. "Cold, sweet, and creamy on your tongue."

Jimmy nods. "And frothy." He takes another turn: "Going up to the cottage for the first long weekend in spring."

I nod. "Victoria Day weekend."

"Yeah," Jimmy replies. "Jumping from the deck into the lake for the first time since the fall before." He laughs a little. It makes his big face crinkle up. "That water would be so frigging cold! It'd just about freeze my balls off, every time. And Barbara would roll her eyes and call me a fool, but she'd jump in right after." His expression falls back into its usual sad grumpiness. Barbara was his wife of thirty years.

Black Anchor says, "Toronto summers, when it would get so hot that squirrels would lie flopped like black skins on the branches, fur side up. So humid that you were sure if you made a fist, you would squeeze water dripping from the air. Your thighs squelched when you walked." Black Anchor's having one of her more conversational days. Apparently, she used to be a poet. A homeless poet. She told me there was a lot of that going on.

I say, "The warm milk smell of my husband's breath after his morning coffee."

"Fucking faggot," grumbles Jimmy. It's an old, toothless complaint of his.

I shrug. "Whatever."

"Hey," says Jimmy, in his gruff, hulking way. I know he's still talking to me because he won't quite meet my eyes, and his face does this defensive thing, this *I'm a manly man and don't you forget it* thing. He says, "That's the closest you've come to talking about a person you used to . . . you know, love. How come is that? Don't you miss anyone?"

His eyes glisten as he says the word "love," like he's crying. Jimmy goes on about Barbara like she was a piece of heaven that he lost. I guess she was, come to think of it.

"Yeah, I miss people," I say slowly, playing for time. Even when you're dead, some things cut close to the bone. Sometimes Baby Boo cries, and it makes my arms ache with the memory of feeding Brandon when he was that little, watching his tiny pursed mouth latch onto the nipple of his bottle, seeing his eyes staring big and calm up at me as though I were his whole world. "I miss lots of people."

Black leans back in her chair and sighs airlessly. "Well, I miss that girl at the doughnut shop who would slip me an extra couple if I went there during her shift."

Jimmy shakes his head. "Doughnuts. Jesus. How did you live like that?"

"I honestly don't know, Sugar."

I shoot Black a grateful glance for getting Jimmy off the subject. When I walk through the darkened mall at night, I try to remember Semyon's touch. The warmth of his hand on my cheek. The hard curve of his arm around me, his hand slipped into my back jeans pocket. I try to remember his voice.

I say to Black and Jimmy, "It's so unfair that we can't see or hear the world. That we can't touch, taste, or smell it."

Black replies, "Maybe being a ghost is a disease."

"What do mean, a disease?" I ask her. For the umpteenth time I wonder, what kind of name is Black Anchor Ohsweygian, anyway? Jimmy thinks maybe she's Armenian. He says that Armenians all have names that end in "ian." Some day I'm going to point out to him that some Armenians have names like "Smith."

"Like maybe we're not dead," she replies. "Maybe we just caught some kind of virus that messed up all our senses. Maybe we're all lying in hospital beds somewhere, and some grumpy cunt of a doctor with a busted leg is yelling at his team that they have to find us a cure."

"And maybe someone used to watch too much fucking television," says Jimmy. He vees his index and middle finger, puts them to his lips. For a second I think he's flipping her deuces, but no, he takes a drag of his imaginary cigarette. Habits. Black glares at him, hacks and spits to one side. Habits. Baby Boo belches a baby belch, then giggles. We don't know Baby Boo's real name. I don't remember how we ended up calling him Baby Boo.

Kitty must have heard us talking. She wanders over, coos at Baby Boo. He gives her a brief baby grin; the kind that always looks accidental, the baby more surprised than anyone else at what its face has just done. Kitty says, "I can smell stuff. Again, I mean. Like when I was alive."

Quickly, I tell her, "You might want to keep that to yourself." She hasn't been here very long. She doesn't know what she's saying. She doesn't know how dangerous it is. I should warn her outright. I don't.

Kitty ignores my lame hint. She says, "I'm serious. It just started to come back a little while ago. Bit by bit."

My heart starts pounding so quickly that my body trembles a little with every beat. Even though I know I don't have a heart, or a body. Even though I know it's just reflex. Jimmy and Black Anchor look just as avid as I feel. The three of us stare at Kitty, our mouths open. She waggles her fingers at Baby Boo. "I thought I was imagining it at first. You know how you can want something so bad it can make your mouth water?"

We know. Jimmy swallows.

Kitty'd only been fifteen. She and a bunch of her friends from school had crowded shrieking and laughing into the women's washroom on the main floor to try on makeup they'd just bought. In the jostling, Kitty fell. On the way down, she hit her head on the edge of a sink.

Kitty whispers, "I can smell French fries. And bacon." She points at Mega Burger, where she'd been standing. "Over there. Someone's burning bacon on the grill."

Black Anchor says fiercely, "What else? Smell something else!" Her voice doesn't sound human any more. It's hollow, mechanical, nothing like a sound made by air flowing over vocal chords.

Kitty looks around her. A slow smile comes to her face. "Somebody just went by wearing perfume. I think it's Obsession. She smells like my mom used to."

Oh, god. She's really doing it. She's smelling the scent trails of the living people all around us in this mall. Black Anchor chews daily over the gristle of a long ago memory, but Kitty just this second took a whiff of someone warm and alive as she walked past us. Life haunts us, us ghosts. It hovers just out of reach, taunting.

Longing is shredding my self-control to tatters. I moan, "Kitty, don't," but she starts talking again a split second after I say her name, so she doesn't hear the warning.

"Mister Kendall," she says to Jimmy, "there's someone sitting right there, in the same chair you are. I don't know whether it's a guy or a girl, but they're chewing gum. You know the kind that comes in a little stick and you unwrap the paper from it and it's kinda beige with these, like, zigzaggy lines in it? I can smell it as the person's spit wets it and they chew. I should be grossed out, but it's too freaking cool. There's someone right there!" She leans in towards Jimmy. She closes her eyes, and no fucking word of a lie, she inhales. Her chest rises and falls, and with it, I hear the breath entering and leaving her lungs. She opens her eyes and looks at us in wonder. "Peppermint," she whispers reverently, as though she's saying the secret name of God.

That does it. The need slams down on me like a wall of bricks, stronger than thought or compassion. I crowd in on Kitty. I dimly notice Jimmy and Black Anchor doing the same.

"Can you smell coffee?"

"Sweat! Can you smell sweat?"

"Is taste coming back, too? Can you taste anything?"

"Can you feel? Can you *touch*?"

Unable to hold the need in check, unable to do anything but shout it in shuddering, hungry voices, we demand to be fed. Kitty, surrounded, looks from one to the other of us, tries to answer our questions, but they come too hard and fast for her to reply. Our hollow shrieks draw the other ghosts. They come flocking in, clamouring, more and more of them as word goes round. We're all demanding to know what she can smell, demanding that she describe it in every last detail, clawing our fingers through the essence of her as we try in vain to touch her. Needing, needing, needing. And through the din is the thin sound of Baby Boo crying. He's only little. He doesn't know how to feed his hunger.

When the frenzy passes and we come back to ourselves, there's nothing left of Kitty but a few grey wisps, like fog, that dissipate even as we watch. The canned music tinkles on about Donner and Blitzen and the gifts that Santa brings to good boys and girls.

Stay long enough in the mall, and you learn what happens if you begin to get the knack of living again. We've used Kitty up. And we are still starving.

Ashamed, we avoid each other's eyes. We step away from each other, spread out through the mall. There is plenty of room for all of us. I go into the bookstore and stare at the titles that appear and disappear from the shelves. I miss reading. Tearlessly, airlessly, I sob. She was only fifteen. At fifteen, Brandon had been worrying about pimples. Semyon and I were coaching him on how to ask girls out. We'd gotten tips from our women friends. I have just sucked from a child what little remained of her life.

I feel it coming on, like a migraine aura. There's a whoosh of dislocation and the world rushes over me. I'm on the clock. My hand slaps down onto the moving rubber handrail. The slight sting of the impact against my palm is terrible and glorious. Sound, delicious sound battered against my ears: the voices of the hundreds and hundreds of people who'd been in the mall on my day. I felt my nipples against the crisp fabric of the white shirt I was wearing under my best grey suit.

There were people near me on the escalator. Below me, a beautiful brown-skinned man in worn jeans and a tight yellow t-shirt. He was talking on his cell phone, telling someone he'd meet them over by the fountain. Beside me was a woman about my age, maybe Asian mixed with something else. She was plump. Girlfriend, don't you know that sage-coloured polyester slacks don't suit anyone, least of all people like us whose waistlines weren't what they used to be? Lessee, I'd gotten a silk tie geometric pattern in greys and blacks shot through with maroon I thought it went nicely with my suit really shouldn't have waited so long to shop for it Semyon was pretty ticked at me for going shopping last minute he's just stressing but we had plenty of time to get to the graduation ceremony just a ten-minute drive and oh look there were Semyon and Brandon now waiting for me at the bottom of the escalator and Brandon's girlfriend Lara that's a pretty dress though I wondered whether she wasn't a little too well dumb for Brandon or maybe too smart but what did I know when I first started dating Semyon my sis thought he was too stuck-up for me but she'd thought the guy before him was too common Mom and Dad were going to meet us at Brandon's school and Sally and what's his name again Gerald should remember it by now he'd been my brother-in-law for over two years hoped my dad wouldn't screw up the directions we'd sent Tati an invitation to the graduation but she hadn't replied probably wouldn't show up you utter bitch he's your grandson Semyon and I had never tried to find out which one of us was his bio dad we liked having Brandon be our mystery child kept us going through his defiant years god I hoped to hell those were over and done with now I mean that time he got mad and decked Semyon it was funny later but not when it happened and look at him nineteen with his whole life before him grinning up at me I was just kvelling with pride and oh shit I should have put the tie on in the store better do that now why'd they wrap it in so much tissue paper there did I get the knot right oh whoops ow my elbow's probably bruised so stupid falling where everybody can see that cute guy turning to lend a hand to the clumsy old fag who can't manage a simple escalator oh crap I'm stuck my tie

The fall by itself probably wouldn't have killed me. But my snazzy new silk necktie caught in the escalator mechanism. And then the lady beside me was screaming for help and the cute guy was yanking desperately on my rapidly shortening tie as it disappeared into the works of the escalator and then my head was jammed against the steps and some of my hair caught in it too and pain pain pain no air pain and then the dull crack and the last face I saw was not Semyon's or Brandon's not even my sister Sally's or Dad's or Mom's or my dearest friend Derek's, just the panicked desperate face of some good-looking stranger I didn't know and would never know now because although he'd tried his hardest he hadn't been able to save my bloody lifemylifemylife.

Broke my fricking neck. Stupid way to go. Really stupid day to do it on. And for the rest of this existence, I'd regret that I'd done it while my son and my husband looked on, helplessly.

I'm standing alone on the down escalator. The canned music chirps at me to listen to the sleigh bells ringing. I'm off the clock. I let the escalator carry me down to the main floor. At the bottom, I step off it and walk over to the spot where I last saw my family. For all I know, no time has passed for them. For all I know, they might still be here, watching me ruin Brandon's graduation day. Maybe I brush past or through them as I walk this way once every day.

I straighten my tie. It does go well with my suit. I walk past the cell phone store, the bathing suit store, the drug store. I turn down the nearest corridor. It leads to an exit. I stand in front of the glass and steel door. I stare at the blackness on the other side of it. I think about pushing against the crash bar; how solid it would feel under my palm; how the glass door would feel slightly chilly against my shoulder as I shoved it open.

Emily Breakfast

Dedicated to Rose, who told me the story of the real Emily Breakfast.

Cranston woke into a bougainvillea-petalled morning, a rosy-fingered dawn of a morning. Soft, pinkish sunlight was streaming its way down from the bedroom skylight, his husband Sir Maracle was sprawled and snoring gently beside him, and Rose of Sharon was crouched on his chest, eyes closed in bliss, the low, vibrating hum of her purring making sleepy syncopation with Sir Maracle's snores. Her bliss was doubtless because she'd found an especially helpful ray of sunshine that not only kissed her with its warmth, but bathed her in glowing light which displayed the highlights in her chestnut fur to a most flattering advantage.

Cranston stretched and sighed, which caused Rose of Sharon to open kiwi-green eyes at him and chirp a single questioning mewl. She wanted her kibble. She always wanted her kibble, and most mornings, either Cranston or Sir Maracle had to stop in the middle of their scurrying about dressing for their j.o.bees to serve Rose of Sharon a big scoopful of kibble into one of her yellow-green bowls (the bowls matched her eyes), and to wash and fill the other with fresh water from the tap in the kitchen.

But there was to be no scurrying this morning. This was the first morning of the blessed furlough that was the weekend. The j.o.bee could go hang for two days, and there was a bedroom full of morning light, his man sleeping by his side, and Rose of Sharon basking on his chest.

With one hand, Cranston shovelled Rose of Sharon gently off him. She made a lazily offended *mraow* and landed *thump* on all fours on the floor. Cranston swung out of bed, grabbed his dressing gown from the hook on the wall, and threw it on. He shuffled his feet into his slippers. He stepped over a leather blindfold and a wooden paddle that had been tossed onto the floor and tiptoed out of the bedroom. He could put the toys away later. Now, it was time for breakfast. Rose of Sharon wove infinity symbols around his ankles with each step he took. This weekend morning, that felt like endearing affection, not exasperating annoyance. Though he still closed her out of the bathroom while he did his morning ablutions.

When he got out of there, Rose of Sharon was busily cleaning and preening herself with her rough tongue, stretching out her pinions till each individual feather at their tips separated from the others. When she saw him, she snapped to and got to her feet. She rubbed herself against his ankles, purring, until he bent to scritch the back of her neck. When he dug his fingers into her scruff and scratched, she closed her eyes in purry bliss. He tried twice to stop, but she butted her head against his hand, begging. So he kept at it a little while more.

But it really was time for breakfast. Cranston straightened up. "Come on, then," he said. Rose of Sharon chirruped a complaint at him for stopping so soon, but she trotted beside him into the kitchen. He scooped her a scoopful of kibble from the big brown paper sack that lived behind the kitchen door. She stalked in circles, her tail an exclamation sign of impatience, until he put her bowl down and she could fall upon it like a hawk upon a mouse. While Rose of Sharon was delicately wolfing down her kibble, Cranston had a look into the 'fridge. There was bacon, there was butter, and the bread was still fresh. There was spinach in the garden. It needed only eggs to make the meal complete. "Time to visit the sisters," he told Rose of Sharon. It was time to let them out of the coop and into their run, anyway.

Cranston let Rose of Sharon out the kitchen door ahead of him, and stepped out into the backyard, along the crazy-paving path that led to the vegetable garden and the chicken coop. He was picturing how he would manage, since of course he'd forgotten to fetch a basket from the kitchen, and of course he wasn't of a mind to go back and get one. He figured spinach first, almost filling one of the big pockets of his dressing gown. One egg cushioned safely on top of that. The second egg in the other dressing gown pocket. He'd have to walk gently then. Once he'd gone too quickly and had had to wash raw egg and eggshells out of his dressing gown pocket. The third egg he would cradle in one hand, leaving the other free to let himself back into the house.

He picked a batch of spinach from the garden, shaking the occasional slug off the leaves, led on by the image of crisp-cooked rashers of bacon, six each for him and Sir Maracle, laid out on the big blue oval serving platter. Bed of barely steamed spinach in the middle of the platter, fried eggs arrayed on top, their edges crispy and their yolks over easy. To keep him company, Rose of Sharon tracked in among the beds of spinach, basil, chives and oregano and pointed out more slugs to him. She didn't eat them. She'd tried that once, gotten herself a mouthful of slime for her trouble, and had never tried it again. The only thing Rose loved more than tracking slugs was getting the back of her neck scritched. "You've got to be part hound dog," he teased her. She gave him a bland stare and switched to chasing butterflies. Problem was, of course, that butterflies flit and flutter, while Rose of Sharon was more the "soar and dive" type of cat. Although she could fly more quickly than they did, the butterflies changed direction on a dime, and she couldn't do that. She almost never caught one. Or perhaps that was part of the fun. When she did catch one, she'd crush it down to the ground under one paw, lift the paw and shake it delicately, and look in a kind of nonplussed way at the brightly coloured smear she'd created. It was as though her playmate had out of the blue chosen to grab his bat and ball and go home.

Cranston layered the spinach into both pockets of his dressing gown, along with some basil and chives. The sweet smell of the basil and the sharp, fresh smell of the chives rose into his nostrils and made his tummy rumble. He got to his feet. "Come along, Rose."

Rose gave a brief, cattish yip, batted ineffectively at one more butterfly, and landed at Cranston's feet. She flupped her wings shut and inquired whether she might have a scritch for the road.

"Not right now, girl."

So she sighed and walked along beside him as he made his way to the chicken coop. As they got close to it, her ears perked. She sniffed the air, and her eyes went avid. Rose loved her some stewed chicken, and ever since Cranston and Sir Maracle had gotten the three hens, she'd suspected she might be partial to raw, recently hunted-down-by-Rose chicken as well. "No, Rose," said Cranston. "I keep telling you, they're not good for you." He gently pushed her aside with one foot while he opened the framed wire gate to the run and let himself in. She sat on the grass outside the run and evil-eyed him, her fur twitching in that way cats have when they're chagrined.

The chicken run was a wire mesh pen with the wooden chicken coop at one end of it. Cranston scooped a scoopful of feed from the big bag they kept under the coop; much like feeding Rose each morning, it was. He opened the little door to the coop and began scattering the feed on the dirt ground of the run. He called out to the three chickens: "Here, Lunch; here, Dinner; here, Emily Breakfast!" The names had been Sir Maracle's little joke. But Emily Breakfast had already had a name when they'd gotten her and her sisters from the animal rescue, so they'd let her keep it, and just added her new name on at the end. Cranston doubted that any of the hens either knew or cared that they had names, but it was the principle of the thing.

Hearing him call, the hens inside the dark coop began to cluck excitedly. Dinner, brick red with white feathers scalloped in amongst the red ones, rushed through the little door first. She almost always did. She hopped down to the ground and started pecking up feed, just as Lunch put in her appearance. Lunch was a kind of yellowish-brown that matched her beak. She was plump and round. "If you don't watch it, girl," teased Cranston, "you won't be able to get out the door pretty soon."

Of course she ignored him and hopped down to the ground with a clumsy half flap of her wings. She started pecking up feed faster than Dinner, keeping one eye on Dinner and rushing her every so often to scare her off a bit of feed that Lunch had had her eye on.

Emily Breakfast was late to the feast today.

"Emily?" Cranston called. No Emily.

"Come on, lazybones. Or are you trying to make sure I don't get your egg?"

He stuck his head inside the coop. In the darkness he could make out the three straw-filled nests, side by each. Lunch had laid a brown egg, and Dinner her usual white one with purple spots.

The third nest was empty. No egg, no Emily Breakfast. Cranston yanked his head out of the coop, banging the back of his skull on the jamb of the tiny door as he did so. He barely noticed. "Rose of Sharon, did you get in here and make off with Emily Breakfast?"

Rose looked hurt. And actually, there were no signs of a struggle in the run; no feathers, no blood. Cranston looked all around the coop and the run, and finally had to admit it. Emily Breakfast was gone. Disappeared. Like the poultry Rapture had come.

Cranston left the henhouse and rushed past a baffled Rose. Yelling for Sir Maracle, he barreled in through the kitchen door. Sir was up and washing the dishes left in the sink from last night's dinner. He was also naked. Ordinarily, Cranston would have stopped to admire his husband's fine brown form: the broad shoulders that narrowed to a lithe waist, the firm swells of his ass and thighs below. Not today. Well, not for long, anyway. "Emily Breakfast's been rustled!" he told Sir Maracle.

"What?" Sir turned away from his washing up to face Cranston.

"She's gone! Gone away clean! Not even an egg, not even a feather! What are we going to do?"

"You're sure she's not hiding somewhere in the coop?"

"There's nowhere in there to hide. The straw's not thick enough to cover a mouse."

"Rose of Sharon didn't get in and cause mayhem?"

"I don't think so, Sir. I think a two-legged miscreant got into the henhouse and took her away from us."

"Chickens walk on two legs," said Sir musingly. "And kangaroos, sometimes."

"That's not—"

Sir frowned. "Let me put some pants on." He came and took Cranston's hand, gave him a kiss. "We'll figure this out."

"We have to find her soon. Before she becomes just breakfast, no Emily."

"I know, love."

While Sir was getting dressed, Cranston started in on making breakfast. He'd forgotten to take the two eggs that had been in the nests, but he didn't have any taste for them right now. Not with Emily Breakfast missing and probably in peril. It'd have to be just bacon and spinach. Cranston laid strips of bacon into a frying pan on the stove. Into another frying pan he put butter, garlic and the chopped herbs.

Sir came back into the kitchen. He ground some coffee beans and put the coffee on to perk.

The butter in the frying pan had melted and was starting to smoke. Cranston tossed in the spinach, covered the pan, turned the heat off.

"Sit," said Sir, pulling a couple of stools out from under the kitchen counter. "Let me serve." He knew that nothing melted Cranston's heart more than when he flipped the script a little.

Cranston beamed his thanks at Sir, but he was too preoccupied to show his full appreciation. "What are we going to do about Emily Breakfast? And the bacon needs turning."

Sir leapt to rescue the bacon before it burned. "I figure we search the yard first, in case she got out of the henhouse somehow." He set out two mugs, began pouring fragrant coffee into them.

Cranston nodded. "Makes sense. And I'll check with the neighbours. She could have gotten over the fence."

Sir flipped the bacon out of the pan onto some folded paper towel. He began serving it onto two plates, then gasped and stopped. He looked stricken. "Have you checked out in the street?"

"Oh, my god." Cranston shoved his stool back and ran out the front door. Sir was right behind him. They went up and down their street, in both directions. There was no Emily Breakfast roadkill to be seen. Sir breathed a sigh of relief.

By now, their neighbours had begun to notice the two of them looking. Sally and Beth offered to call the police. "For a chicken?" said Sir Maracle.

So Sally and Beth sent their eleven-year-old son Juniper to knock on everyone's doors and ask permission to look in their yards for Emily Breakfast. Sabina—Morrigan, June, and Sam's daughter—went with him. She was two years younger, and had a bit of a crush on Juniper. In the meantime, June was broadcasting the news to the neighbourhood via her herd of messenger lizards. Herd?

"What do you call a group of lizards, anyway?" Cranston asked her.

June frowned as she used a length of bright blue ribbon to tie a tiny rolled-up note around the middle of a squirming three-inch-long lizard. "You know, I've never known the official term for it? I just call them a 'scuttle.'" She released the lizard. "Off you go, Baby. When you come back, Mama'll feed you some nice fresh crickets." She sighed. "If it comes back, that is. If it's not losing them to predators, it's message recipients that want to keep them."

Mr. Finkelstein brought out some lemonade for Cranston and Sir Maracle. "Fresh-squeezed," he said proudly.

Cranston muttered to Sir, "I'd really rather have my coffee." But they both politely drank their lemonade while Mr. Finkelstein sat in the rocking chair on his porch and beamed at them.

By the time they got back to their house, half the neighbourhood was either mobilized or alerted in the search for Emily Breakfast, and Rose of Sharon was on the kitchen counter, gobbling down the last of the bacon. Cranston scolded her and shooed her back outside.

Sir sighed. "At least someone got to eat it before it got cold."

"I'll go get the two eggs from the henhouse."

As reports came in from all over the neighbourhood, it became obvious that Emily Breakfast hadn't gone walkabout. Not on her own, at least. Cranston was beside himself. He'd been polishing the padded leather bench in the play room, but his mind wasn't on it. "Who d'you think would want to steal Emily Breakfast?" he asked Sir, who was arranging paddles on the wall in a row according to size.

Sir considered. "Someone hungry?"

"Oh, don't. I can't bear to think about it. Besides, there's probably no one in this city who has a clue how to pluck and"—he swallowed—"gut a chicken."

"I do. My ma used to keep chickens when we lived out Manitoulin Way."

"But you're not the thief, are you?" Cranston was feeling snappish.

"No, of course not."

Cranston sighed. "I'm sorry. I just worry that we're running out of time." He polished a little while longer, then said, "Wanna go sit out in the backyard?"

"You just want to check the yard for her again, don't you?"

"We might have overlooked her somehow. Don't you think?"

Sir thought about it, nodded. "We might have." But he didn't look very hopeful about it. "When we get her back, I'm putting a proper padlock on the door to their run, instead of a latch."

Cranston was already halfway up the stairs to the main floor.

Outside, the early afternoon sun was the soft yellow-white of Emily Breakfast's plumage. Sunlight glowed through the leaves of spinach and the low grass that covered the rest of the backyard. The leaves gleamed a delicious kiwi-green, the same colour as Rose of Sharon's eyes. Sir and Cranston sat in their Adirondack chairs and pretended to be enjoying the sunshine. Rose pestered them for scritches, but they both got tired of it pretty soon. In a huff, Rose wandered off to do cattish things.

Sir said, "Suppose we don't get her back?"

"Let's not get her back first before we think about that, okay?"

Sir thought his way through that twisty sentence, gave an unhappy nod. Then he said, "Silly cat. Stop that."

"What's she up to now?" Cranston turned to look. Rose of Sharon was tracking through the grass in front of the henhouse, her nose to the ground and her head weaving from side to side, picking up the scent.

Picking. Up. The. Scent.

Sir must have been thinking the same thing, because he asked, "Maybe it's you she's smelling? You went to the henhouse this morning."

Rose turned towards the stone paving path that ran along the side of the house to the front. "I didn't go that way," Cranston replied. He and Sir Maracle looked at each other. Rose of Sharon was on the trail of whoever had been in the henhouse last night. Sir Maracle went and undid the latch on the henhouse door.

Cranston stood. "Here, kittykitty." He tried to grab Rose of Sharon and missed. His foot slid on the grass and he went down. Sir Maracle leapt to help him up. He must have pulled the henhouse door open when he did so, and that was the moment that Rose chose to switch directions and dash into the henhouse. "Oh shit!" said Cranston. "Never mind me; get Rose!"

"Screw Rose. Is your ankle okay?"

"Yes, I'm fine. Get Rose!"

But Sir Maracle was already helping Cranston up instead.

A godawful noise came from the henhouse; a cross between a growling and a crowing. It made the little hairs on Cranston's arms stand straight up. Rose was in the middle of the run, standing very still in a stalking pose, one front leg raised to take another step. But she looked more startled than stalkerish; in front of her, Lunch and Dinner had puffed their feathers and drawn their bodies up to full size, which was a good six inches taller than they usually showed. Rose took an uncertain step closer to them. Dinner screeched another challenge. This one came with a small spurt of fire from her nostrils. Her spurs, normally tucked harmlessly against the sides of her legs, descended. Cranston made it into the run just as Dinner and Lunch, snorting Bunsen burner-sized flames, both lunged spurs first for Rose. He pulled Rose out from under. Lunch's thrust gouged a line down his forearm. "Ow!" He tucked Rose under his forearm and hightailed it out of the chicken run. Sir slammed the gate shut behind him. Cranston put Rose down on the ground. She shook herself and stared disbelievingly into the run. Lunch and Dinner, chests out, were stomping around the run, glaring at her. They were still blowing little puffs of smoke from their nostrils.

Sir knelt and stroked Rose. "Now do you see why we don't want you in there?" he asked her. "Chickens are descended from dragons, you idiot."

"Now they're never going to let her in there long enough to get Emily Breakfast's scent."

Sir looked at the chickens that were slowly deflating again as they calmed down. "I'm beginning to think that Emily Breakfast might be able to defend herself."

"Against a cat, yes. But against a human?"

"I don't know what else to do, love. Come. Let's clean out that cut."

"Wait! Check Rose out."

Rose of Sharon was tracking again. They followed her along the paved stone pathway to the front of the house, where she veered off to the wall that ran along the front of their property. She leapt to the top of the wall with a flap of her wings. She sniffed around the top of the wall for a second, then leapt down to the ground outside their property.

"Bastard came over the wall," said Cranston. "Find her, Rose! Go find Emily Breakfast!"

Rose didn't even look up. She just kept following the trail.

Sir put one arm around Cranston. "D'you think that'll really work? It's one thing to track a slug through the spinach patch, but a human?"

"We still don't know that it was a human. Don't foxes get into hen-houses?"

"Damn. Let's hope Rose doesn't corner a fox."

"Shit! I didn't think of that."

But though they went looking for Rose, calling out her name, they couldn't find her, either. They finally gave up and went back home. "We keep this up," said Cranston gloomily, "and we won't have any pets left."

A screech split the air of a peaceful Saturday afternoon. It was coming from down the street. Sir sighed. "What now?"

"Ow! Get off me! Stop that!" June was stumbling up the street towards them. She was waving her hands above her head. "Not the hair, you mange-ridden fleabag!" She was actually being harried in their direction. Rose of Sharon flew above her, dive-bombing her head from time to time with outstretched claws. And worrying at her ankles with spurs extended and the occasional tiny gout of flame—

"Emily Breakfast!" Cranston flung himself through the gate and out into the street.

Emily Breakfast was magnificent. Sunlight glowed white-hot on her feathers. She was at full height, her neck all snaky. She strutted angrily, growl-shrieking her fury at June.

When they got closer, Rose landed on the pavement and butted her head against Cranston's shin, but Emily kept circling June, doing that hair-raising growl and menacing her with her spurs. June's ankles were covered in long red welts.

June stumbled to a halt, her chest heaving. "Those animals are dangerous!" she said to Cranston, doing a little leap to avoid another welting from Emily Breakfast. "I'm going to call the pound to take them away!"

Cranston crossed his arms. "You may want to first explain to them why you trespassed onto our premises to steal one of them. Emily, it's okay. Stop now."

"Why should you guys have all the cool pets?" raged June. "Three chickens! You'd think you could have spared one of them!"

"Excuse me? Who's the one with the trained messenger lizards?"

June scowled. Then she yipped, jumped to one side, and started batting at her ankle. Emily Breakfast had taken one more shot, and had set June's sock on fire with a snort of flame. Then Emily Breakfast turned tail and, squawking, did a waddling run over to Cranston, her wings held out at her sides, for all the world like an alarmed chicken. Which she was, after all. She was just the kind who got feisty when cornered. Cranston was so proud of her! He crouched down, but Emily Breakfast ran right through his welcoming open hands. She crouched under his butt and stuck her head out, quarreling at June from the safe shelter of Cranston's body.

Sir Maracle had come over to join them. "Give it up, June. I'm beginning to think there's a reason that so many of your lizards try to run away and never come back."

"June," said Cranston, "go home. Maybe you'll be the one getting a visit from the animal shelter people."

June huffed. Rose yowled at her. June took a step backwards. "She would have been too much trouble, anyway. Little bitch dropped an egg on my head."

Sir laughed. "Good girl, Emily Breakfast."

June glared at them and stumped off towards her home.

Rose leapt out of Sir's arms. She hunkered down and peered under Cranston at Emily Breakfast. From a safe distance. Emily was back down to normal size. She stepped slowly out of Cranston's lee, towards Rose. Rose got to her feet, ready to flee or fly. But Emily didn't charge, didn't swell. Her spurs remained sheathed. When she got close enough, Rose stuck her nose out and sniffed Emily Breakfast's scent. Emily Breakfast stretched her neck out. With her beak, she scritched the back of Rose of Sharon's neck, the way birds do to show affection to each other. Rose sighed and closed her eyes in bliss. Emily Breakfast kept it up a good, long while.

Herbal

I was once talking online with a group of writers and writing students about tactics for suspending the reader's disbelief in the fantastical elements of a story. I found myself typing something to the effect that one possible strategy was to never give the reader the time to disbelieve. Start the story with a bang, I wrote. Have an elephant . . . then I realized I had a story. I got off the Internet and wrote "Herbal."

That first noise must have come from the powerful kick. It crashed like the sound of cannon shot. A second bang followed, painfully, stupefyingly loud; then a concussion of air from the direction of the front door as it collapsed inward. Jenny didn't even have time to react. She sat up straight on her couch, that was all. The elephant was in the living room almost immediately. Jenny went wordlessly still in fright and disbelief. She lived on the fifteenth floor.

The elephant took a step forward. One of its massive feet slammed casually through the housing of the television, which, unprotesting, broke apart into shards of plastic, tangles of coloured wires and nubbins of shiny metal. So much for the evening news.

The elephant filled the close living room of Jenny's tiny apartment. Plaster crumbled from the walls where it had squeezed through her brief hallway. Its haunches knocked three rows of books and a vase down from her bookshelf. The vase shattered when it hit the floor.

The elephant's head brushed the ceiling, threatening the light fixture. It crowded the tree trunks of its two legs nearest her up against the couch. Fearing for her toes—well, her feet, really—Jenny yanked her own feet up onto the couch, then stood right up on the seat. It was only the merest advantage of height, but it was something. She couldn't call for help. The phone was in the bedroom, on the other side of the elephant.

The animal smelled. Its wrinkly, gray-brown hide gave off a pungent tang of mammalian sweat. Its skin looked ashy, dry. Ludicrously, Jenny found herself thinking of how it might feel to tenderly rub bucketsful of lotion into its cracked surface, to feel the hide plump and soften from her care.

Elephants were hairier than she'd thought. Black, straight bristles, thick as needles, sprung here and there from the leathery skin.

The elephant reached out with its trunk and sniffed the potted plant flourishing on its stand by the window—a large big-leaf thyme bush, fat and green from drinking in the sun. Fascinated, Jenny watched the elephant curl its trunk around the base of the bush and pluck it out of its pot. The pot thudded to the carpet, but didn't break. It rolled over onto its side and vomited dirt. The elephant lifted the plant to its mouth. Jenny closed her eyes and flinched at the rootspray of soil as the animal devoured her houseplant, chewing ruminatively.

She couldn't help it; didn't want to. She reached out a hand—so small, compared!—and touched the elephant. Just one touch, so brief, but it set off an avalanche of juddering flesh. A fingertipped pod of gristle with two holes in it snaked over to her, slammed into her chest and shoved her away; the elephant's trunk. Jenny felt her back collide with the wall. Nowhere to go. She remained standing, very still.

A new smell pulled her eyes toward its source. The elephant had raised its tail and was depositing firm brown lumps of manure onto her carpet. She could see spiky threads of straw woven into each globule. The pong of rotted, fermented grass itched inside her nose, made her cough. Outraged, hardly knowing what she did, she leapt forward and slapped the elephant, hard, on its large, round rump. The vast animal trumpeted, and, leading with its shoulder, took two running steps through the rest of her living room. It stuck briefly in the open doorway on the other side. Then more plaster crumbled, and it popped out onto her brief balcony. With an astonishing agility, the pachyderm clambered out over the cement wall of the balcony. "No!" Jenny shouted, jumping down off the couch, but it was no use. Ponderous as a walrus diving from an ice floe, the elephant flung itself over the low wall. Jenny rushed to the door.

The elephant hovered in the air, and paddled until it was facing her. It looked at her a moment, executed a slow backwards flip with a half turn, then trundled off, wading comfortably through the aether as though it swam in water.

The last thing she saw of the beast, in the crowding dark of evening, was the oddly graceful bulk of its blimp body, growing smaller, as it floated towards the horizon.

Jenny's knees gave way. She felt her bum hit floor. A hot tear rolled down her cheek. She looked around at the mess: the scattered textbooks for the course she was glumly, doggedly failing; the crushed vase in a colour she'd never liked, a grudging gift from an aunt who'd never liked her; the destroyed television with its thousand channels of candied nothing. She wrinkled her nose at the smell of elephant dung, then stood again. She fetched broom and dustpan from the kitchen and started to clean up.

A month later she passed the web design course, just barely, and sold the textbooks. She felt lighter when she exchanged them for crisp bills of money. At the pharmacy, she used most of the money to buy all the lotion they had, the type for the driest skin. After he'd helped her repair her walls, her father had given her another big-leaf thyme cutting, which, sitting in its jar of water, had quickly sprouted a healthy tangle of roots. She'd told him once about the elephant. He'd raised one articulate brow, then said nothing more.

Jenny lugged the tubs of skin lotion home, then went to the hardware store. With the remaining money she bought a bag of soil. Back home again, she transferred the cutting into a new pot that her dad had given her. She put it on the balcony, where it could enjoy the two remaining months of summer. The plant grew quickly, and huge.

She got hired to maintain the question-and-answer page for the local natural history museum. The work was interesting enough, and sometimes people asked about the habits of elephants. Jenny would pore over the curators' answers before putting them up on the web page. It must have been an Indian elephant; an African one would never have fit through her doorway. For the rest of the summer, every evening when she got home, she would go out onto the balcony, taking a container of the skin lotion with her. She would brush her hands amongst the leaves of the plant, gently bruising them. The pungent smell of the herb would waft its beckoning call out on the evening air, and Jenny would lean against the balcony railing for an hour or so, lotion in hand, hopefully scanning the darkening sky.

A Young Candy Daughter

I'm not the only person who's ever asked the question, "What if God was one of us?" But maybe "us" looks a little different from my side of the sandbox.

The Salvation Army Santa Claus wasn't ho-ho-hoing, not any more. He was no longer singing a carol, and he had stopped ringing his bell. He stood on the busy street corner—a thin brown man wearing Saint Nick's heavy velvet-red-and-whites and sweating himself thinner in the tropical heat—and gaped into the brass pot he had hanging in a frame for people to put their coins in.

Only two people stood near him. The young woman's freshness of skin and mischievous smile made it impossible to guess her age. She could have been sixteen, or twenty-six. Her jeans were scandalously tight, and, he noticed as she bent to tie her child's shoelace, showed off her high bottom nicely. Under different circumstances, the Salvation Army Santa Claus would have been using the cover of his cotton wool mustachios and beard to sneak a better glance. The young woman was not so much beautiful as *pretty*. The Salvation Army Santa Claus preferred pretty; he generally found it to be friendlier. Hers shone through despite hair severely processed into rigid ringlets. Her stylized makeup job failed to homogenize and blanch her features. Instead of the sparkling gold chain around her neck, silver or platinum would have complemented her black skin better, but no matter. (The chain supported a pendant with the word "foxy" in gold, followed by a star.) If you were to search for a word for what glowed through her as it did, made you want to laugh with her, and dance, you would have come up with "joy."

The young woman smiled as she placed her hand on the head of the second person standing at the Salvation Army pot; a little boy? Girl? Difficult to tell. An even younger person. The child wore too-big jeans, rolled up at the ankles, with threadbare knees. Its hair was cane-rowed neatly against its head, in even rows that went from nape to neck. It wore a scowl, a Spider-Man t-shirt, and a gold stud in either ear. But earrings were no indicator of gender these days. The child had one foot on a skateboard, up-ending it at an angle. The child pulled a handful of candy out of the Salvation Army pot and, with a look of intense concentration, flung it in an arc away from its body. Other children at the street corner broke free of their parents and scrabbled to collect it. So did one woman, her feet bare and black-bottomed, her body burly only because she seemed to be wearing everything she'd ever owned, in dirty and torn layers one atop the other. She clutched two packets of tamarind balls and five peppermints to her bosom with one hand. In the other hand she held a purple lollipop. As she scuttled into a corner to eat the rest of her prize, she tore the lollipop wrapper away with her teeth.

The Salvation Army Santa Claus stared at the young woman. "It didn't have any sweeties in there before," he said.

In response, she only grinned. *Worlds in that grin; miracles. Somewhere, a leader was shot, and the wondrous creation that was a gull swooped down over the waves and caught a fat fish for its young.* "La'shawna," she said to the child—a girl, then— "people want more than sweeties to fill their belly."

The tomboy of a girl looked up at her, scratched her nose, and said, "So what I should give them?"

"I ain't know," her mother replied. "Some people eat meat but no provisions. Some people eat provisions but no meat. Some people only want a cold beer and some peace and quiet."

The little girl considered. The Salvation Army Santa Claus peered into his brass pot. As far as he could see, it still only held the few coins he had received for singing his carols and ringing his bell. Perhaps the child had put the sweeties in there herself? They were troublemakers, her and her pretty mother. He was going to have to run them off.

"All right," the child said. She tossed her chin in greeting to the Salvation Army Santa. "Mister, tell any hungry people to put they hand in your pot. Each one will find what they want."

"What?" The Salvation Army Santa scowled at the little girl.

"You eat lunch yet?" her mother said to him.

"What that have to do with . . . why?"

"You hungry?"

Her smile was infectious. He found himself beaming back at her. "Yes."

"Then put your hand in the pot, nuh?"

Feeling like an idiot, the Salvation Army Santa did as she suggested. His hand closed over something warm and yielding. A delicious smell came from it. His tummy rumbled. He pulled his lunch out of the pot and nearly dropped it in surprise.

The child laughed. "Mummy, check it," she said. "All he want is a patty and a cocoa bread!"

People were starting to gather round. The woman in all her tattered clothing was tiptoeing nearer. "Only the hungry ones will get anything," the child told the man.

"Come, darling," said the young woman. "We have to go. Plenty to do."

The girl let the skateboard slap to the floor. "What else we must do now?" she asked.

"Well, this nice man going to get more customers than he can handle. So now we have to visit every Salvation Army Santa we can find round here and make their pots into cook pots, too."

"That's a lot of work, Mummy."

"You started it, girlchild."

The little girl made a face and kissed her teeth in mild exasperation. She shook her head, but then she smiled. The smile had something of her mother's about it.

The little girl hopped onto the skateboard and rolled away slowly. She stopped a little way away and did skillful, impatient circles, waiting for her mother to catch up.

Cringing as though she feared violence, the tattered woman snuck her hand into the pot. The thing she brought out was wrapped in banana leaves, tied with string, and steaming. She cackled in amazement, a delight rare and miraculous. *Somewhere, children got a snow day. Somewhere else, a political prisoner died only minutes into his "interrogation," cheating his torturer.* A man stepped up to the pot and put his hand inside.

"Is not this easy, you know," the Salvation Army Santa said to the young woman.

She gave him an appraising look.

"Doing good, I mean," he explained.

She sighed. "I know. She still have plenty to learn, and sometimes I don't know what to tell her. When she help one person, she might be harming someone else." She gestured at the pot, where four people were elbowing at each other to try and get their hands inside. "Where you think all this food coming from?" she asked. "Is somebody hard labour." She clapped her hands to get the attention of the people squabbling over the pot of plenty. "Hey!" she yelled. Faces turned to her. "If allyuh fight, that food going to turn to shit in allyuh mouth one time."

The wrangling subsided a little. The little girl came whizzing up on her skateboard, dipped her hand into the pot, and brought it back out overflowing with penny sweeties, sweet and sour plums, candy canes and gummy bears; only the red ones. She flashed a triumphant grin at her mother, who said, "La'shawna, you have to have more than that for lunch!" The girl put two gummy bears in her mouth and zoomed away again.

The young woman sighed. "I have to go with she," she said. "Yesterday she turned an old man's walking cane into solid gold. He nearly break he foot when he drop it." She waved goodbye to the Salvation Army Santa Claus. Tentatively, he waved back. She began to run after her child. She stopped a little way off, cupped her mouth with her hands and yelled back at the Santa Claus, "Yes, the name is Mary. I ain't have no Joseph. But you nice. I could come back and check you later?"

He nodded.

She ran to catch up with La'shawna.

A Raggy Dog, a Shaggy Dog

In the fall of 2002, I spent two months as writer-in-residence at Green College, a graduate residence of the University of British Columbia in Canada. Green College is a beautiful residence on a beautiful campus in an extraordinarily beautiful part of Canada. I have so many glorious memories of my time there; among them tall pines, gyring crows, taking a bowl out in the mornings to pick wild blackberries for my breakfast, spying shy seals in the ocean, hosting a short writing series, lavender bushes the size of small Volkswagens, the Hallowe'en dance, talking with the grad students about everything from science fiction to religious philosophy, and the weekly word game nights in the dining hall. Though I don't remember which game spawned this next story, it is my fantastical paean to the trials of geek dating, and to imaginatively overcoming them.

> *Have you seen a little dog anywhere about?*
> *A raggy dog, a shaggy dog,*
> *Who's always looking out*
> *For some fresh mischief which he thinks*
> *he really ought to do . . .*
> —from "My Dog" by Emily Lewis

There you are. Right on time. Yes, climb up here where we can see eye to eye. Look, see the nice plant, up on the night table? Come on. Yeah, that's better. I'm going to get off the bed and move around, but I'll do it really slowly, okay? Okay.

You know, I don't really mind when it's this hot. The orchids like it. Particularly when I make the ceiling sprinklers come on. It's pretty easy to do. I light a candle—one of the sootless types—climb up on a chair, and heat a sprinkler up good and hot. Like this. Whoops, here comes the rain. Oh, you like it too, huh? Isn't that nice?

Wow, that alarm's loud. No, don't go! Come back, please. The noise won't hurt you. I won't hurt you.

Thank you.

When the downpour starts, the orchids and I just sit in the apartment and enjoy it; the warmth, the artificial rain trickling down the backs of our necks. The orchids like it, so long as I let them dry out quickly afterwards; it's a bit like their natural homes would be. So when I move, I try to find buildings where there are basement apartments with sprinklers. I've gotten used to the sound of fire alarms honking.

It's best to do the candle trick in the summer, like now. After the fire department has gone and the sprinklers have stopped, it's easy to dry off in summer's heat. In winter, it takes longer, and it's cold. Some day I'll have my own rooms, empty save for orchids and my bed, and I'll be able to make it rain indoors as often as I like, and I won't have to move to a new apartment after I've done it any more. My rooms will be in a big house, where I'll live with someone who doesn't think I'm weird for sleeping in the greenhouse with the orchids.

My name is Tammy Griggs. You can probably see that I'm fat. But maybe that doesn't mean anything to you. Me, I think it's pretty cool. Lots of surface for my tattoos. This one, here on my thigh? It's a *Dendrobium findlayanum*. I like its pale purple colour. I have a real one, in that hanging pot up there. It looks pretty good right now. In the cooler months, it starts dropping its leaves. Not really a great orchid to have in people's offices, because when the leaves fall off, they think it's because you aren't taking care of it, and sometimes they refuse to pay you. That's what I do to earn a living; I'm the one who makes those expensive living plant arrangements you see in office buildings. I go in every week and care for them. I have a bunch of clients. I've created mini jungles all over this city, with orchids in them.

This tat here on my belly is the *Catasetum integerrimum*. Some people think it's ugly. Looks like clumps of little green men in shrouds. Tiny green deaths, coming for you. They're cool, though. So dignified. To me they look like monks, some kind of green order of them, going to sing matins in the morning. After their singing, maybe they work in the gardens, tending the flowers and the tomatoes.

On my bicep is the Blue Drago. They call it blue, but really, it's pale purple too. This tat underneath it is a picture of my last boyfriend. Sam. He drew it, and he put it on me. He did all these tattoos on me, in fact. Sam was really talented. He smelled good, like guy come and cigarettes. And he would read to me. Newspaper articles, goofy stuff on the backs of cereal boxes, anything. His voice was raspy. Made me feel all melty inside. He draws all the time. He's going to be a comic artist. He designs his own tats, indie stuff, not the company toons. I wanted him to tattoo me all over. But he'd only done a few when he started saying that the patterns I wanted freaked him out. He said that at night he could smell them on my skin, smell the orchids of ink flowering. Got to where he wouldn't go anywhere near the real plants. He wanted me to stop working with them, to get a different kind of job. You ever had to choose between two things you love? Sam's dating some guy named Walid now. I hang out with them sometimes. Walid says if he ever gets a tat, it'll be a simple one, like a heart or something, with Sam's name on it, right on his butt. A dead tattoo. When Walid talks about it, Sam just gazes at him, struck dumb with love. I really miss Sam.

I think the orchids, the real ones, like me fat too, like Sam did. Sometimes at night, when I've turned off the light and I'm naked in bed—those are rubber sheets, they're waterproof—and I can see only the faint glow of the paler orchids, I swear that they all incline their blooms towards me, towards my round shoulders, breasts and belly, which also glow a little in the dark. We make echoes, they and I. I like to smell them; the sweet ones, even the weird ones. Did you know that there's an orchid that smells like carrion? I stick my nose right in it and inhale. It smells so bad, it's good. Like a dog sniffing another dog's butt.

Hear that? It's the fire trucks coming. Time to get ready. You going to follow me? Yes, like that. Cool. I'm just going to grab the bigger plants first. Put all my babies into the bathtub where they'll be safe. I have to move quickly. The firemen will burst in here soon, and they aren't too careful about pots of flowers. I learned that the hard way; lost a beautiful *Paph* once, a *spicerianum*. The great lump of a fireman stepped right into the pot. He asked me out, that guy did, after he and his buddies had made sure nothing was on fire. His name was Aleksandr, Sasha for short. I don't get that, but that's what he said. He and I went out a couple of times. I even went home with him once. Sasha was nice. He liked it when I sucked on his bottom lip. But I couldn't get used to the feel of his cotton sheets, and I couldn't keep seeing him anyway; he'd have begun to get suspicious that the fire trucks kept being called to wherever I lived. I need a handsome gentleman butch or a sweet misfit guy who doesn't care how often I move house. Someone with a delicate touch, for staking the smaller orchids and, well, for other stuff. I think the next person I pick up will be like a street punk or something who doesn't even have a home, so they won't barely notice that I have a new flop every few months.

Yeah, it's really wet in here now, isn't it? I'm just going to grab that Lycaste behind you, then put the grow-light on all the plants so they'll dry out. Don't want them to get crown rot. Okay, let's go. Oh, I nearly forgot my new baby! Yeah, it's a pain to carry. The vine's probably about seven feet long now. You can't tell at first cause I have it all curled up. Its flowers aren't quite open yet. I need to take it with us, and a few other little things.

This way. Follow the plant.

I have a routine. Once the plants are safe, I go out into the hallway. No one ever notices. Most of the tenants are usually down in the street already, standing in their nightclothes, clutching their cats and their computers. I'm soaking wet, but if anyone asks, I just tell them that the sprinklers came on, that I don't know why. People expect a chick to be dumb about things like that. I'm careful, though. Almost no electricals in my apartment. Electricity and water don't play nicely together. I use candles a lot. The grow-lights for the orchids are in the bathroom, and there are no sprinklers in there.

This apartment building has a secret. It's this door here, between the garbage chute and the elevator. The lock's loose. Going through this door takes me right up a set of stairs to the roof. The firemen probably won't even look up there. If they did, I'd say that I got scared and confused, just picked a door that had no smoke behind it. Yeah, you have to come up. It's where the plant's going, see?

I'm going to miss this place, with its quiet asphalt roof. This is the second time since I've been here that I've sprinklered the plants, so it's time to move on. I don't like being such a nuisance to the neighbours. One time, in another building, I flooded someone's apartment beside mine. Ruined his record collection. Made me feel really bad.

Up here it stays warm all night, and slightly sticky. I think it's the heat of the day's sun that does it, makes the asphalt just a little bit tacky. Sometimes I lie out here naked, staring up at the stars. When I roll over, there are little rocks stuck to my back, glued there by warmed asphalt. I flex my shoulders and shake my whole body to make them fall off. I like the tickling sensation they make as they come loose.

It's pretty up here tonight. You can see so many stars.

The other night, I put two blue orchid petals right on my pillow, with another petal under my tongue for good measure. It tasted like baby powder, or babies. That's a joke. Because I've got this spiky green hair and the ring through my lip, some people can't tell when I'm joking. They think that people who make holes in their bodies must be angry all the time.

I'd found the orchid petals just lying on the ground out back of my building, by the dumpster. Didn't know who would tear orchids up that way. Lots of people keep them in their apartments, or grow them competitively. The climate here is all wrong for tropical orchids, yet I bet there are almost as many growing in this city as you'd find in any jungle.

Anyway, that night, I laid my left ear—the left side of our bodies is magic, you know—on the fleshy, cool blue of the orchid petals, closed my eyes, and waited for sleep. I sucked on the petal in my mouth. They were a weird, intense kind of blue, like you get in those flower shops where they dye their orchids. They cut the stems and put the flowers in blue ink, or food colouring. The plant sucks it up, and pretty soon, the petals go blue. You can even see veins of blue in the leaves. This orchid had that fake kind of colour.

Not sure why I did that with the petals. You know how it is when you see a dog that someone has tied up outside in the cold, and it's shivering and lifting its paws to keep them from freezing, and all you really want is to saw that chain free and hug that cold dog and give it something warm to eat? Well, actually, you may not know what that's like. You'd probably rather bite a dog than cuddle it. But I'd seen those torn orchid bits lying there, and I just wanted to hold them close to me.

So there I was, with two inky orchid petals crushed between my ear and my pillow, and one under my tongue. It looked like a vanilla orchid.

I think I nodded off. I must have, because after a while, I saw a rat the length of my forearm crawling in the open window.

I didn't want to move. I could see the rat's pointy teeth glinting; the front ones, the ones that grow and grow, so that rats must always have something on which to gnaw, or those teeth grow through their lips, seal their mouths shut, and they starve to death. Its teeth gleamed yellow-white, like some of my orchids, like my belly where the skin isn't inked.

Anyway, I was dreaming, right? So I didn't bother to move. No, stay away from the flower. I know it's almost daylight, but it's not quite ready yet. It blooms in early morning, and I think this is the morning it will open completely. I guess you can tell, and that's why you came.

Anyway, in my dream, I watched while the rat climbed around my orchid pots, investigating. Some of the plants it peered at, then ignored. It only seemed interested in the ones with flowers on them. Those it sniffed at. Maybe rats don't have too good eyesight, huh? Maybe they go more by a sense of smell? Not sure how it could tell how anything smelled, 'cause its own smell was pretty foul. Like rotting garbage, climbing around my room. Could smell it in my sleep.

Finally, the rat seemed to find what it wanted. It nosed at my *Vanilla planifolia*. I was proud of that vine; it was big and healthy, and some of its flowers had just opened a few hours before. The rat climbed up onto the vine, made its way to one of the flowers, and stuck its head inside the flower. Then it climbed back down again and made its way to my window. It stood in the window for a second, shuffling back and forth as though it didn't really want to do something. Then it leapt out the open window and was gone. And this is how I knew for certain that I was dreaming; when the rat jumped, I saw that it had wings. Gossamer wings, kind of like a dragonfly's, with traceries of veins running through. Only more flexible.

That woke me right up. I sat up in bed, feeling really weird, and all I could think was, with four legs and two wings, doesn't that make six limbs? And wouldn't that be an insect, not a rat? There was another thing, too. I couldn't be sure, because it had happened so quickly, but I thought the rat wings had had a faint blueishness to them.

I got myself a glass of water and went back to bed. Next morning, the flower of my lovely *Vanilla*, the one the rat had rubbed itself on, was beginning to brown. That was odd, but not too strange; *Vanilla* flowers close within a few hours and fall off if they're not pollinated. But it now had a faint scent about it of dumpster garbage in the summer heat. Never smelt anything like it on a *planifolia*. Some people would say that's gross. To me, it smelt like a living thing, calling out. Scent is a message.

Look, you can see the firemen milling around outside now. That's the super: the woman with the bright yellow bathrobe. Even in the dark at this distance, you can see that it's yellow. Matter of fact, everything she wears is yellow—everything. I've seen her doing her laundry, and yep, even her undies are yellow. Weird, huh?

She's just let the firemen in. They'll go and break into my apartment, but they won't find anything.

I think the bud's beginning to open. No, you can't rub yourself on it yet. Oh, poor little guy; you're really only about half rat any more, aren't you? You've got orchid tendrils growing up into your brain cells. Does it frighten you, I wonder? Do you have the part of your brain left that can get frightened? I don't think you wanted to jump off that ledge that night, but I think the orchid made you do it. Phew, you stink! I know it's pheromones though, not real garbage.

Even though I'd been dreaming, I closed my window from that night on. Then a little while ago, I stopped to hang with Micheline. She hooks on my street corner on weekend nights; teaching grad school doesn't earn her enough to make ends meet. Sometimes, when business is slow for her, she'll buy me a coffee at the corner coffee shop, or I'll buy her one, depending on which one of us got paid most recently. She told me the oddest thing; how the street kids are starting to tell stories that they've been seeing angels in the city. It's getting to be the end of days, the kids say, and the angels are here to take all the street kids away to heaven. The angels are small and fuzzy, and they have sharp teeth and see-through wings.

You know, I don't know how I'll ever find someone like Sam again. You'd think I'd have plenty of chances. I go out into the world every day, I meet people, I'm friendly, I'm cute—if you like your girls big and round and freaky, and many do. I get dates all the time. Smart people, interesting people. But it's so hard to find people I click with. They just, I dunno, they just don't smell right.

The great thing about orchids is that they have a million ways of getting pollinated. They trick all kinds of small creatures into collecting their pollen and passing it off to other orchids; wasps, ants, even bats. Bee orchids produce flowers that look like sexy lady bees, and when a male bee lands on the flower, ready for action, he gets covered in pollen. A *Porroglossum* will actually snap shut for a few seconds on an insect that stumbles amongst its blossoms and hold the insect still; just long enough for pollen to rub off on its body. Some of the *Bulbophyllum* smell like carrion so they can attract flies.

Us, all us orchid nuts who bring tropical orchids into places where they don't grow naturally, and who cultivate them and interbreed them; we're creating hothouse breeds that thrive in apartments, in greenhouses, in office buildings, in flower shops; all behind doors. They need to find each other to pollinate. They need pollinators. And what small animals get everywhere in a city?

Yes, you, my ugly, furry friend. You only want me for my orchid. Actually, you want me for your orchid, the one that's learned how to travel to where the other orchids are. Most bizarre adaptation I've ever seen. It must have gotten seeds into your fur. Some of those seeds must have germinated, put roots down into your bloodstream. I thought it was wings I saw when you jumped from my window, but it was really the outer petals of the flower, flaring out from your chest in the wind from your jump. It's a stunning blue, for all that it stinks. True blue orchids are rare. Lots of people have tried making blue hybrids. I went and looked it up. One promising possibility right now is to make a transgenic plant by incorporating enzymes found in the livers of animals. Those enzymes can react with substances called indoles to create a bright blue colour. D'you know one of the places you can find indoles? They are the growth regulators in orchids. We even put indoles in the packing mixture we use to transport orchid plants in, to keep them healthy. Your plant passenger there has tendrils in your liver, my friend. When you eat, it gets fed. I can see that you've got a new bloom on your chest there.

Maybe the plant didn't get the knack of it the first time. Maybe when the first bright blue blossom opened, you tore it out, petal by petal, before it could mature into its garbage smell. But eventually, one of the plants put roots down into your spine, travelled up to your brain, found the right synapses to tickle, and you lost the urge to destroy it. Lost the will to go about your own business. Now you can only fetch and carry for a plant, go about the business of orchid pollination. Do you know that "orchid" means "testicle"?

Cool. My flower's opened all the way. Yes, I know you can tell; look how agitated you're getting, or at least, the orchid part of your brain is. Don't worry. I'll let you at it soon.

There's a story that some people from India tell. If you want to bond a person to you forever, you have to prepare rice for them. While it's boiling, you have to squat with your naked genitals over the pot. The steam from the cooking rice will heat you up, and you'll sweat salty crotch sweat pheromones into the pot to flavour it. Make someone eat a meal with that sweat rice, and they're yours forever. Orchids and dogs would understand that trick. Scent is a message.

Here. Come on. Come to the flower. No, I'm not going to let it go. You have to come to me. Gotcha! Don't bite me, you little devil! There. A snootful of chloroform ought to do it.

Jeez, I hope you don't die. I think I got the dosage right; you can find anything on the Web. I just don't want this to hurt you, or you to hurt me because you're scared. Look, I even brought cotton batting to keep you warm in while I do this. Sam taught me how to do a little bit of tattooing. Just inside your ear should do it. Not much fur there, so it's likely that somebody will see it.

Oo, that ear's disgusting. Good thing I brought some alcohol swabs with me. Thank heaven for the gloves, too.

There we go. There's not even a lot of blood. Your ear membranes are too thin to have many blood vessels.

You poor thing. First a chunk of your brain gets kidnapped by a flower with a massive reproductive urge, and now a human being is having her way with you. And you smell like wet garbage in the sun. But for you, that's probably a plus. Probably gets you all kinds of rat dates. I just want a chance. Want to send out my own messages, on as many channels as I can. I mean, who knows where you go in your travels? You might end up in some kind of horticultural lab, and a cute scientist might find you and see your tattoo.

Huh. You're a she rat. Sorry, sister.

I place personal ads, I dress nicely, I chat people up. Nothing. Plants, they just send their messages out on the wind, or via pollen stuck to an insect, or if they're this puppy, they travel a-ratback to wherever their mates are likely to be. Human beings only have a few options. And even pheromones only work so-so with us. Never can tell if the message will get through. So I'm doing everything I can to increase my chances.

There you go, sweetie—the date, my name, my email address, and the name of the new subspecies of orchid that's flowering there on your tummy; *V. planifolia* var. *griggsanum*, after me, who discovered it first.

Please don't go into shock. I think you should be warm enough wrapped up in the cotton. I'll keep dribbling some water on your tongue, keep you hydrated until you wake up. Lemme just have a quick look at this bloom on your chest . . . God, that's creepy.

The firemen are gone now. Pretty soon I'll go in and start packing. I've already put down first and last month's rent on a little place in the market; one of those trendy new lofts they've been putting there recently. It's got the right kind of sprinkler system in all the units. It's probably already got vermin, too, being in the market, but that's okay. The more of you I can find and tattoo, the better. Rats don't live very long, and I bet you that orchid-infested rats live even shorter lives than that.

Oh, hey. You're awake. Good girl. No, no, it's okay. I won't hurt you. The pot's here, with the flower in it, and I'll just step away from it, okay? All the way over here, see? And I won't even move. Yes, you go ahead. Go and pollinate that baby. Though if it can be pollinated, it's no baby.

I didn't squat over a boiling pot of food; I made my room steamy hot, and squatted over an orchid plant; that one right there that you're currently rubbing your body against. Watched my sweat drip into the moss in which it's planted. My calf muscles were burning from the effort by the time I straightened up. That plant's been growing in medium impregnated with my pheromones. It's exchanging scent messages with your flower right now.

You're done? You're leaving? That's okay. Just climb down carefully this time. We're way high up. Atta girl, carry my message; go fetch!

Shift

What do you say when the great Peter Straub comes up to you at a conference and asks you to write a short story for him? You say yes. What do you say when the great Kamau Brathwaite learns that you're in New York City for a few days and asks you to visit the class he's teaching at New York University? You say yes. What do you do when you learn that Kamau is teaching Shakespeare's The Tempest *and is sending his students out into Central Park to look for Caliban? You sit down the night before the class visit and write a rumination about ever-slighted Caliban. You write it from the point of view of perceptive but issue-dogged Ariel. In the telling, you realize that Ariel is also a slave, house negro to Caliban's field negro, equally oppressed by racism, but far too willing to find fault with Caliban's efforts to find love under occupation as best he might than to examine the internalized racism in her own eye. I never liked Prospero, with his entitled sense of ownership of everyone around him. I felt for Sycorax, condemned to literal bondage for the crime of loving her son. I felt for Ariel, the indentured fairy, always doing one more task for master Prospero against the promise of finally,* finally *being set free. I even felt for Miranda, the precious jewel of an overprotected darling daughter. I most certainly felt for Caliban, relegated to the very bottom of the barrel, oppressed by the oppressed in an inescapable chain of contempt. I am similarly a child of historically exploited islands. I know what that shit smells like.*

My father was a Shakespearean-trained actor. Me, I performed a paradigm shift on The Tempest.

Down,
Down,
Down,
To the deep and shady,
Pretty mermaidy,
Take me down.
            —African-American folk song

"*Did you sleep well?" she asks, and you make sure that your face is fixed into a dreamy smile as you open your eyes into the morning after. It had been an awkward third date; a clumsy fumbling in her bed, both of you apologizing and then fleeing gratefully into sleep.*

"*I dreamt that you kissed me," you say. That line's worked before. She's lovely as she was the first time you met her, particularly seen through eyes with colour vision. "You said you wanted me to be your frog." Say it, say it, you think.*

She laughs. "Isn't that kind of backwards?"

"*Well, it'd be a way to start over, right?"*

Her eyes narrow at that. You ignore it. "You could kiss me," you tell her, as playfully as you can manage, "and make me your prince again."

She looks thoughtful at that. You reach for her, pull her close. She comes willingly, a fall of little blonde plaits brushing your face like fingers. Her hair's too straight to hold the plaits; they're already feathered all along their lengths. "Will you be my slimy little frog?" she whispers, a gleam of amusement in her eyes, and your heart double-times, but she kisses you on the forehead instead of the mouth. You could scream with frustration.

"*I've got morning breath," she says apologetically. She means that you do.*

"*I'll go and brush my teeth," you tell her. You try not to sound grumpy. You linger in the bathroom, staring at the whimsical shells she keeps in the little woven basket on the counter, flouting their salty pink cores. You wait for anger and pique to subside.*

"You hungry?" she calls from the kitchen. "I thought I'd make some oatmeal porridge."

So much for kissing games. She's decided it's time for breakfast instead. "Yes," you say. "Porridge is fine."

Ban . . . Ban . . . ca-ca-Caliban . . .

You know who the real tempest is, don't you? The real storm? Is our mother Sycorax; his and mine. If you ever see her hair flying around her head when she dash at you in anger; like a whirlwind, like a lightning, like a deadly whirlpool. Wheeling and turning round her scalp like if it ever catch you, it going to drag you in, pull you down, swallow you in pieces. If you ever hear how she gnash her teeth in her head like tiger shark; if you ever hear the crack of her voice or feel the crack of her hand on your backside like a bolt out of thunder, then you would know is where the real storm there.

She tell me say I must call her Scylla, or Charybdis.

Say it don't make no matter which, for she could never remember one different from the other, but she know one of them is her real name. She say never mind the name most people know her by; is a name some Englishman give her by scraping a feather quill on paper.

White people magic.

Her people magic, for all that she will box you if you ever remind her of that, and flash her blue, blue y'eye-them at you. Lightning *braps* from out of blue sky. But me and Brother, when she not there, is that Englishman name we call her by.

When she hold you on her breast, you must take care never to relax, never to close your y'eye, for you might wake up with your nose hole-them filling up with the salt sea. Salt sea rushing into your lungs to drown you with her mother love.

Imagine what is like to be the son of that mother.

Now imagine what is like to be the sister of that son, to be sister to that there brother.

There was a time they called porridge "gruel." A time when you lived in castle moats and fetched beautiful golden balls for beautiful golden girls. When the fetching was a game, and you knew yourself to be lord of the land and the veins of water that ran through it, and you could graciously allow petty kings to build their palaces on the land, in which to raise up their avid young daughters.

Ban . . . ban . . . ca-ca-Caliban . . .

When I was small, I hear that blasted name so plenty that I thought it was me own.

In her bathroom, you find a new toothbrush, still in its plastic package. She was thinking of you, then, of you staying overnight. You smile, mollified. You crack the plastic open, brush your teeth, looking around at the friendly messiness of her bathroom. Cotton, silk and polyester panties hanging on the shower curtain rod to dry, their crotches permanently honey-stained. Three different types of deodorant on the counter, two of them lidless, dried out. A small bottle of perfume oil, open, so that it weeps its sweetness into the air. A fine dusting of baby powder covers everything, its innocent odour making you sneeze. Someone lives here. Your own apartment—the one you found when you came on land—is as crisp and dull as a hotel room, a stop along the way. Everything is tidy there, except for the waste paper basket in your bedroom, which is crammed with empty pill bottles: marine algae capsules; iodine pills. You remind yourself that you need to buy more, to keep the cravings at bay.

Caliban have a sickness. Is a sickness any of you could get. In him it manifest as a weakness; a weakness for cream. He fancy himself a prince of Africa, a mannish Cleopatra, bathing in mother's milk. Him believe say it would make him pretty. Him never had mirrors to look in, and with the mother we had, the surface of the sea never calm enough that him could see him face in it. Him would never believe me say that him pretty already. Him fancy if cream would only touch him, if him could only submerge himself entirely in it, it would redeem him.

Me woulda try it too, you know, but me have that feature you find amongst so many brown-skin people; cream make me belly gripe.

Truth to tell, Brother have the same problem, but him would gladly suffer the stomach pangs and the belly-running for the chance to drink in cream, to bathe in cream, to have it dripping off him and running into him mouth. Such a different taste from the bitter salt sea milk of Sycorax.

That beautiful woman making breakfast in her kitchen dives better than you do. You've seen her knifing so sharply through waves that you wondered they didn't bleed in her wake.

You fill the sink, wave your hands through the water. It's bliss, the way it resists you. You wonder if you have time for a bath. It's a pity that this isn't one of those apartment buildings with a pool. You miss swimming.

You wash your face. You pull the plug, watch the water spiral down the drain. It looks wild, like a mother's mad hair. Then you remember that you have to be cautious around water now, even the tame, caged water of swimming pools and bathrooms. Quickly, you sink the plug back into the mouth of the drain. You must remember; anywhere there's water, especially rioting water, it can tattle tales to your mother.

Your face feels cool and squeaky now. Your mouth is wild cherry-flavoured from the toothpaste. You're kissable. You can hear humming from the kitchen, and the scraping of a spoon against a pot. There's a smell of cinnamon and nutmeg. Island smells. You square your shoulders, put on a smile, walk to the kitchen. Your feet are floppy, reluctant. You wish you could pay attention to what they're telling you. When they plash around like this, when they slip and slide and don't want to carry you upright, it's always been a bad sign. The kisses of golden girls are chancy things. Once, after the touch of other pale lips, you looked into the eyes of a golden girl, one Miranda, and saw yourself reflected back in her moist, breathless stare. In her eyes you were tall, handsome, your shoulders powerful and your jaw square. You carried yourself with the arrogance of a prince. You held a spear in one hand. The spotted, tawny pelt of an animal that had never existed was knotted around your waist. You wore something's teeth on a string around your neck and you spoke in grunts, imperious. In her eyes, your bright copper skin was dark and loamy as cocoa. She had sighed and leapt upon you, kissing and biting, begging to be taken. You had let her have what she wanted. When her father stumbled upon the two of you writhing on the ground, she had leapt to her feet and changed you again; called you monster, attacker. She'd clasped her bodice closed with one hand, carefully leaving bare enough pitiful juddering bosom to spark a father's ire. She'd looked at you regretfully, sobbed crocodile tears, and spoken the lies that had made you her father's slave for an interminable length of years.

You haven't seen yourself in this one's eyes yet. You need her to kiss you, to change you, to hide you from your dam. That's what you've always needed. You are always awed by the ones who can work this magic. You could love one of them forever and a day. You just have to find the right one.

You stay a second in the kitchen doorway. She looks up from where she stands at the little table, briskly setting two different-sized spoons beside two mismatched bowls. She smiles. "Come on in," she says.

You do, on your slippery feet. You sit to table. She's still standing. "I'm sorry about that," she says. She quirks a regretful smile at you. "I don't think my cold sore is quite healed yet." She runs a tongue tip over the corner of her lip, where you can no longer see the crusty scab. You sigh. "It's all right. Forget it." She goes over to the stove. You don't pay any attention. You're staring at the thready crack in your bowl.

She says, "Brown sugar or white?"

"Brown," you tell her. "And lots of milk." Your gut gripes at the mere thought, but milk will taint the water in which she cooked the oats. It will cloud the whisperings that water carries to your mother.

Nowadays people would say that me and my mooncalf brother, we is "lactose intolerant." But me think say them mis-name the thing. Me think say is milk can't tolerate we, not we can't tolerate it.

So; he find himself another creamy one. Just watch at the two of them there, in that pretty domestic scene.

I enter, invisible.

Brother eat off most of him porridge already. Him always had a large appetite. The white lady, she only passa-passa-ing with hers, dipping the spoon in, tasting little bit, turning the spoon over and watching at it, dipping it in. She glance at him and say, *"Would you like to go to the beach today?"*

"No!" You almost shout it. You're not going to the beach, not to any large body of water, ever again. Your very cells keen from the loss of it, but She is in the water, looking for you.

"A-true. Mummy in the water, and I in the wind, Brother," I whisper to him, so sweet. By my choice, him never hear me yet. Don't want him to know that me find him. Plenty time for that. Plenty time to fly and carry the news to Mama. Maybe I can find a way to be free if I do this one last thing for her. Bring her beloved son back. Is him she want, not me. Never me. "Ban, ban, ca-ca-Caliban!" I scream in him face, silently.

"There's no need to shout," she says with an offended look. "That's where we first saw each other, and you swam so strongly. You were beautiful in the water. So I just thought you might like to go back there."

You had been swimming for your life, but she didn't know that. The surf tossing you crashing against the rocks, the undertow pulling you back in deeper, the waves singing their triumphant song: She's coming. Sycorax is coming for you. Can you feel the tips of her tentacles now? Can you feel them sticking to your skin, bringing you back? She's coming. We've got you now. We'll hold you for her. Oh, there'll be so much fun when she has you again!

And you had hit out at the water, stroked through it, kicked through it, fleeing for shore. One desperate pull of your arms had taken you through foaming surf. You crashed into another body, heard a surprised, "Oh," and then a wave tumbled you. As you fought in its depths, searching for the air and dry land, you saw her, this woman, slim as an eel, her body parting the water, her hair glowing golden. She'd extended a hand to you, like reaching for a bobbing ball. You took her hand, held on tightly to the warmth of it. She stood, and you stood, and you realised you'd been only feet from shore. "Are you all right?" she'd asked.

The water had tried to suck you back in, but it was only at thigh height now. You ignored it. You kept hold of her hand, started moving with her, your saviour, to the land. You felt your heart swelling. She was perfect. "I'm doing just fine," you'd said. "I'm sorry I startled you. What's your name?"

Behind you, you could hear the surf shouting for you to come back. But the sun was warm on your shoulders now, and you knew that you'd stay on land. As you came up out of the water, she glanced at you and smiled, and you could feel the change begin.

She's sitting at her table, still with that hurt look on her face.

"I'm sorry, darling," you say, and she brightens at the endearment, the first you've used with her. Under the table, your feet are trying to paddle away, away. You ignore them. "Why don't we go for a walk?" you ask her. She smiles, nods. The many plaits of her hair sway with the rhythm. You must ask her not to wear her hair like that. Once you know her a little better. They look like tentacles. Besides, her hair's so pale that her pink scalp shows through.

Chuh. *I'm sorry, darling.* Him is sorry, is true. A sorry sight. I follow them out on them little walk, them Sunday perambulation. Down her street and round the corner into the district where the trendy people-them live. Where you find those cunning little shops, you know the kind, yes? Wild flowers selling at this one, half your wages for one so-so blossom. Cheeses from Greece at that one, and wine from Algiers. (Mama S. say she don't miss Algiers one bit.) Tropical fruit selling at another store, imported from the Indies, from the hot sun places where people work them finger to the bone to pick them and box them and send them, but not to eat them. Brother and him new woman meander through those streets, making sure people look at them good. She turn her moon face to him, give him that fuck-me look, and take him hand. I see him melt. Going to be easy for her to change him now that she melt him. And then him will be gone from we again. I blow a grieving breeze oo-oo-oo through the leaves of the crab apple trees lining that street.

She looks around, her face bright and open. "Such a lovely day," she says. "Feel the air on your skin." She releases your hand. The sweat of your mingled touch evaporates and you mourn its passing. She opens her arms to the sun, drinking in light.

Of course, that white man, him only write down part of the story. Him say how our mother was a witch. How she did consort with monsters. But you know the real story? You know why them exile her from Algiers, with a baby in her belly and one at her breast?

She spins and laughs, her print dress opening like a flower above her scuffed army boots. Her strong legs are revealed to mid-thigh.

Them send my mother from her home because of the monster she consort with. The lord with sable eyes and skin like rich earth. My daddy.

An old man sitting on a bench smiles, indulgent at her joy, but then he sees her reach for your hand again. He scowls at you, spits to one side.

My daddy. A man who went for a swim one day, down, down, down, and when he see the fair maid flowing towards him, her long hair just a-swirl like weeds in the water, her skin like milk, him never 'fraid.

As you both pass the old man, he shakes his head, his face clenched. She doesn't seem to notice. You hold her hand tighter, reach to pull her warmth closer to you. But eventually you're going down, and you know it.

When my mother who wasn't my mother yet approach the man who wasn't my father yet, when she ask him, "Man, you eat salt, or you eat fresh?" him did know what fe say. Of course him did know. After his tutors teach him courtly ways from since he was small. After his father teach him how to woo. After his own mother teach him how to address the Wata Lady with respect. Sycorax ask him, "Man, you eat salt, or you eat fresh?"

And proper proper, him respond, "Me prefer the taste of salt, thank you please."

That was the right answer. For them that does eat fresh, them going to be fresh with your business. But this man show her that he know how fe have respect. For that, she give him breath and take him down, she take him down even farther.

You pass another beautiful golden girl, luxuriantly blonde. She glances at you, casts her eyes down demurely, where they just happen to rest at your crotch. You feel her burgeoning gaze there, your helpless response. Quickly you lean and kiss the shoulder of the woman you're with. The other one's look turns to resentful longing. You hurry on.

She take him down into her own castle, and she feed him the salt foods she keep in there, the fish and oysters and clams, and him eat of them till him belly full, and him talk to her sweet, and him never get fresh with her. Not even one time. Not until she ask him to. Mama wouldn't tell me what happen after that, but true she have two pickney, and both of we shine copper, even though she is alabaster, so me think me know is what went on.

There's a young black woman sitting on a bench, her hair tight peppercorns against her scalp. Her feet are crossed beneath her. She's alone, reading a book. She's pretty, but she looks too much like your sister. Too brown to ever be a golden girl. She looks up as you go by, distracted from her reading by the chattering of the woman beside you. She looks at you. Smiles. Nods a greeting. Burning up with guilt, you make your face stone. You move on.

In my mother and father, salt meet with sweet. Milk meet with chocolate. No one could touch her while he was alive and ruler of his lands, but the minute him dead, her family and his get together and exile her to that little island to starve to death. Send her away with two sweet-and-sour, milk chocolate pickney; me in her belly and Caliban at her breast. Is nuh that turn her bitter? When you confine the sea, it don't stagnate? You put milk to stand, and it nuh curdle?

Chuh. Watch at my brother there, making himself fool-fool. Is time. Time to end this, to take him back down. "Mama," I whisper.

I blow one puff of wind, then another. The puffs tear a balloon out from a little girl's hand. The balloon have a fish painted on it. I like that. The little girl cry out and run after her toy. Her father dash after her. I puff and blow, make the little metallic balloon skitter just out of the child reach. As she run, she knock over a case of fancy bottled water, the expensive fizzy kind in blue glass bottles, from a display. The bottles explode when them hit the ground, the water escaping with a shout of glee. The little girl just dance out the way of broken glass and spilled water and keep running for her balloon, reaching for it. I make it bob like a bubble in the air. Her daddy jump to one side, away from the glass. He try to snatch the back of her dress, but he too big and slow. Caliban step forward and grasp her balloon by the string. He give it back to her. She look at him, her y'eye-them big. She clutch the balloon to her bosom and smile at her daddy as he sweep her up into him arms. The storekeeper just a-wait outside her shop, to talk to the man about who going to refund her goods.

"Mother," I call. "Him is here. I find him."

The water from out the bottles start to flow together in a spiral.

You hear her first in the dancing breeze that's toying with that little girl's balloon. You fetch the balloon for the child before you deal with what's coming. Her father mumbles a suspicious thanks at you. You step away from them. You narrow your eyes, look around. "You're here, aren't you?" you say to the air.

"Who's here?" asks the woman at your side.

"My sister," you tell her. You say "sister" like you're spitting out spoiled milk.

"I don't see anyone," the woman says.

"El!" you call out.

I don't pay him no mind. I summon up one of them hot, gusty winds. I blow over glasses of water on café tables. I grab popsicles *swips!* from out the hands and mouths of children. The popsicles fall down and melt, all the bright colours; melt and run like that brother of mine.

Popsicle juice, café table water, spring water that break free from bottles; them all rolling together now, crashing and splashing and calling to our mother. I sing up the whirling devils. Them twirl sand into everybody eyes. Hats and baseball caps flying off heads, dancing along with me. An umbrella galloping down the road, end over end, with an old lady chasing it. All the trendy Sunday people squealing and running everywhere.

"Ariel, stop it!" you say.

So I run up his girlfriend skirt, make it fly high in the air. "Oh!" she cry out, trying to hold the frock down. She wearing a panty with a tear in one leg and a knot in the waistband. That make me laugh out loud. "Mama!" I shout, loud so Brother can hear me this time. "You seeing this? Look him here so!" I blow one rassclaat cluster of rain clouds over the scene, them bellies black and heavy with water. "So me see that you get a new master!" I screech at Brother.

The street is empty now, but for the three of you. Everyone else has found shelter. Your girl is cowering down beside the trunk of a tree, hugging her skirt about her knees. Her hair has come loose from most of its plaits, is whipping in a tangled mess about her head. She's shielding her face from blowing sand, but trying to look up at the sky above her, where this attack is coming from. You punch at the air, furious. You know you can't hurt your sister, but you need to lash out anyway. "Fuck you!" you yell. "You always do this! Why can't the two of you leave me alone!"

I chuckle. "Your face favour jackass when him sick. Why you can't leave white woman alone? You don't see what them do to you?"

"You are our mother's creature," you hiss at her. "Look at you, trying so hard to be 'island,' talking like you just come off the boat." In your anger, your speech slips into the same rhythms as hers.

"At least me nah try fe chat like something out of some Englishman book." I make the wind howl it back at him: "At least me remember is which boat me come off from!" I burst open the clouds overhead and drench the two of them in mother water. She squeals. Good.

"Ariel, Caliban; stop that squabbling, or I'll bind you both up in a split tree forever." The voice is a wintry runnel, fast-freezing.

You both turn. Your sister has manifested, has pushed a trembling bottom lip out. Dread runs cold along your limbs. It's Sycorax. "Yes, Mother," you both say, standing sheepishly shoulder to shoulder. "Sorry, Mother."

Sycorax is sitting in a sticky puddle of water and melted popsicles, but a queen on her throne could not be more regal. She has wrapped an ocean wave about her like a shawl. Her eyes are open-water blue. Her writhing hair foams white over her shoulders and the marble swells of her vast breasts. Her belly is a mounded salt lick, rising from the weedy tangle of her pubic hair, a marine jungle in and out of which flit tiny blennies. The tsunami of Sycorax's hips overflows her watery seat. Her myriad split tails are flicking, the way they do when she's irritated. With one of them, she scratches around her navel. You think you can see the sullen head of a moray eel, lurking in the cave those hydra tails make. You don't want to think about it. You never have.

"Ariel," says Sycorax, "have you been up to your tricks again?"

"But he," splutters your sister, "he . . ."

"He never ceases with his tricks," your mother pronounces. "Running home to Mama, leaving me with the mess he's made." She looks at you, and your watery legs weaken. "Caliban," she says, "I'm getting too old to play surrogate mother to your spawn. That last school of your offspring all had poisonous stings."

"I know, Mother. I'm sorry."

"How did that happen?" she asks.

You risk a glance at the woman you've dragged into this, the golden girl. She's standing now, a look of interest and curiosity on her face. "This is all your fault," you say to her. "If you had kissed me, told me what you wanted me to be, she and Ariel couldn't have found us."

Your girl looks at you, measuring. "First tell me about the poison babies," she says. She's got more iron in her than you'd thought, this one. The last fairy tale princess who'd met your family hadn't stopped screaming for two days.

Ariel sniggers. "That was from his last ooman," she says. "The two of them always quarrelling. For her, Caliban had a poison tongue."

"And spat out biting words, no doubt," Sycorax says. "He became what she saw, and it affected the children they made. Of course she didn't want them, of course she left; so Grannie gets to do the honours. He has brought me frog children and dog children, baby mack daddies and crack babies. Brings his offspring to me, then runs away again. And I'm getting tired of it." Sycorax's shawl whirls itself up into a waterspout. "And I'm more than tired of his sister's tale tattling."

"But Mama. . . !" Ariel says.

"'But Mama' nothing. I want you to stop pestering your brother."

Ariel puffs up till it looks as though she might burst. Her face goes anvil-cloud dark, but she says nothing.

"And you," says Sycorax, pointing at you with a suckered tentacle, "you need to stop bringing me the fallouts from your sorry love life."

"I can't help it, Mama," you say. "That's how women see me."

Sycorax towers forward, her voice crashing upon your ears. "Do you want to know how I see you?" A cluster of her tentacle tails whips around your shoulders, immobilizes you. That is a moray eel under there, its fanged *mouth hanging hungrily open. You are frozen in Sycorax's gaze, a hapless, irresponsible little boy. You feel the sickening metamorphosis begin. You are changing, shrinking. The last time Sycorax did this to you, it took you forever to become man enough again to escape. You try to twist in her arms, to look away from her eyes. She pulls you forward, puckering her mouth for the kiss she will give you.*

"Well, yeah, I'm beginning to get a picture here," says a voice. It's the golden girl, shivering in her flower-print dress that's plastered to her skinny body. She steps closer. Her boots squelch. She points at Ariel. "You say he's colour-struck. You're his sister, you should know. And yeah, I can see that in him. You'd think I was the sun itself, the way he looks at me."

She takes your face in her hands, turns your eyes away from your mother's. Finally, she kisses you full on the mouth. In her eyes, you become a sunflower, helplessly turning wherever she goes. You stand rooted, waiting for her direction.

She looks at your terrible mother. "You get to clean up the messes he makes." And now you're a baby, soiling your diapers and waiting for Mama to come and fix it. Oh, please, end this.

She looks down at you, wriggling and helpless on the ground. "And I guess all those other women saw big, black dick."

So familiar, the change that wreaks on you. You're an adult again, heavy-muscled and horny with a thick, swelling erection. You reach for her. She backs away. "But," she says, "there's one thing I don't see."

You don't care. She smells like vanilla and her skin is smooth and cool as ice cream and you want to push your tongue inside. You grab her thin, unresisting arms. She's shaking, but she looks into your eyes. And hers are empty. You aren't there. Shocked, you let her go. In a trembling voice, she says, "Who do you think you are?"

It could be an accusation: Who do you think you are? It might be a question: Who do you think you are? You search her face for the answer. Nothing. You look to your mother, your sib. They both look as shocked as you feel.

"Look," says the golden girl, opening her hands wide. Her voice is

getting less shaky. "Clearly, this is family business, and I know better than to mess with that." She gathers her little picky plaits together, squeezes water out of them. "It's been really . . . interesting, meeting you all." She looks at you, and her eyes are empty, open, friendly. You don't know what to make of them. "Um," she says, "maybe you can give me a call sometime." She starts walking away. Turns back. "It's not a brush-off; I mean it. But only call when you can tell me who you really are. Who you think you're going to become."

And she leaves you standing there. In the silence, there's only a faint sound of whispering water and wind in the trees. You turn to look at your mother and sister. "I," you say.

Delicious Monster

*When I discovered that the Latin name of the split-leaved philodendron (*Monstera deliciosa*) translates into "delicious monster" in English, I knew I would one day use that in a story. Here is the story.*

The tree was still there. Condos and office buildings growing floor by floor all around formed an organics of the city—urban fractals, patterns repeating, random, but inexorable; yet there in the middle of it was the tree, caged in a small empty lot scattered about with unseasonable thistles and rogue lawn grass.

Looked like that lot was slated for construction too. One of those clapboard condo sales offices had been erected at the other side of it; the kind with a storefront painted to look like a manor house in a magazine. There were stacks of lumber and fat aluminium pipes beside it.

Cars rushed past Jerry on Spadina, speeding irritably to Friday afternoon freedom. The dusky sky spat the occasional dirty snowflake which tumbled onto the sleeve of Jerry's jacket and lay there twinkling for a second, six-clawed, until it melted.

Jerry knelt by the rusting chicken wire that kept the tree in. He peered through one of the fence's rusty diamonds. He reached to steady himself, to twine the fingers of one hand in the fence, but an angry roar startled him, and he yanked the hand back. He looked up to see what had made the noise, so much louder and closer than the fractious bleating of car horns.

There it was. Bloody excavation machines, biting and biting at the ravaged ground. The thing lurched away from the fence, bellowing.

It brandished a toothed hopper, a maw on a stalk. The tree hunkered there smugly, in the lee of its machine protector. "You just wait," Jerry said quietly to the tree. "Pretty soon, it's you the excavator'll be coming for."

Once, as a child visiting the zoo, Jerry'd disobeyed his dad and stuck his hand inside the fencing of the puma cage. There had been no harm in doing so that he could see. The thick wall of clear Lucite that kept the puma penned was a good two feet beyond his reach; the wire fence just an extra precaution in a litigious world. A gaunt great cat had lain panting behind the Lucite, regarding him with a dull, disinterested stare. Its tan coat made it look baked, like biscuits. Glancing to make sure his dad wasn't looking, Jerry'd waggled his fingers at the puma.

Later, thinking about what he'd done, he couldn't say what reaction he'd hoped for, exactly, from the puma. Something. Some acknowledgement that it'd seen him. His dad had barely said a word to him all weekend. Jerry'd knelt and stared hard at the puma. Look. Look over here. He hadn't seen the other one flying at him until it was a big golden blur in the corner of his eye. A millisecond later it slammed against the Lucite with a heavy thump. Jerry'd thrown himself backward onto his behind. That's when his dad had turned and asked in a puzzled voice why Jerry was sitting in the dirt. Jerry hadn't been able to take his eyes off the puma that had charged him. It had looked at him, licked its bruised nose. A fixed, hungry stare. The sunlight had played in its fur, making it glow.

It'd been a few years since Jerry'd walked this far north on Spadina. The tree's swollen middle still flowed in rolls like lava down to the ground. He could see the cincture that bit into the tree's trunk about two-three feet from the ground. Something had been chained there, tight around the tree, years ago, then abandoned. Must have been only a sapling then. It was sturdy enough for climbing now. It had grown, the living tissue of its wood welling and swelling around whatever it was that it now held trapped. Same as he'd done last time he'd passed the tree, Jerry peered closer, trying to see what it held in its folds.

"Mister, you got any change you can spare? I'm trying to get a coffee." The guy standing, jittering, with his hands in the pockets of a shredding jeans jacket was young. He'd shaved off all the hair on his head, except for a limp tuft of it at the front, dyed green, that flopped into his eyes.

"Uh, yeah," Jerry said, lurching to his feet. "Think I got some here." He started fumbling in his pockets. Had he put any change in there? He usually did when he was flush, to give to homeless people who asked for it. Sandor always teased him for being a softie when he gave change to beggars. Teased him and then rewarded him with a kiss or a squeeze of his hand.

"Thanks, man," said the guy. "Really 'preciate it."

Sandor didn't give money, but he always seemed to have extra smokes in his pocket to give away.

Something was funny about the way this guy stood. One shoulder was clearly higher than the other. One hip canted up at a sharp angle.

Damn. Empty pockets. "Hang on." Flushing with embarrassment at the delay, Jerry took his wallet from his coat.

While Jerry fumbled, the young man looked politely off to one side. "God, is that ever freaky-looking, eh?" he said.

He was looking at the deformed tree.

"Yeah," Jerry replied. "Well . . ." There was a twenty. He wasn't going to give the kid that. He tried to surreptitiously shield the contents of his wallet from view, to riffle through the remaining bills with his other hand.

There were more snowflakes falling now. The young guy was shivering in his thin jacket. "It's a monster, that tree," he told Jerry. He said it with a familiar air. If this was his beat, he'd seen this tree before. "A monster like me, right?"

"Delicious monster," Jerry heard himself mutter. The young man had a gnarled beauty about him, like a skinny rock star who cut his own body with razors, or like a bonsai tree.

"What'd you say, Mister?"

Shit. "Uh, nothing." Perversely, the twenty kept jutting up out of the pile of grocery receipts and bus transfers in Jerry's wallet. He sighed, yanked it out. "I mean, uh, here. Hope you have a delicious dinner."

He handed the twenty to the guy, whose face brightened in delight. "Shit, thanks, man!"

"No problem."

The young man pocketed the money, then looked inquisitively at Jerry. "Not a lot of people stop to really look at stuff in the city. Not ratty old growing stuff, anyway."

"I'm curious about it, is all."

"Flower gardens, maybe. They'll look at the neat, pretty things."

"I mean," Jerry continued, "what's that thing stuck inside it?"

The young guy shrugged, his green hair tumbling onto his beautiful face. He looked at the tree's bulge, looked up at the sky. "It'll be during the eclipse," he said. "That's when it happens." Then he lurched away into the darkening day, one hip hitching higher than the other, one foot hitting the ground sooner than the other, arms windmilling awkwardly to propel him forward.

Delicious monster. That's what Jerry's dad had really taken him to the zoo to see; *Monstera deliciosa*, the massive Swiss cheese plant that flourished in the South American Pavilion. It had been warm in there, and damp. It'd smelt green, a stuffy fetor of growing, living and dying things that clung inside the nose. Jerry'd taken his coat off. The heat had baked into his skin, his hair. It had felt like moisture was condensing on his eyelids. He'd gone heavy, slow. His dad was finally animated. "This stuff comes from my part of the world," he'd said. "From Guatemala."

When he was young, Jerry'd thought his dad had lived in the middle of a jungle, in a tree house, or something. Had thought his dad had spent his days feeding orangutans, the gentle old men of the forest, and wrestling massive boa constrictors that could consume an entire child; swallow a whole person until all you could see of them was a series of lumps in the constrictor's middle. Dad was forever on about centipedes the size of snakes and eels that could electrocute you with a touch. But . . . "No," Jerry's mother had said, "orangutans are from Borneo, whatever they call it now. That's Asia. Your dad's from South America." But Jerry still hadn't really understood. From his northern city home, where the biggest trees were the low, cultivated rowan trees that shed their orange berries in the fall, Borneo might as well be Guatemala. It wasn't until Mum had shown him pictures of Dad's family's house in Guatemala City, where she and Dad had gone on their honeymoon, that Jerry had realised that his dad was a city boy, too. Probably the only electric eel Dad had ever seen was the one right here in the Toronto zoo.

The excavator was quiescent now, crouched beside the condo sales hut. The snow was heavier, but melting as it fell. Beads of freezing water hung off the thistle leaves. If he looked carefully at the water droplets, he could see car brake lights reflecting red in them. Spring was pouncing in like a lion, all right.

No use putting it off any longer. Jerry turned north towards his dad's condo. The snow was turning into biting hail.

"How's your mum?" Jerry's dad took Jerry's coat, hung it in the hall closet. Jerry followed him into the living room.

"She's fine. Says she's got a new plant cutting for you, and you should go by and get it. Dunno where you'll put it, though." A ficus rioted in one corner of the living room, nearly touching the ceiling. The spider plant hanging from a nook was a veritable cathedral of foliage. Trifoliate, an ornamental shamrock blushed hugely purple. Dad grinned.

Sudharshan rose from the couch, came and gave Jerry an awkward hug. "Good to see you," he murmured. Jerry gave a kind of grunt back.

"And how's Sandor?" Dad asked.

Jerry sat on the arm of the plush burgundy couch. Sudharshan frowned.

"He's great. Settling into his new apartment."

A trilling noise came from over by the dining table. Jerry turned to see what it was. He was up and standing beside the cage before he knew it. He reached to touch the wire bars. "Yikes. Dad, what the hell is that thing?"

The bird—Jerry figured that's what it was—tilted its head at the sound of his voice. It sidled on its perch, closer to Jerry, one eye beady on him. Jerry pulled his hand back from the cage. The thing was tiny, bald and fucking hideous. No feathers on its head, none on its wings. Looked like something out of the grocery's freezer. Probably no feathers on its body, either. Hard to tell, in the weird little suit it had on it. "And what's that it's wearing?"

Sudharshan laughed. He came over and stroked one of the cage's wires with a beautifully manicured hand. "You like his jumpsuit?" he asked Jerry. Sudharshan's face always made Jerry think of chocolate brownies, dark and sweet. "I crochet them for him. He'd freeze to death otherwise, wouldn't you, my numbikins?" Sudharshan cooed at the disgusting little thing. It screeched back at him, tossing and tossing its beak up into the air.

"Why doesn't it have any feathers?"

"Birdie alopecia," his dad said, coming up behind Sudharshan and putting his arms around Sudharshan. Sudharshan put his hands on top of Dad's, smiled. He leaned back into Dad's embrace. Jerry looked away.

"It's a rare condition my birdie has," Sudharshan told him. "He'd have died in the wild."

Jerry snuck a look back at his dad and Sudharshan. They were still cuddling. He sighed and deliberately kept his eyes on them, trying to look cool. His gaze slid back to the creepy bald bird in its bright green wool jumper. "How does it, you know?"

"Hole in the base of the suit," Sudharshan told him. "Want some chai?"

"Uh, yeah." Something to do.

"I'll get it." His dad headed for the kitchen.

"Not too much cardamom, okay, sweetie?" Sudharshan called after him. Jerry could feel his face heating up.

Sudharshan pulled chairs out for himself and Jerry. They sat. Then he leaned over the cage, made more smacking noises at the bird. His long nose with the dip in it echoed the bird's hooked beak. He opened the cage door, reached a hand in. "Come, darling, come. Say hello to Uncle Jerry."

The bird mumbled its beak against Sudharshan's brown hand. Jerry held his breath, afraid that it would peck. The bird climbed onto Sudharshan's hand, windmilling its wings for balance. "Where'd you get it?" Jerry asked. In the kitchen, the kettle began whistling off key.

"They've been in my family for years," Sudharshan said. "His grandparents' parents belonged to my grandparents. Each new generation of children looks after the new generation of birds. It's kind of our duty. How's work?" He carefully brought the bird out of its cage. It screeched loudly. Jerry put his hands over his ears.

"Work's going okay," he said. "Sold a big mansion up in Aurora. Rich couple, one kid. Six bedrooms, that house has."

Jerry went silent. Sudharshan said nothing. The bird crab-walked up Sudharshan's arm, perched on his shoulder and nibbled at his ear. Sudharshan giggled and chucked it under its chin. It still looked to Jerry like plucked freezer chicken, walking. He swallowed and looked around the room. One whole wall of the apartment was painted with images of suns. They flared and wheeled through space. Each one was different. They seemed hand-done. "Your art work?" he asked Sudharshan.

"We did it together," Jerry's dad said, coming out of the kitchen. He was balancing a tray, a white lace doily on it under a teapot, three mugs and a saucer. The mugs were a fat, sunny yellow. He put the tray down on the table. Jerry recognized the doily. It was part of a set that his mum used to save for when they had company. "Three sugars, right, Jerry?"

"I don't take sugar, Dad."

"You like sugar."

"I never liked sugar. You always gave me too much, and I never liked it."

Sudharshan busied himself with his ugly pet. Jerry watched the way that his long black hair caught the light, gleaming. Looked at Sudharshan's handsome face, sucking in light and reflecting gorgeousness, and hated him.

With a squawk, the bird threw itself off Sudharshan's shoulder and onto the table. It started stalking Jerry, its tiny body strutting. It stared him down. Sudharshan laughed. "Rudy, stop it." The bird ignored him. It was almost to the edge of the table where Jerry's hand was. It was bigger than he'd thought. Jerry pulled his hands away, into his lap. Sudharshan scooped the bird up and cupped his other palm protectively around it. "Stop it, I said." He beamed at Jerry. "That's his snake-eating glare." He tucked the bird back into its cage and locked the door.

"A parrot that eats snakes?"

Jerry's dad began pouring chai. "It's not a parrot, son. We never said that it was."

Jerry took the yellow cup that his dad held out. He sipped the chai. It was too sweet. "What the fuck is it, then?"

"Jerry. Language."

"I don't know the word for it in English," Sudharshan told him. "I just call him Rudy. He knows his name. They all do."

Dad poured chai for himself and Sudharshan. As he lifted the teapot, his biceps swelled against the rolled-up sleeve of the tight white t-shirt he was wearing. He looked better nowadays, Jerry had to admit. He hadn't heard his dad complain once about his bunions. Blunt-toed army boots had replaced the pointy Italian leather shoes. Well-worn jeans sat better on his hips than the polyester dress pants that used to be his uniform. His gut had shrunk. It was now just this cute little suggestion of paunch, yet another manly bulge beneath his form-fitting t-shirts. A chain of fat silver beads encircled his neck. They shone against the warm yellow-brown of his skin. Jerry wondered where the tiny gold cross on its sallow gold chain had gone. The stiff brush cut in which Dad now wore his black hair suited his solid, square face. The lines in the corners of his eyes were the friendly signs of someone who smiled a lot, not the creases with which Jerry'd become familiar as a child; the disappointment and anger that had once been incised there. Now Dad's brown eyes were happy. Who was this man?

Dad offered Sudharshan the cup of chai along with a tender gaze. Jerry felt a lump forming in his solar plexus. The mug disappeared behind Sudharshan's long, wide hands. There was just a little bit of yellow china gleaming out from between his fingers. He sipped from his cupped hand. The colour of the mug made his chin glow. Jerry thought of butter, of chocolate brownies, warm and sweet in the mouth. He pushed the thought away. Sandor thought it was all very cute. Your dad's one of the boys now, he'd said. Hey—maybe the two of them can come to the Box with us some day. Jerry'd told him to shut the fuck up.

"Eclipse soon," Sudharshan said. "You going to watch it?"

"That's why I came," Jerry reminded him. "That's why you invited me." His dad only looked at Sudharshan, stricken.

"Where will you go?" Dad asked Sudharshan.

"I thought we'd go up onto the roof," Sudharshan replied. "We can see the sky more clearly from there."

His face remained open, friendly, but Jerry'd been looking at his dad, so he knew that Sudharshan hadn't answered the question Dad had asked. Dad stared into his mug like someone had hidden the sun in there. He looked up at Jerry, baring a too-bright smile. "Hey, Jer; you seen my *Monstera*?"

"Say what?"

Dad pointed to a shady corner of the apartment. Sure enough, there was a Swiss cheese plant there, a static explosion of large, oval leaves riddled with holes. Jerry hadn't really noticed it before, huddled in the dark like that. "Wouldn't it be better in the sun, Dad, like the rest of the plants?"

Dad sucked back the rest of his chai, put the cup down. He had an angry look. He pointedly didn't direct it to Sudharshan. "It prefers to have its roots in the shade. But it gets more than enough sun. Look at where it's growing to."

With his eyes, Jerry followed the trailing growth of the plant. It
had made its way along the bottom of the wall to the big picture
window, and sure enough, was climbing to the light, using a thick,
succulent tree in a pot there as its ladder. The leaves of the *Monstera*
were so mixed in with the leaves of the tree that Jerry couldn't tell
what the tree was.

"It's a banana plant," Sudharshan told him. "The *Monstera* needs it,
but it's strangling it. I'll have to have my cousin get me a new one."

Dad reached for Sudharshan's hand, but Sudharshan pulled away.
"Delicious," Sudharshan said. "The chai, I mean. It was perfect, lover."
He smiled at Dad, hesitated, took the outstretched hand, kissed it.
The longing on Dad's face! And now Jerry was afraid, like when he
was a kid. Like when his parents would fight, and then try not to
fight, try to make up, but one of them would be closed, arms folded,
the light shut from their face, and the other would look with longing,
would try to touch, would be rebuffed and then finally taken in
again, reluctantly, and the child Jerry would feel relief, but with a hard
little stone of fear left there, below his breastbone.

"Isn't it about time for that eclipse?" he asked Dad and Sudharshan.
In his cage, peeled Rudy screamed and flapped his raw limbs, swinging
back and forth on his little trapeze.

Sudharshan checked his watch. "Yes, soon." He went to a beautiful
pale wooden cabinet, all carved—the doors looked like strips of
bamboo—and got out three pairs of goggles. The eyepieces had a
funny gold sheen to them. "Welders' glasses," he said. "Rated safe for
looking at the sun." He handed one to Jerry.

"I'm not coming," Dad told them. He sat at the table, mug in his
hands, staring at the window where the banana and the *Monstera*
plants wrestled.

Sudharshan just stood there, looking at Dad. His face did
something complicated, moved through shock and sadness to an
unbending calm. "Carlos," he said softly, "don't you want to see what
happens? I don't know when I'll see you again."

"Why?" Jerry asked. "Where're you going?"

"He's leaving me," Dad told Jerry.

"I am not." Sudharshan went to the front door, began pulling on his boots. "I'll come back."

"When?" Dad asked.

Sudharshan reached into the hallway closet, pulled out a long, black wool coat. He shrugged into it, stuck the two pairs of goggles into a pocket. "As soon as I can, lover."

"Where are you going?" Jerry asked again. Rudy swung harder and harder on his trapeze, warbling a harsh and complicated song. Sudharshan reached into the closet, pulled out something round and shiny, about the size of a Frisbee.

"I'm travelling for work. I have to go."

"You're leaving me."

"What's that thing you're holding?" Jerry asked. What in hell was going on?

"If you don't come outside with me now, we won't be able to say goodbye."

"You're leaving after the eclipse?" Jerry asked. Rudy hit an ear-piercing note. Dad's eyes were wet with tears. Sudharshan walked over to him, touched his shoulder.

"Please, Carlos. It's about to happen. Please come."

"Will someone tell me what's going on?" Jerry said. They didn't even look at him. Dad stood, got his coat, a sexy biker jacket in heavy brown cowhide. Jerry hated it that his dad looked sexy.

"Let's go," Dad said. "Jerry, why're you just standing there?"

Sudharshan did something to make the gold disc disappear into the inside pocket of his coat. It should have been too big to fit. Jerry slipped into his own coat, and when he turned back, Sudharshan had Rudy out of the cage again. He put the bird inside his coat and cinched the belt of the coat tight. Rudy shifted around inside, stuck his creepy little head out. "Ready?" Sudharshan asked.

"You're taking Rudy to see the eclipse? Won't it damage his eyes?"

"He'll be okay," Dad told him. "Come on."

As Sudharshan unlocked the front door, Jerry's eyes fell on the

picture window. The *Monstera* was fruiting. The spike that it thrust
up towards the light would plump. In a year, it would be a scaly
fruit with pale yellow flesh. It would taste delicately sweet to some,
like a mix of banana and pineapple. To others, it would irritate
their throats and make them cough in vain efforts to dislodge the
miniscule hairs with which the fruit was filled.

The three men and the bird went out into the hallway of the
apartment building, heading for the elevator. Jerry remembered
something. "Dad? I thought that *Monstera* never fruits if you grow it
in a pot?"

Grumpily, Dad replied, "Strange things happen around Sudharshan."

In the elevator, no one spoke. Rudy peered around him with
interested, birdseed eyes. Jerry wondered what Sudharshan would do
if his pet pooped in his coat.

They stepped out onto the roof. The cold, bluish light of late
afternoon made Jerry squint. There was a fractious wind. It poked
fingers down his collar, up his sleeves. "There's the sun," Sudharshan
said, pointing.

"I know where the sun is," Dad responded. But he didn't look
where his lover was pointing. Instead he went to the side and looked
over. They were thirty-two floors up. There was a ledge, but it'd be
easy to leap. Jerry moved towards his dad.

"Carlos, come over here and put your goggles on," Sudharshan
said. "You too, Jerry."

Rudy punctuated the command with a high note. Both Jerry and
his dad obeyed. The goggles made everything a calm, non-reflective
yellow. The sun no longer bit at Jerry's eyes. Dad looked bug-eyed,
strange. Jerry went back to the ledge, looked over. He could see the
construction site, the excavator, the gravid tree.

Dad said to Sudharshan, "Aren't you going to put your glasses on,
too?"

"I don't need them."

"And did you bring a pair for me?" said a voice from over by the door to the elevator. Jerry looked. It was the man from the street. He tossed the lick of green hair out of his eyes and hitched his way over to Sudharshan, scowling.

Sudharshan only nodded. "Good to see you, Gar. You'll be fine, you know that."

"You two know each other, then?" Jerry was way out of his depth. He only wished he knew whose waters he was floundering in.

Gar regarded him bitterly. "His family knows my family."

"I'd take care of Gar, if he'd let me," Sudharshan said.

"I just bet you would." This from Jerry's father. "It's him you're going away with, isn't it? The rest was just some story."

Sudharshan replied, "Carlos, it's not what you think." The sky began to darken.

"I don't know what to believe any more, Vick."

Vick? Victor? Wasn't his name Sudharshan?

Dad let go of Sudharshan's hand. Or Vick, or whoever he was. Dad adjusted his goggles more comfortably on his face. "Gar. That's your name, right?" he snarled.

"Yeah."

"Well, you should cover your eyes or something."

"I'll be okay," the young man replied gently. He turned his angry face full on the darkening sun. Jerry was frightened. People went blind like that, staring at eclipses.

"Hey, Gar," he whispered, but the young man ignored him.

A whistling sound came from the front of Sudharshan's coat. Rudy worked his way right out into the open, and with a happy warble, jumped onto Gar's shoulder. Gar looked to see what had landed on him, and his face softened. "Hi there, little brother," he said to the bird. He reached an open palm to Rudy, who leapt into it, chirping. The bird nibbled lightly at one of Gar's fingers, a gesture of avian affection. Gar grinned broadly down at Rudy, then up at Jerry. "He's just a fucking little sport, isn't he? He and I."

"I'm sorry, Gar," Sudharshan said. "Sometimes it happens that way." The sky was blackish-gray now. "Pollution, toxins leach into the eggs. You know." The air rushed, whooshed around them. "We look after you. All of you." Looking up at the sun, Jerry's dad gasped, put his hands to his mouth. Jerry didn't dare look. The wind beat like wings.

"Yes, you do, O King," Gar replied. "You extend the hand of charity to us broken ones, whether we're any use to you or not."

"Well I would, if you would take it. You don't have to beg in the streets."

"You don't get it," Gar told him.

Jerry, too unreasonably terrified to think, kept his gaze resolutely down. There, in the building lot; the tree with its swollen middle. The wrecking machine crouched over it, crane-like. As Jerry watched, a shadow washed over it, over half the city.

Out of the dusklight Gar muttered, "I could live with you and be fed serpents' tongues and sweet water."

"Amrita."

"Whatever. Sugar. I could, but I'm not Rudy. I won't die without your care. I don't have to stay with you."

Rudy screamed. It was almost full dark now. Whatever was arriving was big enough to blot out all the light, to eclipse the sun. Jerry's dad cried out and crouched against the roof, cowering. "I believe you, I believe you," he whimpered.

"It's all right, Carlos," Sudharshan shouted over the rushing wind. He pulled the disk out of his coat. It glowed with light. He held it high and twirled it, signalling.

There was a huge cracking sound from the construction site. By the light of Sudharshan's disk of fire, Jerry could see that the swollen tree had finally burst at the belly and split apart.

Jerry refused to look at Sudharshan's hand with its spinning circle. He felt the weight of air above them rush down. Something was coming. He threw himself over his dad. And finally, finally, he looked up.

Pinions wide enough to span creation. A keel of a chest, deeper than the oceans. A man's body with the dimensions of a god. Backlit by the sun it eclipsed, the bird-headed man-thing swooped down, roaring. *Talons that could grasp an elephant and bear it away. A raptor's beak long enough to spear a sun.* Jerry cried, but couldn't look away. Small, he was so small. The thing swept past them, the wind of its passing nearly knocking them over. The sun peeked back out. The thing's awful cawing stopped.

"Long time no see, Daddy!" Gar called out to the creature. Then: "Oh. Would you look at that? A healthy hatchling at last."

Jerry's dad mewed under him. Jerry hardly heard it. He had to know. He stood on noodle legs and looked over the side.

The massive bird-thing looked briefly up at them. Its deep gaze, absently hungry, sucked Jerry in. A pointed tongue the length of a car snaked out and licked a hooked beak. Then it looked back down. It had folded itself up to sit in the construction site like a brooding hen in a nest. The tree stuck out from among its breast feathers; the creature was nesting on top of it. If the skeleton building or the excavator were still there, they were hidden somewhere under its body. On the street, cars were gathering to ogle. As though it bit on a toothpick, the thing pulled the top of the swollen tree away.

A smaller, ugly head covered in pinny green feathers poked out from beneath the bird-thing's breast. Crazily, Jerry thought of Rudy sticking his head out of Sudharshan's—Vick's—coat. The smaller thing opened its beak wide. It was all red inside there. The big bird-thing retched and vomited into the ugly baby bird's mouth. Frantically, the baby gulped it down. The father fed his child.

"The long, thin scrawny ones stick between your teeth, and the short thick ones just squirm . . ." sang Gar. "Whaddya figure my new brother's dining on, Vishnu?" Vishnu, not Victor. "Pre-digested cobras? King snakes? I remember how that tastes."

"He can't do it by himself," Sudharshan murmured.

Jerry's dad had stood up. He was looking down at the insane spectacle in the construction lot. Wonder made his features gentle. "That's some growing boy," he said. "How often will he eat?"

"About a ton of meat, every other day," Sudharshan said. "Garuda will need to hunt down a lot of snakes over the next five years or so. I have to help him. The baby is my new mount."

"So you're going to go away after all," Jerry's dad said. "You're leaving."

Sudharshan looked exasperated. "I told you; not for long!"

"Five years isn't long?"

"Not when you're a god, it isn't," Gar told them.

Jerry looked at his father's eyes filling, at his father bowing over again, shrinking in on himself again. He looked at Sudharshan, at the grief on the god's face. He remembered the picture albums that his mother had shown him, of his dad as a little boy in khaki shorts, grinning for the camera, proudly holding up—

"Dad," he said.

"He's leaving me, Jerry."

"Dad. Listen. Look at me."

"I'm going to be alone again."

"Dad."

"What."

"You used to hunt snakes, Dad," Jerry told him. "As a boy. Remember?"

And through his gold-lined goggles, Jerry's father looked at him, really saw him clearly. "My god," Dad whispered. "I did." He reached for Jerry and pulled him into an embrace, laughing, crying. Surprised, Jerry hugged back. His dad's shoulders were broader than they looked.

Over Jerry's shoulder, Dad said to Sudharshan, "I'll help you with your Garuda. You and me, okay? It's perfect."

"No," responded Sudharshan.

Stricken, Jerry's dad released him. From the street below came the sound of sirens. Jerry glanced over the side. Two fire engines were converging on the construction site. As if.

"No," said Sudharshan again. "It won't work, Carlos."

"Why not?" Jerry's dad cried out.

"It's too dangerous."

"I don't care. We'll be together. I can protect you."

The incarnation of an immortal didn't even bother to point out the flaw in his partner's logic. "You can't leave your job."

"Like they'll miss one lousy bureaucrat."

"Rudy, then. I can't take him, he's too frail. I need you here to look after him."

And now, Jerry's dad was at a loss for words. His face began to crumple.

Sudharshan was crying now, too. "Rudy's my responsibility, Carlos. All the garudas are. I thought you'd help me take care of him. Please, lover."

Jerry saw Dad's broad shoulders bunch, the twist of his hip, before he realised what was happening. Dad turned, Sudharshan screamed, "No!" and Jerry reached his hands out to catch Dad, to hold him, but Dad was vaulting over the ledge before any of them could move.

"Fuck!" Gar cried out. Someone in the street screamed.

Dad spread his arms and legs. He plummeted, landed on Garuda's broad back, rolled. Jerry tried to keep breathing. Dad fetched up against a boulder-sized shoulder. He pushed himself to a sitting position. Jerry could see the moon of his upturned face, looking at them. He waved.

Garuda turned its eagle's head, peered down at its new rider. It opened its beak and struck. Carlos barely danced out of the way in time.

"Please, please," Sudharshan whispered. "He's my love. Please don't hurt him."

A god was begging for his father's life.

"Hey, Dad!" Gar called down. Garuda met his gaze. "That's Carlos! He's gonna help you feed the little one there."

Garuda closed its beak. Twisted its head sideways to regard Jerry's dad with one eye. Carlos reached a hand up, stroked the tip of its mane of feathers, each longer than Carlos was tall. Garuda allowed the touch. Turned back to feeding his son.

Sudharshan threw his head back, eyes closed. He let a breath out.

His shoulders relaxed. "Oh, you smart-mouthed monster's son, you," he said to Gar. "Thank you."

"Any time I can be of assistance."

Sudharshan looked at him. Calmly, Gar gazed back. "Yes," the god replied. "I'll remember."

"You do that."

Sudharshan regarded the scene below them, his gaze fond. "Now, what am I going to do with that stubborn man? He can't come with me. Rudy needs . . ."

Gar laughed. "Is that all? Don't sweat it, Vishnu. I can housesit. Keep Rudy in birdseed and earthworms, yeah?"

Rudy skreeked.

Sudharshan glared at the two of them, the two failed garudas. He scowled down at the construction site, where Dad was stroking Garuda with one hand, and trying to wave the firemen away with the other. They had ringed Garuda and stood, uncertainly, holding limp hoses. Sudharshan sighed. "All right, then," he said.

Jerry laughed. Sandor'd never believe this in a million years.

"Look, we'd better be going," Sudharshan told them. "Those people down there could get hurt. We'll send word."

Vishnu didn't so much jump as float down into the cushioning of Garuda's feathered body. His dad and Vishnu pulled the ugly baby bird into a cradle between them on Garuda's back. Garuda purred at them as they struggled. Its child was bigger than the two men combined. But they managed.

The police had arrived. They bullhorned at them to get down, pointed rifles. Dad shielded Vishnu with his body. Garuda roared again, and the people on the ground crouched and covered their ears. It gathered its taloned feet under itself and leapt into the air, its wings pumping. They flew. In seconds they were too small to see.

"You'll have to care for the *Monstera*, too," Jerry told Gar.

"What's that?"

"It's beautifully ugly. I'll show you."

Sitting in Gar's palm, Rudy made a chirping noise.

"Yeah, but he never remembers," Gar told his brother.

"Never remembers what?" Jerry asked.

"My dad. Garuda. We don't like king snakes. They have this weird sweetish taste to them."

Jerry laughed, trying to make out the speck in the sky. "He forgets, huh? Yeah, I know what that's like."

Snow Day

The Canadian Broadcasting Corporation runs an annual radio event called "Canada Reads," in which a jury has an on-air debate about five books by Canadian authors. Ultimately, the CBC chooses one book each year that they suggest all Canadians read and discuss. I was one of the jurors for the very first Canada Reads. (Who knew that becoming a writer would eventually mean getting to debate with our former and first female Prime Minister, Kim Campbell?) A few years later, CBC called me, as they did a number of previous jurors. They were running Canada Reads again, and they wanted to commission us to each write a story that incorporated the titles of that year's five shortlisted Canada Reads novels. The only catch: we weren't allowed to use the titles as titles. Once they told me what the five titles were, the idea caught my fancy so strongly that I had my story written within a matter of hours. "Snow Day" is that story. (The five titles and their authors are listed at the end of the story.)

The shovel bit through the foamy snow on the top stair of my front porch, then stopped with a clang. I scraped away the snow to see what was beneath. Ice. Served me right for not shovelling after the snow had fallen last night. It had thawed, then the temperature had dropped into the deep freeze, and now the steps and the sidewalk were frozen solid.

On the street, a few cars and a bus slewed through the slush. The city had declared a snow day, so there wasn't much traffic out.

I sighed and began shovelling in earnest. I'd have to scoop all that snow into the road, then crack the layer of ice and start in on that.

The small of my back was already twinging in anticipation of pain. I scooped the shovel under a big load of snow.

"You need to lift with your legs," said a voice behind me. It managed to sound both squeaky and hoarse. I turned. No one there. Just a raccoon, perched on my green organic waste bin. Damned things had been trying to figure out how to open it for months. Almost every week the bin had new tooth marks.

"Scram!" I shouted. I dropped the shovel, clapped my hands together to frighten the raccoon away.

The raccoon jumped off the bin and hid behind it. It peeked out at me. "Jeez, no need to get snarky. I was just giving you some good advice." Its mouth wasn't moving.

"All right," I said, looking around. "Who's the ventriloquist?"

I couldn't see anyone. Most of my neighbours were at work. And Granny Nichol, who usually spent the day at her window watching the world go by, had her blinds drawn today.

The raccoon stepped out from behind the bin and sniffed the air in my general direction. "Lady, it's no fun being able to understand you, either. It's creepy inside a human's head. Got any scraps? It's slim pickings out here in this weather."

"Shoo." I waved my shovel at it. If I could get it to go away, the prankster's trick would be spoiled.

The raccoon backed up out of the way of the shovel, but stood quietly watching me, though I could see its snout twitching in the direction of the green bin. I'd had fish for dinner, and the bones and skin were in there, right on top. I thought I could smell them, and they made my mouth water. I could imagine how they would taste, how the bones would crunch in my teeth, how I would save the head for last, holding it in my little black paws . . . euw. As if.

Suppose the raccoon was rabid? Should I call someone from the City?

The raccoon went over to the fence, swung itself up onto the palings, climbed to the top and crouched there unhappily. "You're just going to let them take that fish head away, aren't you?"

I ignored it. I scraped the snow off the icy steps, trying to pay no attention to the way I hungered for the offal I'd thrown away, the splintery feel of the wood palings under all four of my paws, the way that my eyesight seemed fuzzy and the sounds of the cars too loud. I wasn't thinking in raccoon, I wasn't. When I was done, I stood at the bottom of the five steps and looked up at them. The glare from the ice coating them hurt my eyes. I turned my head, backed up a bit.

"Watch out!" came the smoky voice. I heard a scraping, screeching sound and leapt out of the way just as a car skidded up onto my sidewalk, missing me by inches. My front steps stopped it. The stairs shook, but held, although all the ice splintered away. No crystal stair, not any more.

A man leapt out of the driver's side. "My god, I'm sorry!" he said. "Are you all right?"

"I'm fine," I told him. But really, I wasn't paying him much attention. I looked to the raccoon, still crouched on the fence. "Thank you."

"You're welcome," it growled. "Just consider it payment for the tomatoes."

"That was you, then. You destroyed all my plants."

The raccoon shrugged.

"Lady," said the man, "I'm so sorry."

By then, a teenager had climbed out of the passenger side. "It's the brakes," she muttered. "Your brake shoes just went." She looked at me and rolled her eyes. "1999 Passat. The rotors are crap. I told Dad he'd soon be singing the Ancient Volkswagen Blues."

"Never mind that," her father said. "Look. It's the same here, too." He was pointing to my back yard. From out of it—from everyone's yard, really—squirrels were climbing down from the trees and converging on the street. Raccoons came too, and the occasional deer. Mice. Rats. Cats and dogs. A moving carpet of snails and slugs. More bugs than I wanted to think about. Birds were massing in the sky, flocking to the electric wires and the lintels of houses. I saw a gazillion sparrows, a million pigeons and gulls. Even the hawks were flocking. Hawks don't flock. "It was like this on our street, too," said the man. "I got us out of there, but it's the same everywhere."

"What's going on?" I asked.

"Beats me, lady," warbled a starling from the railing of my abused stairs. "And can you open that plastic thing, already? Some of us are hungry here."

I heard a hollow crash and a tiny metallic tinkle. A bear had cracked the bin open with one swipe. Cautiously, the smaller animals near it moved in on the feast.

Now the people were showing up; in cars, on foot through the snow, in wheelchairs, on bicycles. They gathered by the side of the road, leaving the street itself clear. That was important; I knew it somehow.

Granny Nichol's door opened. She let her dog Trevor out. "Good morning, everyone!" she said. She stepped onto her porch. She was carrying a bird cage. In it, a parrot shrieked and hopped from its swing to the floor of its cage and back again. "Shh, Billy, shh," she crooned.

"Get me the bleep outta here, lady!" it cawed. "It's time, can't you tell?"

"Yes, I can, dear. Just hold your horses."

Granny Nichol put the cage on the floor of her porch and creakily opened its door. The parrot leaped out. "Finally!" it hollered. Its wings were clipped, so it climbed, beak and claws, to join its avian cousins perched on Granny's eavestrough. Pets were exiting from all the houses, freed by their owners, who were also coming out onto the sidewalk.

"What about people's tropical fish?" the teenager asked. "They can't come out into this cold."

Nobody answered her because just then, the sky directly above us went dark. "Is it the Apocalypse?" cried someone.

"Don't be an idiot," replied someone else.

If it was the Apocalypse, it was taking the form of a row of lumpy, somewhat spherical objects, each about four storeys high, landing soundlessly in the street in either direction as far as the eye could see. You know when an orange goes bad, and gets this kind of pretty blue fuzz on it? They looked like that. Funny; I always thought spaceships would be shiny and metal. Like in the movies. These looked like something I'd throw into my composting bin.

A bulge appeared in the side of each object. I wasn't scared. I don't think anyone was. We all just waited. The raccoon kept gnawing on the fish head it had retrieved.

Each bulge split open, and an animal or two stepped, slithered or flew out. I saw a hippopotamus, and a lynx, and I think a cassowary. A colourful butterfly clung to the alligator's brow, like a bow-ribbon. A human being came out of one ship, leaning on a goat for support. She was old—the human, I mean—and her features were African, and she was smiling. They all came out, and behind them, their ships sealed, like those cool bandages. They all started talking to us, though no one's lips moved.

The ship in front of my house had disgorged some kind of cow, or antelope, or deer. No, too chesty for a deer, and too graceful for a cow. It had close, tawny fur, with deep brown stripes on its face and sides. Two long, thin horns stuck out from the top of its head. On its shoulder was a bird. The bird was smallish and plump, almost round. Its feathers were a deep grey with whitish flecks. It had a yellow beak with a reddish bit around its nostrils.

The beast picked its way carefully towards us through the snow. The bird on its shoulders wobbled, but hung on. They got close to us, stopped, looked us over. We looked back.

"So," said the antelope thing, "anybody wanna ride?"

"In that?" asked the bear. It got down on all fours, sniffed at the rotten orange ship.

"Yeah," said the bird. "You can come if you want to. It's a hoot."

An owl on a telephone pole above us hooted. The pigeons laughed.

"Where does it go?" asked the raccoon.

The antelope thing looked thoughtful. "Best I can describe it is, next door. You can visit, and if you like it, you can stay. Or you can come back here. Whaddya say?"

"Can we think about it?" asked the man who'd crashed into my front stairs.

"No. No time." The bird was addressing us over its shoulder. The antelope thing was already heading back to the ship. "Now or never. One-time offer only."

"Wait!" yelled a cat, turning in fretful circles at my feet.

The beast stopped and turned around. "We've discovered," it said, "that there are two kinds of creatures. The ones who come with us, we call them the Adventurers."

"And the others?" hissed the cat.

"We call them the Beautiful Losers. Because this Earth is beautiful and fearful, and it's a brave choice to stay, to never see anywhere but it. Just touch the skin of the ship, and it'll open for you." They disappeared back inside.

"Oryx and crake created He them," whispered the young woman.

"What?" I said.

"That was a spotted crake, and the thing it was sitting on was an oryx."

Birds were streaming into the ship. Granny Nichol was making her way to it as quickly as she could go. Her parrot, however, had clambered down to the porch and was headed determinedly back inside the house.

"Honey," said the man, "I really want to go. You coming?"

The young woman smiled at her father. "You go, Dad," she said. "I like being rockbound."

He hugged her tightly.

"But you have to come back, okay?" she said. "So you can tell me all about it." She stood and waved while he disappeared into the ship's side. "Aren't you going?" she asked me.

Nearly every creature had made its choice. I saw smaller rotten-orange pods flying out of windows and doors. The tropical fish, I thought. And the shut-ins and the babies. I guessed that some of the

ships had gone into the rivers, lakes, and seas. I looked at the snow
shovel in my hands. Stay and shovel snow, or go and see what lay next
door to this world?

The young woman gave my shoulder a gentle shove. "Go on," she
said.

THE FIVE TITLES:

Beautiful Losers by Leonard Cohen
No Crystal Stair by Mairuth Sarsfield
Oryx and Crake by Margaret Atwood
Rockbound by Frank Parker Day
Volkswagen Blues by Jacques Poulin

Oh, hell yeah. I used "oryx and crake" in a sentence.

Flying Lessons

The first time I heard Antoine de Saint-Exupéry's novel The Little Prince *in the original French was in Jamaica, in my high school French class. The reading was from an actual 33 ⅓ rpm vinyl record, being played on a portable record player that our French teacher had brought into class. I believe the reading was by de Saint-Exupéry himself. I remember my initial astonishment because I, an A student in French, couldn't understand a word of it. Neither could any of my classmates. We'd been studying French for years, but we'd never heard whole blocks of text spoken at anything like normal speed by a native speaker.*

It was Mister Gonsalves who taught Carol how to fly, when she was nine. Come, he'd said, I'll show you my little cat.

Afterwards, in her junior school carved into the red dirt of a Diego Martin hillside, she'd practise her flying during lunch break. Would stand on the part of the schoolyard below the tuck shop: the wide, paved part that sloped down to the high gate at the entrance. The other children would be playing and zooming around on the level dirt playground that had been carved out further up the hill, not on this steep leaning bit that rolled all balls out into the street. Sometimes you could find quartz crystals on that rough playground, marvellously faceted under God's loupe. Carol bet that the jewels Ali Baba had found in the story didn't look like the sharp, shiny ones in Daddy's jewellery shop, but all soft and white and gleamy inside, like the quartz you could find in the playground dirt.

But when Carol wanted to feel herself flying—when school lessons had been too hard and she had got all her sums wrong and Miss had called her up to the front of the class and told her in front of everybody that she must stop daydreaming—Carol had no time at break for digging for magic jewels in red dirt, or for Red Rover, Red Rover, send Carol right over, or for skipping Double Dutch. She would stand at the very top of the steep paved part of the school grounds and close her eyes, raise her arms out to her sides, and lean forward until if she leaned any further, she'd tip and fall. She would close her eyes and wait. You had to trust that the feeling would come. Do you like my cat? Mister Gonsalves had said. Would you stroke him for me, Carol?

When she flew, it was quiet up in the air, it was like Peter Pan. The breeze flowed under her eyelashes and trickled out the corners, making them feel cool and wet. She could go away, wherever she wanted: to a magical island where there were only children, and they played right through the day and night, as late as they wanted, and had toolum sweeties for breakfast and plantain tarts for dinner; or up high in the jamoon tree outside Mister Gonsalves's bedroom window, to crouch in the branches, eating sour jamoon berries till her hands and mouth turned purple from their juice. From the treetop you could see everything: the silly bald top of Mister Gonsalves's head where he lay with somebody on his bed. And across the road was her house with its red flagstone porch, where Mummy and Daddy wouldn't be home from work until six o'clock.

When the school bell rang and she had to go back inside, it would be time for English class. She was good at English, so Miss wouldn't have to tell her to concentrate. They were reading about the Little Prince. Carol figured that the pilot in the story was going to help the little boy to fly home to his asteroid where his friend the rose lived.

Mister Gonsalves's cat had been warm and brown and hairless. It had raised its blunt head up for kisses. Carol didn't remember what else; she was flying. It was nice that she had learned how. Because now, whenever she could get everything to work just right, it would come, the feeling of lifting off, of leaving her body and floating gently away; up, up, up into the warm Trinidadian sun.

Whose Upward Flight I Love

When I moved to Toronto from the Caribbean as a teenager, the winters were among the hardest things to get used to. More than three decades later, I still haven't quite managed it.

That fall, a storm hailed down unseasonable screaming winds and fists of pounding rain. The temperature plummeted through a wet ululating night that blew in early winter. Morning saw all edges laced with frost.

In the city's grove, the only place where live things, captured, still grew from earth, the trees thrashed, roots heaving at the soil.

City parks department always got the leavings. Their vans were prison surplus, blocky, painted happy green. The growing things weren't fooled.

Parks crew arrived, started throwing tethers around the lower branches, hammering the other ends of twisted metal cables into the fast-freezing ground to secure the trees. Star-shaped leaves flickered and flashed in butterfly-winged panic. Branches tossed.

One tree escaped before they could reach it; yanked its roots clear of the gelid soil and flapping its leafy limbs, leapt frantically for the sky. A woman of the crew shouted and jumped for it. Caught at a long, trailing root as the tree rose above her. For a second she hung on. Then the root tore away in her hand and the tree flew free. Its beating branches soughed at the air.

The woman landed heavily, knees bowing and thighs flexing at the impact. She groaned, straightened; stared at the length of root she was clutching in her garden glove. Liver-red, it wriggled, like a worm.

Its clawed tip scratched feebly. A dark liquid welled from its broken end. "We always lose a few when this happens," she said. The man with her just stared at the thing in her hand.

The tree was gaining altitude, purple leaves catching the light as it winged its way to its warmer-weathered homeland. She dropped the root. He tried to kick dirt over it, his boot leaving dull indentations in the earth. Then he gave a shout, not of surprise exactly, rushed to another tree that had worked most of its roots whipping out of the soil. She ran to help. Cursing, they dodged flailing foliage, battened down the would-be escapee.

He panted at her, "So, you and Derek still fighting?"

Her heart tossed briefly. She hogtied the faint, familiar dismay. "No, we worked it out again."

And Derek would stay, again. They would soldier on. And quarrel again, neither sure whether they battled to leave each other or to remain together.

A burgundy gleam on the powder-dusted ground caught her eye. The severed root was crawling jerkily, trying to follow in the direction its tree had gone.

Blushing

Does the blushing bride have the first idea what's in store for her?

"All the keys to my house are yours," he said. The rowdy sounds from the bar kitty-corner across Bellevue Park were muffled by the brick walls of the house. In here, it was quiet as breath.

He touched my cheek. His fingers pressed softly in, the way a chef tests a steak for doneness. He was as flushed as I knew I must be. My husband of three hours. My pale, precise love. Anything that excited him made his skin blossom shell-pink. I took the hand that held the large brass ring bristling with keys, and kissed his palm. We were at the top of the spiral staircase. The slippery satin train of my wedding gown spilled in a cascade down the stairs. It pulled at me. It was trying to slither downwards. I put a firm foot on the material. Heard the soft, explosive pop as the heel of my pump went through it. That'd hold it still.

I cupped the weight of the ring of keys in my hands the way I'd cradle the back of a baby's head. "All of these," I whispered, "mine?"

He smiled. "Except this one." He plucked a small key from the bundle and held it up for me to see.

It was brass, ornate. Its handle was a plain ceramic egg shape, like an eyeball, ending in a gold band. I touched the egg. It warmed under my fingers like skin.

"Another eye joke?" I asked with a teasing smile. "You optometrists."

That earned me a frown. "Be serious," he said. "You know which room I mean?"

I did. After the fire, after I'd accepted his proposal, he'd had the house gutted and remade to prepare it for me: the exterior sand-blasted to bring out the Victorian façade's plummy pink Credit River sandstone and rich red brick; the burnt couch replaced with a vintage settee in dark, knurled wood. In some precious import store in the market he'd found antique locks and keys taken from India, their greasy brass mottled blue-green with verdigris. He'd had the workmen install them in all the doors. I would visit every weekend to inspect the work with him. He'd given me my engagement ring under the lead-crystal-paned dome of the sun room, had playfully nipped blood from my earlobe on the Canadian Shield granite of the kitchen counter. Over the weeks, we had entered every room in his house one by one, wet some surface in each room with our fluids. Made them jointly ours. Except one.

I chuckled and put my arm through his. "C'mon," I said. "Show me your secret room." I still thought we were playing a game, that this would be the final deflowering of the last room of the house.

He shook his head. "I'm not kidding. Don't go in there. I'll need to have somewhere in our home that's just for me. You have your studio, after all."

I pulled out of his arms, let chill air whisper through the space between us. "Don't you trust me?"

"It's only healthy, you know. You don't want to become like those boring couples who might as well be the same person?"

I pouted, but said nothing.

He pinkened, smiled. He waved the little key in front of my face. "Atta girl. Promise me you will never use this key?"

I shrugged.

He hugged me, nibbled at the soft skin of my upper lip. "I knew I could trust you," he said.

But the day he returned to work, the key was gone from the ring. I tested the lock on the forbidden door. It was secure. I returned to bed. The smothering grandeur of the house made me want to lie cradled in Egyptian cotton forever. That, or run screaming into heavy traffic, cackling into car windows and gouging my eyes out. I chose to doze and dream, must have fallen asleep. I woke a few hours later, groggy, with a muddy headache. I couldn't figure out the coffee maker. My wedding gown had fallen off its shelf and was pooled on the bedroom floor. I stepped on a tube of Cadmium yellow in my studio, squeezing a long worm of it out onto the new oak flooring. It was late afternoon when I finally managed to leave the house. The sky was already beginning to darken into a still winter evening. The market air smelled like a meat locker. My tummy rumbled.

The Jamaican patty shop on one corner and the shop that sold used leather wear arm-wrestled for musical supremacy, dance hall vying with hard rock through tinny speakers that blared out over the heads of the passers-by.

A health food shop had a hand-lettered sign in its window, advertising a sale on dried mountain berries that I knew I could buy for a tenth of that price in the Chinese market over on the main road. The telephone poles were spackled with the motley of old posters: band appearances; dog-walking services; grainy, nth-generation photocopies of the faces of missing women.

At the precious little import store a perky Goth girl with bouncy Pollyanna braids told me that they'd sold the last of the antique locks. A job lot. To make room for new stock. "Old wooden teeth," she said. "With hinges. Masses of them. Gross."

"Who'd you sell the locks to?"

She lifted the coin tray out of the till, rummaged around some pieces of paper beneath. From one of them she wrote me an address on a piece of receipt paper she tore from the credit card charger. She reached into a fish bowl on the counter that was full of small, slim cylinders. She handed one to me. "Mace," she said. "No charge. It's getting dark."

The used office furniture warehouse on Spadina Avenue only had three of the locks left that they'd bought from the import store. A man with a receipt book and a worried look said, "I can give you a deal on those." I bought them, just in case. He tried to sell me a backless kneeler chair, too. "Great for your core strength," he said, patting the soft little tummy spreading above the waistband of his jeans. I wished him a good evening as I left.

"You be careful out there," he replied. He flopped into a padded steno chair with a sigh.

I wandered back through the market. The incense store was shutting the scent of sandalwood away for the night. The blinds on the big fish market snapped down like eyelids. In the bakery, bread was half price. I bought a loaf of something a rich chestnut brown. I tore pieces off it and chewed as I went. How could he call it total love if he kept any part of himself hidden from me?

The butcher shop was closed. A knob of bone rolled in the gutter outside it. I kicked it across the street and sulked along, thinking of lamb chops.

I passed the window of a bar, its black-painted storefront garish with commissioned graffiti. A man in a bulky hand-knit sweater was lugging a mannequin into the window. The mannequin was nude except for a chastity belt, complete with lock and key. The key jutted rudely from its crotch. The handle of the key was ivory, egg-shaped.

I rapped on the door until the man in the sweater opened it. "We don't open till six." His teeth were long and yellow.

"How much for the chastity belt?"

I twisted the ovoid handle. The key turned in the lock to the secret room like a knife scraping against bone. I pushed the door open. It resisted me, this last secret. It was very heavy, and padded. I stepped inside.

The coppery smell prickled the flesh of my arms.

The sight dropped me to my knees. It was all red in that room; red as blood. My slippers slushed in red. Red painted the walls and dripped in clotted gouts to the floor. The missing women had been given an extra throat apiece, and surplus orifices. As payment, the giver had taken an organ or two: a womb here; a tongue there. The women's eyes. Oh, their eyes.

I dropped the key. I had to dabble knuckle-deep in blood to retrieve it. I rubbed it against my dress to clean it, but that only spread more of the stain onto me. Trembling, I slid my hand across the congealing mess. Raised my palm to my nose.

The door creaked further open. There he stood, his colour high. "I didn't promise," I said.

He grabbed my hair, cranked my head back to a painful angle. "I told you not to come in here."

He probably thought my laughter was weeping. "It's all right," I said.

He went still.

"I will play your games with you."

He released me. Looked past me to the meat locker inside. "There were—" he began.

"—only two bodies when you left here this morning. I know."

Staring at him, I licked a salty drop of blood from my fingertip. "Apple of my eye," I said, "we don't need to keep secrets from each other."

His face took on the open wonderment of a child's. A locked door opens for the right key.

The third woman, her eyes mace-reddened, writhed against the gaffer tape that bound her up like a sausage. Her Pollyanna braids were less bouncy now. She tried to scream through the tape across her mouth.

It was a pity about her eyes.

Ours Is the Prettiest

The first shared-world anthology I ever encountered was the Thieves' World series. The next was the Bordertown series originally created by Terri Windling, about a city on the border between the lands of magic and the lands of the mundane world. The idea with a shared-world anthology is that the authors may use one another's characters created for the world of the anthology. You're not supposed to kill off another writer's character, but beyond that, all bets are off. So when Ellen Kushner and Holly Black revived the Bordertown series after a thirteen-year hiatus and asked me to submit a story for it, I knew that part of the fun for me would be messing with some of my favourite characters from the original series. I chose Ellen Kushner's Screaming Lord Neville. Though he'd never been described as a Black man, enough about him and his shop fit the bill. And since Blackness comes in every possible skin shade, it was easy to make him be a brother for my story. Ellen delightedly gave me permission to have at; Bordertown was multi-ethnic from the very beginning, even if that was often more in the conception than the execution. I also took the opportunity to gently tease Stick, also a Black man, and one of Charles de Lint's characters. Stick may take himself too damned seriously, but his pet ferret Lubin knows how to have fun. Though maybe Stick does have a hidden sense of humour; after all, who gave Lubin her outfit, if not him?

The thing about Bordertown that's always bugged me is that while the human side of the Border opens out to the whole world and all its cultures and races, the Fairie side seems largely monocultural and monoracial. There's apparently only one country on the Fairie side of the Border. I decided to hint at other magical races, other Fairie ethnicities, lore, and nationalities. Holly and Ellen were pleased. Though of course there was pushback. Readers who didn't feel *comfortable admitting that the only way they like their fairies is British as bangers and mash and white as a snowstorm made vague comments along the lines of "Ours Is the Prettiest" not feeling like a Bordertown story. I understand; I do. But the World is bigger than that. Why then would the world of magic be any smaller?*

If you're confused about the backstory to "Ours Is the Prettiest," I recommend you read the Bordertown anthologies and novels. They are things of beauty.

"Damiana!" Beti used her hands to part the veil of rag strips she'd strung from the cone-shaped hat she was wearing. The veil covered her face completely. I didn't know how she could see where she was going in that costume of hers. "Juju in the air this morning, oui?" she shouted over the brassy music from the camel-drawn omnibus. It'd been repurposed as a moving platform for some of the musicians in the parade.

I smiled. "Juju weather for true, yes!" Beti and I had only met four days ago, but she'd already learned the phrase "juju weather" from me. She mangled my accent, though.

I scanned up and down Ho Street as far as I could see. Which wasn't very far, what with the parade floats and banners and, apparently, all Bordertown spilled into the street to celebrate. Around us, people were dressed up like devils, like dragons, like whatever the rass they pleased. All of us were dancing, strutting, jamming, chipping, rolling, and perambulating down Ho Street however we might to the rhythms blaring from the various bands marching the parade route. The racket was tremendous.

I couldn't see Gladstone anywhere near us. I blew out a sigh of relief. Beti wanted nothing more than to find Gladstone, her new girlfriend, in all this comess, but Gladstone was pissed at Beti and was cruising to do some bruising.

The camel bus had a black banner draped around it. The lettering on it was made to look like bones, and read "We Dead Awaken." Through the windows we could see the musicians, all of them wearing funereal black suits, including top hats tricked out with black lace veils. Even the musicians were playin' mas'. It was a brass band, instruments shouting out the melody to a song I almost recognized.

Today was Jou'vert; the daylong free-for-all we were pleased to call a "parade" ushered in the week of bacchanalia that was Bordertown's more or less annual Jamboree. Word had gone around town that this year's theme was "jazz funeral." I was dressed as a Catrina from the Dia de los Muertos—a gorgeous femme skeleton in sultry widow's weeds, complete with a massive picture hat.

I suppressed a sneeze; my sinuses were tingling. Juju breeze for true, blowing a witchy front of magic from the Realm into Bordertown. Juju weather always made things in Bordertown especially . . . interesting. My fellow human friends made mako on me when I said I could sense the pools and eddies of magic as they wafted through Bordertown. Only Gladstone, half Blood as she was, had ever backed me up. And now her new girlfriend Beti, too. Or possibly her newly *ex*-girlfriend Beti. Beti, who might be from the Other Side, or who might just be a young brown girl playing out her own personal power fantasy.

Gladstone's life could get complicated.

Gladstone could deal. It was Beti I was concerned for, so young and so naive. Newbies to Bordertown never believed they were as out of their depth as they really were.

Beti swung a turn around me. She was completely covered by multicolored strips of old clothing that Gladstone had helped her collect from the discard bins at Tatterstock, the trashion clothing place in Letterville. Her voice growled softly from her whirling dervish center: "Do you see Gladstone?" It made my heart ache. Poor baby butch Beti. In the few days I'd known her, I'd already learned that her gruff voice came out lowest when she was trying to play it cool.

"Come," I replied, "lewwe go further down the road. I sure we going to buck up on Gladstone soon." Over my dead body. Glads was gunning for Beti, certain that Beti'd betrayed her. Striding to the beat, I set off down the road, weaving my way through the other mas' players. Beti followed me obediently, a little devil dustling sticking close to its mummy.

When I ran into Gladstone last night, she'd been propped up at a table at the Ferret, well into the snarly phase of a drunken bout with her favorite flavor of self-pity in a bottle—Mad River water chased with anisette. Gladstone sober was the best friend a person could hope to have. Gladstone on a binge was a snake-mean nightmare best avoided. I had a scar on my chin to keep me from ever forgetting that. I intended to make sure that this town—and Gladstone, my dearest friend—wouldn't ride roughshod over Beti, shiny as a new copper penny, with not the slightest hint of silver to her eyes or her hair. It was kinda funny the way the three of us had bucked up on each other just four days ago:

Screaming Lord Neville sashayed over to greet the customer who'd just stepped tentatively in through the doorway of the Café Cubana. "Table for one, sweet thing?"

The sweet thing was a sturdy, burnished brown tomboy with that leonine Bob Marley face you find on a lot of Jamaicans. She gave him a shy nod. She was wearing fancy runners with the laces not exactly tied, a plain baggy T-shirt, and jeans two or three sizes too big, her hands slipped into their back pockets. One of the newest styles to hit Bordertown since people had started flooding into it from the World last month, claiming that Bordertown had disappeared for thirteen years.

"This way, sugar." He led the way, practically voguing as he went. He had reason to show off. He was a tall, light-skinned brother with the

kind of figure that could carry off any look. Today he was decked out in a shimmering purple confection of a satin gown, an off-the-shoulder number with deep décolletage—I had to admire how he pulled that off—a nipped-in waist, and a full, bouncing poodle skirt made even fuller by a froth of lavender and sage petticoats peeking out from under it.

The girl slouched along behind him as he led her to a booth. She glanced at me, and more than glanced at Gladstone, who didn't notice. I was on the alert, though. Any rude gesture from that girl, any comment about Gladstone's halfling looks, and I'd be on her like a dirty shirt.

Instead, she said, "A good day to you both." She smiled at me, practically beamed at Gladstone. I nodded a greeting. She was almost to her table before Gladstone realized someone had been talking to her and mumbled a hasty "Good morning."

I leaned over and whispered to my friend, "How you figure baby girl keeps her pants up?"

That barely earned me a smile. Gladstone had a fragile look to her this early Noneday morning. The skin around her eyes seemed thin, the blue threadworm of veins there showing even through the rain-soaked-earth-brown of her skin. Outwardly, Gladstone looked anything but delicate. She was sporting the usual threads: black leather boots; loose faded jeans encasing her strong, flared thighs; a worn red flannel shirt with the arms cut raggedly off to display broad shoulders and biceps sculpted by her work as a navvy. All topped off with a close-cropped nap of silver hair, thick as a silverback's pelt, and a—usually—shit-eating grin that flashed a single gold tooth. Her eyes were also silver, from the Trubie side of her family, and they only strengthened her overall studly glamour. Many a femme and the occasional butch went all weak-kneed and tongue-tied in Gladstone's presence. Me and Gladstone had had a thing once. That was long over—too many years between us, two different worlds of experience. Now our thing was that kind of staunch, comfortable friendship where neither one of us had to mince words. No, me and Gladstone story done. It's Beti's story I'm telling you now.

I swung aside the skeletal bustle that was the skirt of my gown just in time to get it out from underfoot of a staggerline of Trubies, everyone of them dressed to pussfoot in gleaming white canvas bell-bottoms, sailor shirts, and beanies. All that silver hair only made the white suits seem even whiter in the Jou'vert morning sunshine. The line of them careened toward me in time to the road march tune. What was that chorus? It was nagging at me, half remembered. *The prettiest . . . the prettiest . . .*

A twenty-foot-tall stilt-walker wearing horns, red body paint, and not much more did a nonchalant daddy-long-legs step over the Trubies and proceeded on down the parade route, her bud breasts bouncing as she went. Two of the Trubies grinned at me and called out, "Jamboree!"

I gave them back the response, *"En battaille-là!"* and swung my noisemaker around on its stick so its racket sawed at the air. I shook my head at the silver flask one of them slid out of a back pocket to offer me. She was only being friendly, but they had a way of forgetting that some of the things they drank for pleasure could cause humans serious pain. The line of them changed direction, stumbling cate-a-corner off in the opposite direction, zigzagging through the crowds of people doing the jump up to the music. I said to Beti, "True Bloods playing Drunken Sailor mas'! What a thing!"

Beti stopped her dervish whirling long enough to peer at me through the strips and tatters of torn cloth and reply, "But they are not masquerading as the dead. Shouldn't they have obeyed the edict?"

"It was a *suggestion,* not an edict. Too besides, some of them had white skull faces painted on. Not that you could notice white face paint so easily on that lot."

Beti was pogoing now. I picked up the hem of my gown and followed her, chipping down the road to the music. Edict! Jeezam peace. I was getting used to the weird-ass things that ti'Bet could come up with. Is not like anyone was going to police what people wore. Nobody coordinated or organized the Jou'vert parade; it just happened. Nobody picked an official theme for each year's parade;

word just got around. And half the masqueraders completely ignored the theme and wore whatever pleased them. I even saw someone dressed up as a cell phone. The new, teeny kind. New to Bordertown, anyway. We'd learned about them last month, when newbies started flooding into the town again after a three-week absence. Only all the newcomers swore it had been thirteen years that Bordertown had disappeared from the World. And now here they were, chattering on about tweeting and MyFace and complaining that they couldn't "text" anyone with those ridiculously tiny portable phones they carried everywhere.

I said, "Neville, we ready to order over here." I'd tried making conversation with Gladstone, but I was only getting one-word answers.

"You mustn't address me as Neville today," announced Neville as he came over.

I turned my face to one side so he wouldn't see me roll my eyes. Always some drama with Neville. He slipped a pencil from behind his ear and produced a small, neat notebook from somewhere amongst the frills and flutters of his outfit. "Today, my darlings, I am the Beneficent Miss Nell. Your order, sweet children? I just put a pot of the house special blend to steep—fresher than your old uncle Charlie with the wandering hands! And the raisin cake is good today. The cook was in a nice, nice mood this morning." He leaned in closer. "Only whatever you do, darlings, don't order the scones. Cookie was never any good at those. He say is English people's food, all starch and no flavor. I mean to say, Cookie is a sweet man, sweet can't done." In a stage whisper he continued, "But he have his little blind spots, you know?" Then he burst into a gleeful cackle. He was the selfsame cook, but he never ceased to tire of his joke.

A gruff voice called out, "What is in the house blend?" It was the handsome mannish girl, sitting alone in her booth. I couldn't place her accent. Not Jamaican, then.

Neville—Miss Nell—beamed at the question. "Oh, sweetheart. The house blend have ginger grated fresh by the nimble fingers of a certain handsome young man; dried nasturtium petals, squash blossoms, and rose petals, all grown when magic permits in the summer garden of the best-looking negro this side of Soho; and nuggets of dried apple as sweet and lingering as that brown man's kisses. The house blend will fix anything troubling your heart, darling daughter. And for finger food, too besides, we have ripe banana dipped in sweet batter and fried, and green banana to boot. Cookie does fry them up nice-nice in olive oil, sprinkle them with a little coarse salt and some cayenne, then drench them in so much butter, you going to be licking your fingers and wiping grease from your mouth with the back of your hand and belching one rude belch, and thanking the stars in the heavens that you find your way to Café Cubana at long last."

By the girl's frown and her baffled look, Miss Nell had lost her early on in that flight of language. She pointed at Gladstone and said, "I want what that one has." Her two eyes made four with a startled Gladstone's. Not a bit of shyness to the butchling's gaze this time. It was Gladstone who blushed and looked down. I ordered our usual: roasted hazelnut and hemp tea for Gladstone, with fried ripe bananas. Madagascar Muckraker for me, with fried green bananas, extra butter. No scones for either of us.

Like a seven-foot hummingbird, Neville—Miss Nell—flitted and flashed from customer to customer, taking orders and giving banter. From what I could tell, he did so in at least five languages, including High Middle Elvish and La'adan, which was popping up everywhere now that the River Rats had for some reason taken a shine to it.

A tinny tinkle of a tune came from somewhere about the girl's person. She pulled a cell phone out of the kangaroo pocket of her sweatshirt, flicked it open. She spoke a greeting into it, in a language I didn't know. All around the cafe, people smiled, shook their heads. Another newbie come to check out Bordertown now that it was open to the World again. She would find out soon enough; over here, a cell phone might take it into its head to dance a jig, to loudly broadcast the audio from the last time you'd had sex, even to ring. What it would not do was allow you to have a conversation with another person. Not for long, anyway.

Gladstone, still looking like someone had stolen her puppy, muttered,

"*Last year, me and Charlotte marched in the Jamboree Jou'vert parade together. I was dressed in Pierrot Grenade, and she was my Pierrette.*"

I closed my eyes. "And two weeks after that, she left you. Don't tell me that is what all this moping and sulking is about."

She looked at her hands. "This time of year is just reminding me, you know? Everyone's gonna be at the parade, all coupled up and shit. Not me, though."

I sighed and rubbed the scar on my chin. "Gladstone, you know I love you, and I sorry to be so harsh, but Lottie's not your girlfriend anymore. Not for nearly a year now. Good thing, too."

I opened my eyes. Gladstone's face had gone ashen and completely still, as though someone had slapped it. Feeling like a shit, I continued, "Let me guess: you got drunk out of your mind again, you probably tried to get violent, and she'd finally had enough, and she left you. Same old story, doux-doux." Okay, so that was the real reason I'd broken up with Gladstone. Same blasted reason everybody did. "She broke up with you, and she been hanging out with Nadine from since. The two of them happy like pigs in mud. She not coming back to you."

Gladstone sighed. "The pretty ones always leave."

"Yes, if we want to remain pretty." I managed to pull my fingers back before they touched the jagged place on my chin.

The tomboy girl was babbling into her cell phone. Unusual for the conversation to have lasted this long. I couldn't place the language, but she looked distressed. Her voice was getting louder.

Gladstone muttered, "I give them my heart and they toss it back in my face and it just makes me crazy, you know?"

The girl barked a panicked question into the cell phone. Agitated, she started arguing before she could have heard much of the answer.

Gladstone wailed, "Lottie left, you left. They always leave."

I sighed. "Where's Nelly with that blasted tea?"

Beti had stopped dancing for the moment. From the torque to her pitchy-patchy costume, I could tell that she was turning this way and

that, trying to peer through the crowd. "Can you see . . . anyone?" she
asked me.

"Not yet," I answered.

She seemed to shrink into her already-small self. I felt like a shit for
the dance I was leading her on.

Over there. Was that a nap of silver hair on a burly body? Yes, but it
wasn't Gladstone. I let out the breath I hadn't realized I was holding.

I spied out Stick on the sidelines, leaning against a telephone pole,
wearing his usual grim and faintly disapproving sour face. Wouldn't
hurt him to come and join the bacchanal. He was even dressed
right for a jazz funeral: black jeans, black boots, black T-shirt. But
for all his grace when beating people up in his self-appointed role
as Bordertown's helper of the helpless, I was sure that dicty negro
couldn't shake his groove thang if his life depended on it. His ferret
Lubin was doing it for him, weaving around his ankles for joy of the
music, and occasionally standing on her hind legs to do a little ferret
jig. Lubin just loved to dance, oui?

But wait—was Lubin wearing something? I squinted, but the
blasted myopia wouldn't let me see clearly. Trailing a swirling Beti, I
casually chipped my way closer to Lubin and Stick. A troupe of man-
bats blocked the view for a few seconds until, with a swish of their
leathery outstretched wings, they moved past. Lubin stood up on her
hind legs again and began to hop about. I busted out laughing.

"What?" asked Beti, mid-pirouette.

"Stick's ferret. That guy, see? His pet is wearing a Carmen Miranda
costume." Lubin wore a tiny layered miniskirt, each layer a different
color, and a little purple cotton halter that left her midriff bare. Each
front leg sported a yellow armlet ruffle, high up. I couldn't make out
the details of the colorful hat secured under her chin with an elastic
strap, but I'd bet it was a mini cornucopia of tropical fruit.

Beti looked where I was pointing. "That man comes from across
the river," she said.

"Who, Stick? I can believe he's crossed the Big Bloody."

From the movement of the motley covering her top half, she must have shaken her head. "Not the Mad River. The one running through my town. He has a look to him like the people who live on the other bank."

Uh-oh. Tickle in my nose, and that sensation like my hair was lifting up off my scalp.

From since I was a small girl back home—back *home* home, that is, not my second home of Toronto, Canada—I used to know when it was going to rain, even before the rainflies came out to fill the sky, to flit and dance in the air until the rain came down and washed their wings from their bodies so they could transform into adults. In Bordertown, I could sense magic weather as well as the regular kind, and right now, there was big magic heading our way. Gladstone on a tear could send a stormwash of the stuff on ahead of her like a shock wave. Only Gladstone's juju could give me the kind of migraine that was suddenly a threatening whisper behind my left eye. When I'd seen her last night she'd muttered, "Bitch thinks she's too good for me, huh? I'll show her." She hadn't seemed to be particularly aware of who I was. She was just announcing her pique to the general air.

I put my hand on Beti's back to urge her forward. "We gotta go."

"Very well. But I wanted to watch the small woman dance some more."

"Small woman?" I kept moving us through the crowd. Over there, was that a broad shoulder in a red plaid jacket with the sleeves cut away? Best as I could, I ducked us behind a very tall, thin girl wearing a very tall, thin cardboard box that had been decorated to look like a coffin.

"The one you just showed me," said Beti, sounding frustrated. "The tiny one in the plenty skirts. With the guy from over the river."

"Lubin?" I nearly tripped over my own bustle in surprise. "But Lubin isn't a woman."

"She's not a girl?"

"She's a *ferret*, ti'Bet. An animal."

"A woman animal. Like you."

Weird kid. "Sure. I hear the Horn Dance has their own crew planned for today. Lewwe go see if we can find them."

The Beneficent Miss Nell returned from the back-room kitchen, apron and cap abandoned so she could show off her ensemble to advantage. She was holding aloft two trays loaded with orders. And she was singing, in a booming, tuneful bass, the old calypso about Frenchmen and their predilections for cunnilingus. I thought I could see the browned, crushed-baton shapes of fried green bananas on a saucer on one of those trays, and a saucer of golden rounds of batter-dipped, fried ripe bananas. I sat to attention, hopeful. Sure enough, Nell began sweeping in our direction, and then it was like slow motion, like the way things happen when you're in a car that's about to collide with another, and you can see

it

happening, but

it's too late

to stop, and you're thinking, oh shit this is going to hurt, and then everything speeds up and the butch girl was striding toward Nell, out of her line of sight, but she was chattering on her cell phone, not looking where she was going, and before I could shout out a warning, bam! And then there were spilled bits of bananas and broken crockery everywhere, and Miss Nelly was down on the ground, her tiara askew, and the girl was looking shocked and dismayed at her and was shaking banana bits out of her short dreads, and Gladstone was already out of her seat and on the way over there.

Gladstone asked them both, "Are you okay?" The girl turned those marsh-green eyes toward her, and I swear that Gladstone gasped. The girl smiled at her, and there it was; Gladstone get tabanca just so. Just like the last time, and the time before. A big believer in love at first sight, Gladstone was. So of course it happened to her all the time. It was the first step in her personal dance of self-destruction.

The girl slid the cell phone back into her pocket. In the quick glimpse

I got, it looked more like a shell than a cell—white and crenellated on the outside, pinkening to a deep rose centre. When I left the World nineteen years ago, there were cell phones with superheroes on them and cell phones that lit up in the dark. Looked like there was a fad for organic now.

Gladstone and her new crush helped Miss Nell to her feet, the girl apologizing the whole time in that accent I couldn't place. She really was astonishingly striking. Small and sturdy and muscly, a one-person puppy pile of energy and enthusiasm. By the time Gladstone and the girl were done cleaning up the mess that Beti's carelessness had made, the two of them were good, good friends, and Gladstone was introducing her to me (her full name was something unpronounceable that apparently meant "a blessing on our house"—I made do with Beti, the part of it I could say) and offering to show her the best places to get a last-minute outfit to wear to the Jou'vert parade, since she was so new in town and Gladstone knew her way around. They scarcely noticed me paying both sets of bills.

"Gladstone, man," I complained when we left the Café Cubana, "I never got to taste my green banana."

Beti gasped. "I am so sorry," she said. She touched my arm briefly. "This is my fault. We must go back and get you another meal."

Both gracious and graceful. "Nah, is all right, never mind that," I said, smiling. "What I really want to know is how come you were getting reception on your cell phone."

"My cousin called me."

Gladstone's lips twitched. "From the Other Side?"

"Whoa, wait," I said. "You're from the Realm? A human from the Realm?"

"She says she's not human," Gladstone replied. "Elvish." She and I shared a covert, amused smile. New in town with a bad case of the elf wannabees. Most of them got over it. I had, and was still grateful for Gladstone's patient indulgence in those years I'd swanned around in gauze skirts festooned with what I'd fancied to be Elvish runes.

Beti had the grace to look abashed. "Not from the Realm. From . . ."

The syllables landed on my ears and slid away, like marbles rolling in oil. Gladstone's face did something peculiar. Interested, hungry, and resentful, all at once. "Wow. Really? I've heard about you guys."

Beti simply nodded. "What's that?" She was pointing above our heads. Gladstone replied, "What? Oh. That's Jimmy."

I asked, "What's that place allyuh talking about? That unpronounceable place?"

Gladstone looked embarrassed for me. "A country across the Border."

"The Realm, you mean?"

"No, a different country. There isn't only the one, you know."

I hadn't known.

"Jimmy?" Beti reminded her.

I answered this time. "The stone gargoyle. He lives there on top the Mock Avenue Church tower."

Gladstone cut in. "I could take you to see him. They say that if the bell ever strikes the right time, he'll come to life. I could take you and show you. If you'd tell me more about . . ."

I started herding us toward where Gladstone and I had chained our bikes. "A different country? Wow. Live and learn. Okay, but if cell phones don't work in Borderland, they sure not going to work on the Other Side, either." Why was Gladstone going along with Beti's story?

Beti said, "It's kind of like texting, okay? Except with kola nuts. Though jumbie beads work just fine, unless you want to get all self-righteous and ancestral and shit."

The common-class stylings combined with her odd accent were cute as hell. "Kola nuts. Jumbie beads. Right."

Beti didn't reply, just turned those mossy eyes on me with a sweet smile. For the next four days, that's how she responded any time we bucked up against some mystery about her.

That's how it all started. Bordertown was a place of collisions that led people's lives in new directions. For the four days before Jamboree, Gladstone wandered everywhere with Beti. The two of them were just totolbée over each other. They were holding hands within minutes of meeting, kissing within hours. Gladstone took her to see Jimmy, and to hang with her skateboarder friends at Tumbledown Park. Plus shopping

for a Jou'vert costume. I bet if I had said "Lottie" to Gladstone them days,
she would have replied, "Who?" She would have forgotten me, too, had
it not been for Beti. Gladstone told me; every little trinket Beti found,
every sight she saw, it was, "We must tell Damiana!" and she would drag
Gladstone to come visit me at Juju Daddy's.

Stick saw me looking at him and Lubin. He nodded gravely at me.
I swear the man knew who I was even under my skull makeup and
the big picture hat decorated with small gravestones and teeny crows.
Stick gave me the creeps.

Beti lifted some of the motley from her face and looked around.
"When will Gladstone be here?"

My heart ached for the poor kid. "I don't know, ti'Bet."

She frowned the way you frown when you're trying not to cry.
"But I want to see her before this is all over. I want to dance with her
while I still can."

"Plenty of time, doux-doux. The last lap around the market isn't
till sunup tomorrow. Come, lewwe try and find some other Catrinas."

"Like you?"

"Yes, like me." She and I had given up trying to dance for now.
Too many people. We kept pushing on through the thronging bodies,
the laughter, the dancing. Through the musk-salt sweat of human
bodies and the lavender-salt sweat of Trubie ones. Through the sense-
memory of me lying with my head cradled on Gladstone's chest, both
of us damp from the exertion of fucking. My musk-salt sweat and her
complicated lavender-musk-salt one. I wondered what ti'Bet's sweat
smelled like: salt, or sweet? Or maybe both? What was she, really?

A breeze tugged at my hat, horripilated the little hairs on my arms.
Jumbie weather. Coming in on little cat feet, like those light sun
showers of sweet rain that can turn in a flash into a full-out storm.

For all the pushing and shoving and comess, I nearly jumped right
out of my skin when a howl cut through the music, and a figure
tumbled past us, throwing itself into a triple somersault. Whoever

or whatever it was landed on its feet facing us. It was wearing a pallbearer's suit, complete with top hat. A wolf skull peeked out from under the brim of the hat. I drew back. I swore I could see through the empty spaces amongst the bones of the skull to the paraders dancing on the other side of the person. Then he pulled the mask and hat off in one to reveal his own lupine head and furry snout. The mask was solid again. Juju weather, making me see things.

"Ron!" I squealed. "Jou'vert, sweetheart!"

Ron the Wolfboy sketched a deep bow at us, flourishing with his hat and mask. He bruised the air with another howl that just might have been the words, *"En bataille-là!"*

Ti'Bet launched into a ululation of her own. Which only increased my horripilation. She started dancing around him. He grinned, reached to take her hands. Instead, she clapped her hands onto his shoulders. He took her by the waist. Together, man-thing and mystery woman, they capered through the crowd, barreling into revelers, who greeted them with cries of "Jou'vert!" and *"En bataille-là!"*

"Jeez, girl. Look at how all these colors fighting with each other, nah?" With thumb and forefinger, I sorted through the pile of discarded rags Beti and Gladstone had dumped on the kitchen floor of my squat. "You couldn't find anything nicer than this?"

"They are from people who may be dead. That's the theme, right? To celebrate your ancestor spirits?"

"I guess."

"I will make an egungun, then. Spirit of the ancestors. It beats people with sticks to remind them to be good."

"My granny used to threaten to do that to me. She never did, though."

"The sticks are also to keep people away. To touch the egungun is to die. Only Gladstone says I mustn't beat anyone with sticks during the parade."

I made a face. "Shit, no. That used to be the tradition centuries ago, back home. 'En bataille' means 'Let's rumble.'"

"I do not understand."

"Never mind," I said. "Nowadays the 'en bataille' is only pappyshow. No real fighting supposed to happen." Sometimes she worked too hard at this being an elf thing. So did Gladstone, but she at least had a reason. She was half elf, after all. Half elf and all Bordertown. Beti was probably neither.

"You realize most of these clothes too mash up to mend?"

Beti grinned at me. "I'm going to, uh, mash them up even more." She took a crumpled and stained linen dress shirt from me and began tearing it into long strips. Her hands were strong. "Today I walked through your marketplace, and I visited a place across the Mad River," she said happily. "Lots of people brown like me and Gladstone. And I ate jerk chicken."

"You were in Little Tooth, then. The Jamaican section."

"Yes. Tonight, Gladstone is taking me dancing."

"Like you trying to experience all of Bordertown at the same time!"

"I have to go soon."

"After only a few days? School must be out for the summer by now."

Beti hesitated. Then she said, "I would like to stay longer, but someone is coming to take me away."

Damn. I'd been hoping a casual mention of school would get her to make a slip one way or the other about this elf business. I'd just have to keep trying to get the real story from her. I held one of the rags up against her. "This purple is good on you. Bordertown don't let everybody in. This person who wants to take you away may be the wrong kind of person."

For a second, hope lit her face. But the light went out. "This one, borders cannot stop him."

"Who is he?"

"My brother. Do you really think he might not be able to come here?"

Gladstone whisked into the room, her arms full of more gaudy rags. "Who might not be able to come here?"

Beti turned to her. "My fiancé," she said.

I chuckled. Wherever she was from, English was certainly not her first language. "Ti'Bet, you just told me he was your brother. He can't be your fiancé, too."

She went still, then gave a dismissive laugh. "Brother, betrothed—I always get them confused."

Gladstone dumped her armful on top of the one I was already sorting. "So which one is he?" I could tell she was trying not to let her suspicion show.

"My brother. My blood, yes? He's coming soon to be with me."

Before I could ask her about the difference between "take me home" and "be with me," she tackled Gladstone, knocked her down into the mound of rags on the floor. Giggling, they began to wrestle. Gladstone had Beti pinned in under a minute, but Beti laughed her growly teddy bear laugh and somehow managed to twist her body and use her legs in a scissors hold around Gladstone's waist. The wrestling turned into groping and the giggling was silenced by kisses. I watched them. Only for a little while. When buttons started being unbuttoned by eager fingers, I left the squat and went for a walk. It was high time I had a girlfriend again.

Beti and Ron were still dancing their jig. They'd been joined by Sparks, Ron's girlfriend. Briefly, I wondered whether Ron had dog breath. I used to give Glower those soft cakes of raw yeast for his. But I wasn't really paying them too much mind, oui? I was busy keeping a watch out for Gladstone. Too besides, the turreted shape of Beti's pitchy-patchy costume had finally jogged my memory. The song that the chorus of the road march was sampling was:

> *In a fine castle, do you hear, my sissie-oh?*
> *In a fine castle, do you hear, my sissie-oh?*

So long I hadn't played that game! Not since small girl days back home. We'd form two circles of children. The circles would haggle with each other in song:

> *Ours is the prettiest, do you hear, my sissie-oh?*
> *Ours is the prettiest, do you hear, my sissie-oh?*

The response, a simple expression of longing that even when I was a child had struck me as endearing in its brave vulnerability:

> *We want one of them, do you hear, my sissie-oh?*
> *We want one of them, do you hear, my sissie-oh?*

But suppose it hadn't been a plea, but a threat? *Give me one of your pretty ones, you hear me? Or else.*

Or else what? And was the first team's reply an act of generosity, or a capitulation?

> *Which one do you want, do you hear, my sissie-oh?*
> *Which one do you want, do you hear, my sissie-oh?*

No. Not Beti. They didn't want our Beti, did they? All that talk about having to leave soon, not having much time. Beti was jumpy as a cricket in a chicken coop today. And where the hell had she gotten to? I'd lost her in the crowd.

My left eye twitched. Oh, god. Juju heading our way. That twitch in my eye; in the bad years, that's how I'd learned to tell when Gladstone's nature was running high. How to tell when to stay away from her.

Gladstone slouched casually against her bicycle and mine. We'd leaned them against the bus stop where we'd arranged to meet Beti. Mine was chained the usual way. Gladstone's had only a piece of old rope looped around the fork, trailing untied to the ground. The way she put it was, if the bike believed it was tied up, nobody would be able to steal it. Seemed to work, too. In any case, no one had ever stolen her bespelled bike. I'd lost five bikes to thieves since I came to Bordertown. Gladdy and I were going to take Beti mudlarking along the banks of the Big Bloody. Sometimes you found cool trash to keep or trade.

Gladstone looked up and down Chrystobel Street. "You see her yet?"

I sighed. "No, girl. But I sure she going to come."

"I just want her to be safe, is all."

I nodded. If you didn't have your own wheels in Bordertown, there was always what passed for a transit system; you found some simulacrum of a bus stop—this one was a dead tree still standing at the curb of Chrystobel Street, the length of its blackened trunk painted shakily in green with the words "The Bus Stops Here." And you waited. There was no schedule, no official transit system. Anyone with any kind of vehicle could take it into their head to set up a route and charge whatever they pleased. You never knew what would show up. A rickshaw pulled by a wild-eyed youth with spiky red hair and the shakes from Mad River withdrawal. A donkey cart, complete with donkey. There was even a bus pulled by a unicorn that only let virgin passengers on.

"I'm actually having a hard time keeping up with her," said Gladstone. "Beti, I mean."

"Like I used to with you."

"She keeps wanting me to take her to all this stuff I've never heard of."

"Like what?"

"She wants to see a movie about a guy wearing an iron suit. The second one, she says, 'cause she's already seen the first and the third. She wants to try something called an ecsbox. She wants a Hello Kitty vibrator." Gladstone blushed.

Me, I thought my belly was going to bust from laughing. "You mean, Sir Gladhand's flashing fingers not doing it for her? Like you slowing down in truth, gal! Oh, don't be like that. You know is only joke I making." Then it dawned on me. "Wait one second; those things she wants, they're all from the World. Things from the time when the Way to Borderland was closed."

Gladstone was still sulking. "So?"

"Why would a newbie come here for things she can get out in the World?"

A bitter chuckle. "You still don't believe she's from across the Border?"

"Do you?"

She shrunk in on herself a little. "I've heard about . . . you know? That place she says she's from?"

"It's a real place?"

"It may only be stories. My da used to tell me them." She looked at me, longing making her face vulnerable. "A country on the Other Side where people have both my skin and my magic."

Huh. Maybe Beti was telling the truth, then. I wasn't convinced, though.

A team of boys riding three tandem bikes pulled up to the stop, off-loaded two guys with backpacks and a woman carrying a live chicken by its bound legs. No Beti. The guys paid for their ride with smokes. The woman paid with the chicken. They wandered off in separate directions. The bikes moved on.

"So you going to go there?" I asked. "To Unnameable?" I tried to keep my voice light, to prepare my heart for yet another loss.

She stared at her shoes. "She won't tell me anything about it. Nothing that counts, anyway. Just like all those other Bloods who think they're better than us halfies."

"Girl, get real. I see how she looks at you. If she not telling you anything, maybe she can't. Is you self tell me that people from beyond the Border are forbidden to talk certain things."

Gladstone scowled. "Yeah . . ."

"Well, then." She wasn't going to leave me. Relief. Triumph. Guilt.

"Damy, all that stuff she wants that I've never heard of, I can't give it to her." Shame burned deep in those silver eyes, banking to anger. Outcast in the World, outcast over the Border. Gladstone would probably live out her life in Bordertown, and she knew it. And even here, she had to steadily battle closed doors and sniggers behind her back. "Beti can go wherever she wants, in the World and out of it. Comes here flaunting it, slumming with the halfie."

I sneezed. "Don't go sour on this girl the way you do, okay? I like her."

Gladstone huffed and stared at the ground.

"Beti!" I called. I pushed between a scary clown wearing a T-shirt that read "Why So Serious?" and a near-naked Trubie. The Trubie was ancient as the hills and thrice as wrinkled. He had a boa constrictor draped over his arms. Age had blanched the two braids hanging down his back from silver to pure white. They were each nearly as thick around as the snake, and their tips tickled his dusty ankles. His eyes were an opaque fish-belly pale, but they followed me all the same.

The snake charmer was suddenly blocking my road. Blasted Trubies could move quicker than thought. He leaned in toward me and croaked, "What will you give her, do you hear, my sissie-oh?"

I sneezed. The man looked startled, as though someone had just shaken him out of a dream. He smiled at me. "Excuse me, cousin," he said, his vowels liquid with the accent of the Realm. "I did not mean to bar your way." He stepped aside.

"Don't fret," I replied. My skin was still crawling with the surprise of the first thing he'd said to me.

"Did I misspeak you, cousin?" he asked. "It seems to me I said something, though I don't remember what."

"No. Nothing much, anyway. It was nothing."

I could lie with words, but never with my face. He studied the polite fib he saw written there, and probably my fear, too, besides. He gave me a rueful smile. "There is a wild magic in the bloods of both our races, my friend. We must give it sport from time to time, yes? And sometimes the bacchanalia calls our spirits forth in ways we do not ken."

I wasn't sure what he was talking about. I needed to find Beti. I gave him the Jou'vert greeting, though my voice cracked midway.

"To battle, then," he replied. The response didn't sound so light-hearted in translation. I shuddered. As I moved on, he was crooning at his snake, which had raised its head to his and was flicking its tongue over his lips, scenting his breath.

"Beti! Where you dey? Beti!"

Into my left ear, the juju breeze whispered something that sounded like: *We will beat her with green twigs, do you hear, my sissie-oh?*

I yelled, "That don't suit her!" The general commotion swallowed up the sound of my voice. I muttered, "Do you hear that, my fucking sister dear?" I pressed on, calling out Beti's name. And I found myself muttering under my breath, "You didn't come to Bordertown for this, oui? Playing mother hen to baby dykes and sullen butches with substance abuse issues." But is lie I was telling.

In truth, I'd never planned to come to Bordertown at all, for any reason. People don't believe me so I don't talk it much, but I swear I didn't leave Toronto. It left me.

It had been a bad year, is all. My girlfriend at the time had just left me. Something about me being smothering. I'd had to put my nineteen-year-old dog down once his heart trouble was too far gone. Then Grandma died back home, and I couldn't afford to fly down for the funeral. And the last straw: I'd been temporarily laid off yet again from my job at the forever precariously funded crisis center.

The Change happened slowly, in the weeks that followed. At some point it crossed my mind that the flashily overlit Honest Ed's Discount Emporium seemed to have seamlessly metamorphosed into a store called Snappin' Wizards Surplus and Salvage—More Bang for the Buck, More Spell for the Silver. Sure, the words on the sign had changed, but the place still sparkled with enough lights festooning its outside to illuminate half the city, and was still piled to the ceiling with everything from army parachutes to sex toys. And sure the Swiss Chalet chicken place across the street had been replaced by a club named Danceland, but that was construction in downtown Toronto for you; they were always bulldozing the old to replace it with something else. The little import shop where I bought my favorite fair-trade dark chocolate ran out of it, and then chocolate was scarce everywhere. I didn't drink coffee, so is not like I missed that.

And as to the presence in the city of fine-boned people with fancy hair, high style and higher attitude? Toronto'd always had its share of those. By the time I had to accept that I was no longer in Toronto and those weren't just tall, skinny white people with dye jobs and contact lenses, it didn't seem so remarkable. People changed and grew apart.

As you aged, your body altered and became a stranger to you, and one day you woke up and realized you were in a different country. It was just life. I hadn't needed to travel to the Border; it'd come to me. I'd settled in, found a new job, started dating Gladstone. Life went on, if a little more oddly than before.

I got used to it: to dating a truly magical mulatress, to reading by candlelight when the power outed, to riding a bicycle everywhere, in any weather. I even rigged up a Trini-style peanut cart: a three-foot-cubed tinning box attached to the front of a bicycle, with a generator powered by the action of cycling. Or by a spellbox, when electricity wouldn't manifest. Peanuts roasting inside it. The outlet chimney was a whistle, so the escaping steam would sing through the whistle as I rode. That and the smell of roasting peanuts would make people run come. Daddy Juju loved it. He painted the store name and address on the side of the tinning box, and I rode the streets of Bordertown and served out fresh roasted peanuts in little rolled cones of newspaper.

I made a good life here. Working at Juju Daddy's was my job, true. But it wasn't what I did. There was a reason I'd worked at a shelter in Toronto. A reason my Toronto ex had said I was smothering. I watched out for newbie baby dykes and shy hunter fairies (human or elf) as tough as nails and as brittle as glass; I kept an eye on bruised halflings who didn't realize they were already whole in and of themselves. I smoothed ruffled feathers and mediated lovers' quarrels, and fed the ones who couldn't feed themselves, and tried to keep the people I loved from hurting each other too much.

"Beti!" I shouted.

The street took a sharp turn, and when I rounded it, for an instant I had the crazy thought that Beti had somehow multiplied. I was in the middle of a crew of Betis, a proliferation of Betis. Cone-shaped masses of rags and tatters danced all around me, and jesters in motley, and hobo clowns in torn jackets and pants and crumpled top hats. A pitchy-patchy crew! No matter her fancy name for her costume, it was a plain old pitchy-patchy mas'. I laughed, relief making my voice a little too wild and hyenalike. The dancers didn't have musicians, but were making their own music by singing: *"We will give her a wedding ring, do you hear, my sissie-oh?"*

With a clomping of hooves, the camel bus drew to a halt at the crumbling curb. Gladstone's face brightened. "She's here!"

Through the windows of the bus, we saw Beti stand and take the hand of a pretty Trubie girl, tall and slim with big cat eyes and a complicated fall of silvery hair. Laughing, they headed for the bus's exit. I didn't have to look at Gladstone to know the change that had come over her face. The shocked shift from eager anticipation to self-protective sullenness.

"Gladhand Girl, don't jump to conclusions, okay?"

"You see? Like always calls to like. Why stay with the half Blood when you can have another purebreed?"

"They may just be friends."

"Friends. Right. I gotta go."

And that was the last Beti and I had seen of Gladstone. At least, that's what I was telling Beti. I hadn't mentioned running into Gladstone last night.

The other girl had been just a friend in truth; someone Beti had met on that same bus that had picked them both up as they were wandering around the outskirts of Bordertown, trying to figure out the way in. Beti'd only wanted her new friend Lizzie to meet her new love Gladstone. And the real kicker? Beti told me that Lizzie wasn't even a Trubie. Just one of the rare humans who kinda looked like one.

Someone spun me around. I recognized the particular configuration of strips of cloth. "Beti!"

She grabbed me around the waist, spun me so my back was against her front. We went into a classic dutty wine like the people all around us, hips gyrating together. She caught on fast, this one. She'd been watching how back home people danced to soca music. It was sexual, yes, but it didn't have to mean sex. It was a pappyshow of sex, a masquerade. Sex is powerful and beautiful and dangerous. Is bigger than peeny humans. To wine up dutty with somebody else is like playing mas' in corpse makeup. Is like saying, these things have power over us, but right now, we can laugh after them. First time Gladstone saw me dance like this with someone else, we'd had one big mako row. She'd been convinced I was about to lie down right there on the floor of the club and start getting nasty with the fella I'd been wining with. With some fella who wasn't her, never mind that he was a stranger I'd only clapped eyes on five minutes before, and a fella to boot!

That was the first time she'd given me blows. And like a fool, I'd gone back for more. Hadn't protected myself, hadn't insisted she find a way to stop trying to own me with her fists. All those years in my previous life I'd worked to help battered wives, husbands, parents, children. But of course, when I was the one getting beat up by someone who loved me, I decided I didn't need help. I was the expert, right? I could handle this all by myself. I could manage Gladstone, oui? Be her lover and her therapist.

Gladstone wasn't the only one who needed to learn that control is something you might try to exercise over a runaway train, not over a lover.

The revelers started bellowing out the song about not giving a damn, 'cause they done dead already. So long I hadn't heard that kaiso! From the big standard the two Frankenstein flag-bearers were dancing with, the crew was called the Jumbie Jamboree. Dead mas' all around us. Vampires. Ghosts. Even douen mas'—small children dressed as the spirits of the unbaptized dead, wearing panama hats that hid their faces, and shoes that made it look as though their feet were turned backward. If you hear the sound of children laughing in the forest, don't follow their footprints. Because they might be *douens,* luring you deeper into the forest when you think the footprints are leading you out.

I leaned back into Beti's embrace. I turned my head toward her. "Why you disappeared like that?"

"I can hide with these people," she said, her voice rough. Like she'd been crying? I turned and took her in my arms.

"Don't worry, child. I won't let Gladstone find you."

She pulled back, pushed some of the motley away from her face. "Gladstone? You're keeping Gladstone from me?"

Oh, shit. "She want to hurt you," I blurted.

Beti reared back, startled. "Why?"

"She's real mad at you for hanging with that girl from the bus. She thinks the two of you been cheating on her."

She looked confused. "Cheating . . ." Light dawned. "You mean making sex with each other? But we haven't."

"Don't matter. When Gladstone get like this, all she want to do is lash out. You have to stay away from her till she calm down. Believe me, girl, I know. Same thing she did to me." I turned my face, showed her my scarred jaw.

The fear, the distress on Beti's face tore my heart out. "She doesn't realize," she said. Through the prang-a-lang of the music, I thought the next words she said were, "She should be the one scared of me."

"What?"

She smiled sadly, touched my arm. "Don't worry. Things change." Then she looked back behind us, crowded close to me. "What is that?" she cried.

Cold fear-sweat was crawling down my spine before I even turned to look. Whatever it was, I could feel it coming, feel it in my sinuses, in the savage change that had come upon colors.

Something parted the crowd like a wave, leaving me and Beti exposed in the middle of the road. The air had gone dark around us, damp and cold. I heard screams from the crowd. But the spectacle approaching us did so in silence. No sound from the pounding of the horse's hooves, the baying of the dogs that weren't dogs, the harsh, rasping breath of the quarry that they were chasing down the very middle of the Jou'vert parade, in what had been broad daylight a second ago. Beside me, Beti gasped. I hustled her over to the sidelines. We watched the Hunt approach. They were moving in slo-mo.

Beti asked, "What are those?"

Beside her, someone in a Phantom of the Opera costume replied, "The Wild Hunt. Here. Not the band. The real thing." His voice shook. "We're all in some deep shit now."

"Why?" asked Beti.

"Anyone who sees them dies."

A deep voice cut in. "We are. We're all going to die. Someday."

I turned. It was Stick. Lubin was riding on his shoulder, all a-bristle as she stared at the spectacle approaching us.

The quarry didn't seem to be really there. I mean, we could see her. But her feet didn't exactly touch the ground as she ran. They either landed a little bit above it or a little bit beneath the surface. For all she was of the Blood, exhaustion had blanched her face even whiter. Her hair hung in sodden ropes of merely gray that swung in dead weight whenever she looked over her shoulder to see how close the hounds were. Sweat had glued her once-gorgeous flowing dress to her body, and its streaked color was more mildew now than the pale green it probably used to be.

"Linden," muttered Stick. "So that was her punishment."

I hoped I would never again see anything like the dogs that were chasing that woman. Black. Small, about the size of terriers. But their heads and snouts were ratlike, only with the dangling, eager tongues of dogs hanging out from between their fangs. Too many legs. They ran more like centipedes than dogs. They swarmed over the road, red eyes intent on their prey.

As she drew level with us, Linden stumbled. People in the crowd cried out. She put one hand down to break her fall. It didn't quite touch the ground, but some invisible solid surface just a hairsbreadth above the disintegrating asphalt of Ho Street. There were rings of silver and sapphire on three of her outspread fingers. One of the hounds leapt, caught the hem of her dress, but she was up again. She bounded away, leaving the hound with a scrap of sodden silk in its mouth.

Behind the hounds came the hunters themselves. Leading them

was a Trubie on a motorcycle, her beautiful face grim. The rest were on horses, on goats, and I think I saw one riding a tapir. Silently, the whole mess of them bounded by. As the last few passed, the day grew bright again, and the wetness left the air. For a few seconds, we were all quiet. Some people were crying, some still just standing with their mouths hanging open, catching air. Stick muttered, *"Love wealth and glory more than life itself, and starve in splendor."*

Then someone in the crowd started clapping, followed by others. People began shouting "Jou'vert!" and *"En bataille-là!"* Pretty soon there were noisemakers going, and whistles. The Phantom of the Opera shouted, "Glamour! It was just a crew with a glamour!" The band began playing again. The Phantom put his arm around the waist of a chunky, purple-haired woman in a skeleton catsuit, and they careened into the steps of a jig.

Somewhere in the comess, Beti had lost her headpiece. "That was . . . pretend?" she asked.

Stick narrowed his eyes. "Could be."

Me, I didn't business with him and his constant suspicion. My headache was gone and my nose had stopped tingling. Real or make-believe, the Wild Hunt had been the source of the juju weather—not Gladstone, after all. Jubilant, I fumbled for Beti's hand amongst her rags and patches, and we started dancing to the music again:

> *We will frighten her half to death, do you hear, my sissie-oh?*
> *We will frighten her half to death, do you hear, my sissie-oh?*

Bellowing out the verse, I swung the hoop of my skirt in a circle. It crashed against Gladstone's leg. My two eyes made four with hers. Hers were rimmed with red, her face blotchy. She narrowed her eyes. Heart thumping, I pushed Beti behind me, but I was too late. Beti squealed, "Gladstone!" She ducked around me and flung herself into Gladstone's arms.

Blasted child was going to get herself a black eye this Jou'vert afternoon. "Gladstone, wait!" I yelled. I leapt toward the two of them to try to intervene.

Gladstone shoved me away. I landed hard on the ground, heard the balsa wood frame of my skirt crack. "Leave us alone!" she said. She enveloped Beti tenderly in her arms. Beti twined her legs around Gladstone's middle. The two of them gripped each other's shirt backs, held each other like they would never let go. They swayed like that for long seconds, to their own music, ignoring the driving beat all around them. My heart cracked open, just like my fragile costume. I stood up.

Gladstone hefted Beti back to her feet. Beti started toward me. "See, Damy?" she cried out. "It's all ri—"

Gladstone reached me first, grabbed the front of my blouse, yanked me to her. "It's been you the whole time, hasn't it?"

"Wha-at?" I squeaked. We were being buffeted about by revellers. No one to notice the drama going down in their midst.

Beti said, "Gladstone, what are you doing? Come and dance with me."

But Gladstone only had eyes for me.

"Dowsabelle just got all withdrawn," she said. "I started fighting more and more with her. Trying to get some reaction from her, I guess. Hated myself. Couldn't stop. But who'd been whispering warnings in her ear every day, scaring her half to death?"

I drew myself up tall. "You *are* scary, damn it!" I tried to yank my blouse out of her hand. She held on.

"I got murder-drunk the night Lottie left me," she continued. "*After* I came home and found she had moved out. Couldn't find out for days what had happened. Where did she go, Damiana?"

I squeaked, "You were going to blow any minute. I could feel it." Juju Daddy had let me put Lottie and her stuff up for a few days in a room above his shop, until she'd found her own place. When the juju weather headaches of Gladstone's ire had faded, I'd told Lottie it was safe to move.

"And now you're trying to frighten Beti away."

"She doesn't frighten me," Beti answered. "You don't frighten me. What's coming frightens me, but it has to come"—she burst into tears—"and then you and Damiana both will turn your faces from me!"

We turned to her, startled. "Oh, Beti," said Gladstone, bending and folding her into a hug. "We would never turn away from you."

We. Did I deserve that "we"? Had I been minimizing the damage Gladstone could do when she was out of control, or had I been causing it?

It happened so quickly. A voice shouted something in a language I didn't understand. An arm pushed me out of the way and grabbed Beti's shoulder. A hand peeled Beti away from Gladstone as easily as peeling the skin from a ripe banana. Beti turned, saw who it was, and angrily spat out more words I didn't understand. A young black man slipped in front of Beti, between her and Gladstone. He tried to shove Gladstone away, but Gladstone held her ground. "Fuck I will," she said. "Get away from my girlfriend."

"Go away!" Beti cried out, backing away. But I couldn't tell whether she was talking to the youth or to Gladstone.

The young man was a sturdy tumpa of a thing, short and muscled and pretty. He wore his jeans and T-shirt as though they were a costume. His eyes were sad, longing. They were Beti's eyes. He reached for Beti again, same time as Gladstone lurched at him. Magic smell filled up my nostrils.

"No!" Beti shouted. Quicker than thought, she slapped Gladstone's hand away from her brother's. He must be the brother come to take her home, right?

That blow had some serious power behind it. Gladstone grimaced in pain, covered her wrist with her other hand, pulled her hands in close to her chest. "But I love you," she said to Beti.

Beti slung her arm through the crook that Gladstone's made. "I know," she replied sadly, pulling Gladstone away from her brother.

He followed them. Beti stopped, said something to him that sounded like a plea. He snapped angry-sounding words at her, reached for her hand. She pulled it away. She looked scared. Gladstone tried to reach around her. Beti grabbed Gladstone's sleeve. "No!" she shouted. Little as she was, she was strong. She was holding Gladstone off with one arm and the weight of her body, backing them both away from her brother and arguing with him same time. I started forward.

Stick lifted a warding hand in front of me. "Stay out of this," he muttered. He called out something in the language that Beti and her brother were speaking. The two of them turned, looking startled.

And then I saw something I never thought I would. Stick bowed the knee to them both.

Gladstone said, "What the hell?"

Stick raised his head and asked Beti and her brother a question.

Beti replied, pointed at her brother and Gladstone.

Her brother cut her off with sharp words.

She responded to him with sad, pleading ones.

He begged, scolded.

Stick stood.

He shouted angrily at them both. He gestured at the crowd.

I sneezed, then slapped my hands to either side of my head as an eyeball-melting migraine hit me. Like a friction charge, some deep juju was building up between Beti and her brother.

Stick's eyes went wide with alarm. He snapped an order, pointed a finger northward, in the direction of the Border. *Go,* he was saying to Beti and her brother. *Go back now.*

Beti protested.

Stick turned in a panicked circle. Stick never panicked! There were people thronging all around. "Run!" he yelled to the crowd. "Get the fuck out of here!" One or two people started backing away, looking confused, but most didn't even notice him.

Then the old snake charmer elf was by Stick's side. Lubin sniffed curiously in the direction of his snake. The snake benignly tasted her air. The Trubie said something to Stick, turned, and began urging people to move away from Beti and her brother.

Stick yelled at Gladstone, "Let her go! Now!"

Gladstone shook her head, swung a protective arm around Beti's shoulder. Beti shrugged it off.

I saw the hurt on Gladstone's face, smelled the juju tide come rolling down. Blinding headache or no, I kicked off my shoes and ran toward my friend. "Gladstone, no!"

Beti turned sorrowing eyes on Gladstone, blew her a kiss. "It's time," she said.

Beti's brother reached his hands out. Beti stepped forward and clasped them with both of hers.

Gladstone reached their sides, grabbed his forearm in one hand, Beti's in the other.

Beti shouted, her voice so large and gonging that it exceeded sound. All the Jou'vert action went still with the shock of it.

Beti and her brother exploded into shards of prismed light . . .

I was still running, still screaming Gladstone's name, though all around me was only painful brightness and I couldn't feel my body, couldn't hear, couldn't see.

. . . and coalesced again. Not as a thick-bodied black boy and his sister, but as one faceless something. A something tall as a tower. A something cone-shaped with many-colored tendrils that flared out from it as it spun. A something that made a sound like monsoon winds through the branches of a dead tree. Like the whistle through the air of withies just before they struck bare flesh. But loud, so loud. People fell to their knees, those that weren't running. Even Stick stepped back.

Not me, for I couldn't see Gladstone anywhere. I ran right up to the thing. "Beti!" I screamed.

It kept spinning, whistling, clacking.

The old elf ran to stand between it and the crowd. He held up warding hands. The thing began to move away, but one of its flying tendrils whipped across the snake charmer's face. He convulsed and fell, his snake with him. He was frozen in rigor by the time he hit the ground. Oh, god; death had come to Jou'vert for true.

I planted myself in the path of the thing. It came on toward me. "Ti'Bet, stop it!"

It hesitated.

"Where's Gladstone?" I screamed at it. "What you did to her?" The thing dithered from side to side in front of me. I howled, "Bring them back!"

Gladstone, the snake charmer; they couldn't just be gone.

The tip of the thing leaned its deadly self toward me. I didn't give a damn. I'd done deaded already, just like Stick said. Whether now or later, who cared? I'd meddled in my friend's life, and now two sweet beings were gone.

The Beti-thing's body smelled like dry rot, like carrion. It smelled like Granny's perfume, like my old dog Glower's breath, like grief and regret and resignation and goodbye.

And finally, it smelled like peace. It pulled back. It moved away, and there where it had been lay Gladstone, only Gladstone. Her clothes were torn, there was blood coming from her nose, and half her hair had been singed off. I dropped to my knees, felt her neck for a pulse. She was still alive. "Gladstone?" I said. No answer.

"Lemme see to her, sweetness." It was Screaming Lord Neville, dressed in the tiered plantation gown and Madras cotton head wrap of La Diablesse, the devil woman. "I know a few little things," he said. He folded his long length down to sit beside us. Below the hem of his gown peeked one red sequined pump and one cow's hoof. He saw me staring at it and smoothed the gown over his feet.

The pitchy-patchy thing spun away, in the direction of the Nevernever. People tried to reach the old snake charmer. His snake had coiled itself protectively around his body and wouldn't let anyone near. Please God I never again hear a snake scream in grief. And I won't, for it wasn't a snake. It drew itself up to man-height, howled that terrible howl once more, and became a searing red flame of wings with a dragon mask of loss. In seconds, it and the dead elf were only ash, dissipating on the breeze.

For the next few minutes, as my headache faded, I dithered around

Miss Nell. She checked Gladstone in case there were internal injuries. Stick brought water. People offered cloaks to keep Gladstone warm and tore costumes into bandages for her. When she opened her eyes, it was like somebody had turned the sun back on.

"I'm sorry," I said. "I thought you were coming to hurt her."

She smiled weakly. "Truth? I might have." Gently, she touched my chin. "Thank you for keeping me from being an ass even when I'm too stubborn to ask for help."

"What was she?"

"A rainfly, I think."

Gladstone had never seen rainflies, but I'd described their life cycle to her. How joyfully they danced in the air before a rainstorm. How when the pounding rain came it drove them to the ground and pulled off their wings. How they wriggled and wriggled and then crawled away, metamorphosed into their adult forms.

Beti had been doing her last dance as a child. She and her brother had needed each other in order to move on to the next stage of their development. No wonder she confused the word for "brother" with the word meaning "two who will become one."

"So she was really from beyond the Border?" I asked Gladstone. "Some kind of egungun for true?"

"Some kind of what?" Gladstone was staring longingly in the direction of the forest.

Lord Neville said, "Whatever she was, doux-doux, she knew she couldn't hide it forever. Brave, proud child. You two did right to care for her."

He slid his platform shoe off one foot and massaged his toes. He kept the hoof concealed beneath his gown.

Men Sell Not Such in Any Town

My fascination with Christina Rossetti's twincesterrific Nineteenth-Century poem "Goblin Market" would eventually be played out in more detail in my novel Sister Mine *(Grand Central, 2013). In this next story, only the title—and perhaps the protagonist's obsession with evanescent fruit—have much to do with the poem.*

"Did you hear? Rivener has created a new fruit!"

"How very dull. Her last piece was a fruit, too."

"Not like this one!" Salope said. She sat me at the table, murmuring the evening benediction as she did so. She draped my long sleeves artfully against the arms of the chair in the first pattern of the benediction ritual. She took my hat and veil, hung them on the peg. She plucked the malachite pins from my hair, one by one. She shook the dark, springing mass free, and refashioned it into a plait down my back. I endured as long as I could, then leaned back and stared up into her cool granite eyes.

"Tell me of Rivener's creation," I commanded her.

She came around to my side. She slipped her fingertips into the pockets of her white apron and composed herself for the tale. She stood quite straight, as was proper. My blood quickened.

"Rivener's previous fruit," she said, "*only* sang like a rain forest full of parrots; *only* enhanced the prescient abilities of those who ate it. This one is the pinnacle." She stopped, though she didn't need breath. I felt a single drop of sweat start its slow trickle between my breasts. The heavy silks were stifling. "Stop dawdling; tell me!"

She caught her bottom lip between gleaming teeth. She came and draped my sleeves into the second pattern; this evening, she'd chosen the shapes of mourning doves. I gritted my teeth. She continued: "It is the colour of early autumn, they say, and the scent lifting off its skin is a fine bouquet of virgin desire and dandy's sweat, with a top note of baby's breath. It fits in the palm, any palm. Its flesh is firm as a loving father's shoulder."

She stopped to dab at my face with a cutwork linen handkerchief from her pocket, and I nearly screamed. She resumed: "The fruit shucks off its own peel at a touch, revealing itself once only; to its devourer. A northern dictator burst into tears at the first taste of its pulp on his lips, and begged the forgiveness of his people."

"Poet and thrice-cursed child of a damned poet!" Her father too had played this game of stirring exalted cravings in me. I lifted my bodice away from my skin, fanned it to let air in. It wasn't enough.

Salope squatted in her sturdy black shoes, square at heel and toe. This exposed her strong thighs, brought her face level with my bosom. "I'm making you hungry, aren't I? Thirsty?"

"Bring me some water. No, wine."

"At once." She left the room, returned with a sleek glass pitcher and a glass on a silver tray. The golden liquid was cold, and beaded the pitcher. Salope poured for me, tilted the glass to my lips. I tasted the wine. It was dry and dusty in my mouth. I turned my head away. "What does Rivener call this wonder?" I asked.

"'The God Under the Tongue.'" Salope put the glass down on the table and took the appropriate step backwards. "There are one hundred and seventeen, limited edition, each one infused with her signature histamine."

"The one that makes the fingertips tingle?"

"The very same."

This heat! It distracted one so. "I wish to purchase one of these marvellous fruit."

"To taste it?"

"Of course to taste it! Bring me my meal."

"Instantly." She went. Returned with a gold dish, covered with a

lid of sleekest bone. It had been fashioned from the pelvis of a whale;
I knew this. She put the dish down, uncovered it. A fine steam rose
from it. "Here is your supper, Enlightened."

I picked up the golden spoon. "Contact the auction house."

Salope barely smiled. "I already have. It's too late. All one hundred
and seventeen of 'The God Under the Tongue' are already spoken
for."

I slammed the spoon back down onto the table. "Tell them I will
pay! Command Rivener to make another! Just one more!"

Salope looked down at the ground. When she returned her gaze
to mine, she was serene. "It's too late, Enlightened. The Academy has
decided. Rivener has been transmigrated to Level Sublime. She is
beyond your reach."

"Machine."

"There is no need for insult, Enlightened."

"Go away."

Salope bowed, returned the spoon to my hand, and dissipated into
black smoke. I preferred a pale rose mist, but Salope kept stubbornly
reverting to black. It had been her father's favourite colour.

Her father had finally pushed me too far. I'd ordered him to dissolve
himself permanently from my aura. I had grieved for two voluptuous
years, then sought everywhere for his like. Nothing. Eventually, in
desperation, I had his daughter created. Perverse poet's child; how she
could arouse the senses!

I am Amaxon Corazón Junia Principia Delgado the Third, and I
bent over my meal and wept luxurious tears into my green banana
porridge. It was a perfect decoction, and it now would never satisfy
me. Only the poet's daughter, and her father before her, ever saw me
so transported.

The room spoke with Salope's voice. "Thank you, Enlightened. I
consider myself well paid for today's session. Please recommend my
services to your acquaintances."

I would. Oh, I would.

About the Author

Nalo Hopkinson was born in Kingston, Jamaica, and also spent her childhood in Trinidad and Guyana before her family moved to Toronto, Canada, when she was sixteen.

Hopkinson's groundbreaking science fiction and fantasy features diverse characters and the mixing of folklore into her works. Of her writing she says, "I frequently use Afro-Caribbean spirituality, oral history, culture, and language in my stories, but place my characters within the idioms and settings of contemporary science fiction and fantasy. When I was starting out, it was my way of subverting the genre, which speaks so much about the experience of being alienated, but still contains relatively little writing by alienated people themselves." Hopkinson also helped to found the Carl Brandon Society, which strives to bring people together to discuss the issues of race and ethnicity in science fiction and fantasy.

Hopkinson's novels include *Brown Girl in the Ring*, *Midnight Robber*, *The Salt Roads*, *The New Moon's Arms*, *The Chaos* and most recently, *Sister Mine*. Her early short fiction was published in the collection *Skin Folk*. She has edited four anthologies, including *Whispers from the Cotton Tree Root: Caribbean Fabulist Fiction*.

In 1997, Hopkinson won the Warner Aspect First Novel Contest for *Brown Girl in the Ring*. *Brown Girl in the Ring* was also nominated for the Philip K. Dick Award, and received the John W. Campbell and Locus awards for Best First Novel. Her second novel, *Midnight Robber*, was a *New York Times* Notable Book. Her collection *Skin Folk* received the World Fantasy Award and the Sunburst Award for Canadian Literature of the Fantastic. *Salt Roads* received the Gaylactic Spectrum Award for positive exploration of queer issues in speculative fiction. *The New Moon's Arms* won the Sunburst Award, making Hopkinson the first author to receive the award twice, and the Prix Aurora Award. She has been awarded ten grants for her work, including an Ontario Art Council Foundation Award.

Hopkinson has faced many obstacles, including suffering from anemia and fibromyalgia. She spent a few years too sick to read or write, and was sometimes homeless. Her view on these dark periods can be humorous: "But every so often I'll go through an old notebook or find a file I don't recognize and open it up, and there's a page or two of writing that I did during that time that I do not remember. At some level I was still writing. The cool part about it is, the writing is pretty good!" (*Locus*, September 2013)

Hopkinson currently resides in Riverside, California, and teaches in the Creative Writing department at the University of California, Riverside.